Also by Michael McBride

NOVELS

Ancient Enemy
Bloodletting
Burial Ground
Fearful Symmetry
Innocents Lost
Sunblind
The Coyote
Vector Borne

NOVELLAS

F9
Remains
Snowblind
The Event

COLLECTIONS

Category V

MICHAEL McBRIDE

PREDATORY INSTINCT

A THRILLER

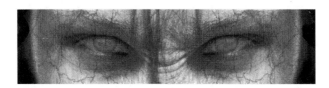

FACTOR V MEDIA

Predatory Instinct copyright © 2012 by Michael McBride

All Rights Reserved.

This book is a work of fiction. Names, characters, places and incidents are either products of the author's imagination or used fictitiously. Any resemblance to actual events, locales, or persons, living or dead, is entirely coincidental. All rights reserved. No part of this publication may be reproduced or transmitted in any form or by any means, electronic or mechanical, without permission in writing from Michael McBride.

For more information about the author, please visit his website:
www.michaelmcbride.net

Dedicated to the Delirium Family

RIP

Special Thanks to Shane Staley, David Marty, and Steve Souza; Brian Keene; Gene O'Neill; Jeff Strand and "the great race"; Bill Rasmussen; my amazing family; and, most importantly, all of my readers, without whom this book would not exist.

Fossil skull DNA identifies new human ancestor

By RADLEY DUNHILL
Associated Press Writer

NEW YORK (AP) – Scientists have identified a previously unknown ancient human through the analysis of mitochondrial DNA from fragments of skull bones unearthed in a Siberian cave.

A team of archaeologists investigating the Seima-Turbino Phenomenon, a spontaneous rapid and massive exodus of the indigenous peoples of the Altai Mountains into distant parts of Europe and Asia during the second millennium BCE, exhumed the fossilized remains from one of twenty-two distinct layers of strata. Thermoluminescent and radiocarbon dating of the surrounding sediment suggest that this unclassified hominin (human-like creature) existed a mere 35,000 years ago at a time when both primitive humans (*Homo sapiens*) and Neanderthals (*Homo neanderthalensis*) cohabited this isolated region of Central Asia, raising the possibility that these three distinctive forms of human could have met and interacted.

Researchers at the Douglas Caldwell Institute for Evolutionary Anthropology in New York extracted the mitochondrial DNA, which is inherited only through the maternal line, from the bones and compared the genetic sequence with those of modern humans and Neanderthals. The analysis revealed that the three last shared a common ancestor more than one million years ago, proving that the Altai individual, referred to publicly as the "Siberian Hominin" and as "Enigman" by the scientists in internal emails, represents a previously unrecognized African migration.

"Whoever carried this genome out of Africa is some new creature we never even suspected might exist," said Dr. Geoffrey Melton of the Caldwell Institute. "The evidence is convincing. We are dealing with a hitherto unclassified hominin, and quite possibly a new species entirely."

Without a more complete fossil record, scientists can only speculate as to what the Siberian Hominin may have looked like or how it may have behaved or intermingled with early modern humans. However, based on the size of the skull fragments, it more closely resembles its larger and more heavily muscled Neanderthal cousins than its human contemporaries.

"Paleontologists are scouring the northern region of the Altai Mountains for further evidence of the Siberian Hominin," Melton said. "While the cold weather helps preserve ancient DNA, the constant presence of so much snow at the higher elevations makes it like looking for a needle in a haystack the size of Texas. We're dealing with thousands of acres of the most inhospitable terrain in the world, and it's blanketed by snow and ice year-round. We may never find any sign of this miraculous new species again."

While archaeologists remain hopeful that their diligence will be rewarded, for now they can only look down from the sheer icy peaks like their ancestors must have done tens of thousands of years ago, and imagine a time when creatures simultaneously familiar and alien moved through the blizzarding snow.

I

What but the wolf's tooth whittled so fine
The fleet limbs of the antelope?
What but fear winged the birds, and hunger
Jewelled with such eyes the great goshawk's head?

—Robinson Jeffers

ONE

Altai Mountain Range
Siberia
Friday, October 5th
3:02 p.m. NOVST
(2:02 a.m. PST)

The wind screamed across the sheer granite face of Mt. Belukha. Its peak hid behind a white shark's fin of blowing snow, still five hundred meters above them. There was no sky, only the blizzard that assaulted them from all directions at once and threatened to sweep them from the ice-coated escarpment, upon which the new flakes accumulated in a layer as slick as greased glass. Progress was maddeningly slow as even their crampons and ice axes hardly secured tenuous purchase. They had passed the point of no return hours ago. There was no choice but to continue higher and pray that their ice screws held in the fractured ice. With the ferocity of the sudden storm, a descent under darkness would be suicide.

Four days ago, a chunk of ice the size of an office building had calved from the mountain with the sound of cannon fire and thundered down the northwestern slope. From their base camp in the upper Katun Valley to the south, they had watched in horror as fragments the size of semi trucks lay siege to the timberline, exploding through the wall of evergreens as though it were no more substantial than tissue paper. Two kilometers to the north, and they would have been pulverized to such a degree that their bodies would have been unrecognizable, if they were even found at all. But fear metamorphosed into excitement when the binoculars revealed the mouth of a cave roughly one hundred and fifty meters below the nearer of the twin summits. Lord only knew how long it had been sealed behind the ice.

It had taken several days to plot their ascent to coincide with the ideal weather forecast, which hadn't predicted the freak storm that swept up the valley three hours ago like a tsunami of blowing flakes.

Dr. Ramsey Ladd, Director of the Center for the Advanced Study of Hominid Paleobiology, had to pause to summon the last of his failing strength. His arms and legs trembled as he clung to his axe handle and rope, balanced on his toes. The ledge beneath him couldn't have been more than four inches wide, but it was the largest he had encountered in quite some time. The wind whipped the fur fringe of his parka hood into his face, which felt as though it had frozen solid even with the full neoprene balaclava facemask. Ice accumulated in the corners of his goggles, narrowing his already constricted field of view. It was hard to imagine feeling claustrophobic so exposed on the mountain, and yet his chest tightened to the point that he had to concentrate to keep from hyperventilating the already thin air. He didn't dare risk shifting his weight to glance over his shoulder to confirm that the others were still behind him.

Just fifty more meters, he assured himself, and again forced his trembling body upward.

He nearly sobbed when he hooked his axe over the precipice and hauled himself up into the cave. Every muscle in his body ached. His throat was stripped raw. Ice knotted his lashes and beard, and clung to his chapped nostrils. He crawled deeper into the darkness, away from the blizzard shrieking past the orifice. When he could crawl no more, he collapsed to the granite floor, rolled out of his rucksack, and desperately drank the water from his thermal hydration bladder. His breathing eventually slowed, and he listened from the darkness as the others clambered up with the clamor of axes and crampons and performed the same exhausted ritual.

Saved from the elements, the cave had to be at least twenty degrees warmer. The echo of their slowing exhalations gave some indication of its size, which was far larger than he would have guessed from the valley below. He removed his flashlight from his pack and clicked it on. The beam shoved back the shadows and limned the granite walls.

"My God," Ladd whispered. He stood and turned a complete circle, watching in awe as the beam spotlighted ancient pictographs distorted by a layer of glimmering ice. There were angular lines and abstract representations of stick men and beasts he couldn't immediately identify. "Can you guys see this?"

He heard the clatter of spiked cleats behind him, but couldn't tear his eyes from the wall. The state of preservation was miraculous. He couldn't begin to fathom how old these finger-painted images were.

"Judy?" he whispered.

"The designs are different than any I've seen at the other proto-human sites we've discovered," Dr. Judith Rivale, Professor of Anthropology at The George Washington University, said. She shed her goggles and her mask to more clearly see. Her chestnut bangs were crisp with ice and hung in front of her brown eyes and wind-chafed brow. "I hesitate to even speculate until we're able to accurately date the strata. The level of preservation is so staggering, thanks to the ice, that this could just as easily be a hundred thousand years old as twenty."

She glanced back at the man behind her, whose parka was lined with so much fur he appeared more animal than man.

"Don't look at me," Dr. Carlos Pascual said. As Head of Paleoarchaeology at the Smithsonian National Museum of Natural History, he had been called upon to authenticate and evaluate discoveries predating the Upper Pleistocene Era on every continent. Were it possible to be an expert on the inexplicable, he was as close as one could get. "This is all positively modern to me. Whoever painted these did so long after all of the other hominin branches died off."

"Wait a second," Rivale said. She stepped closer to one of the walls and carefully chiseled away a section of the ice with her axe blade. "This can't be right. These markings almost look Sumerian, like an early form of cuneiform."

"Take pictures," Ladd said. "Maybe our Kyrgyz guide has seen more like this elsewhere in these mountains."

Nelson Spears, a doctoral candidate from the University of Pennsylvania who had insinuated himself onto their expedition team, due in large measure to his father's company's financial backing and political connections, removed his digital camera from his backpack and began the process of documentation.

Ladd wandered deeper into the cave. The strobe of the flash distorted the shape of the granite walls, making them appear to alternately expand and contract, and throwing shifting shadows across the smooth stone. At the furthest reaches of his vision, he glimpsed a pyramidal stack of stones. As he neared, it drew contrast and resolved from the darkness. They weren't rocks. Vacant-eyed skulls of all shapes and sizes stared back at him from the column of light. There had to be at least fifty of them. All of their faces were turned outward, so that no matter where he stood, they always seemed to be looking at him. He stepped closer. His beam spotlighted fossilized bones long since absolved of their flesh and aged to the color of rust. Fracture lines coursed through their sloped, elongated craniums like spider webs.

"Get a shot of this," he said.

Once Nelson had taken several pictures from various angles, Ladd carefully tried to lift the uppermost skull, but it wouldn't budge. The pyramid had petrified in that form.

"These are the most remarkably preserved remains I've ever encountered," Pascual said. "Look at this. The flat frontal bone, the prominent brow ridge, the protuberance of the occipital bun, the suprainiac fossa. Some of these are undeniably Neanderthal. And the rest? My God. A combination of archaic and modern human traits? Astounding. Do you realize what we're looking at here? This could be the most important paleontological discovery of our lifetimes."

Another flash illuminated two more pyramids against the rear wall, between which a fissure split the granite. The shadows receded from his beam. As he approached, he realized that it was more than a mere alcove.

The crevice was barely wide enough to allow him passage. His jacket rubbed on the walls with the repeated sound of a quickly drawn zipper. Five meters in, the ceiling lowered and he had to duck. The circle of his beam reached a flat surface ahead, and focused smaller and smaller as he advanced. He felt the subtle movement of air against his face and smelled the damp breath of the planet: the aged scents of crumbling stone, dust, and possibly the trace residues of smoke and something unpleasantly organic.

Before he reached the terminus, a hole opened in the ground. He knelt and shined his light down into a smooth chute that descended beyond the light's reach. One side had evenly spaced half-circles of shadow. He had seen similar markings before. They were handholds, chiseled into the stone, smoothed by time and frequent use.

"What do you see?" Rivale asked.

Ladd shrugged in response.

"I'm going down," he said, and swung his legs over the edge.

"Let us belay you. If you fall and hurt yourself, we'll never be able to get you back down the mountain."

Ladd was in no mood to argue. The moment his toes found the grooves, he tucked his flashlight into his coat pocket and started down. Rivale did her best to shine her light onto the primitive rungs. It barely provided enough illumination to navigate the small ledges, which had been carved in a zigzagging fashion. He realized he should have been counting the handholds, but it was too late now. All he could do was continue until he stepped down onto solid ground. Rivale's flashlight was the pinprick of a distant star high above him when he finally stepped away from the wall and into the waiting blackness.

*   *   *

"Are you all right down there?" Pascual called. His voice echoed around Ladd, who turned and directed his light into the darkness.

"Yeah," he said in little more than a whisper. The cavern was so large that his beam was about as effective as a candle's flame. It diffused to nothingness before it encountered the far wall.

"Ramsey! Is everything okay?" Pascual shouted, louder this time.

Ladd could only nod as he started forward with the clacking sound of his cleats. The cool breeze followed from the tunnel at his back. It waned as he pressed deeper into darkness that grew warmer with each step. Water dripped unseen around him with discordant plipping and plinking sounds, beneath which he heard faint scritching that immediately brought rats to mind. A vile stench permeated his balaclava, forcing him to take several deep breaths through his mouth to keep from retching. Something must have crawled in here to die. He imagined a festering bear carcass crawling with rodents and felt his stomach clench.

The clatter of crampons echoed from the chute behind him.

He drew wide arcs across the chamber with his beam. Petroglyphs spiraled up a cluster of stalagmites, which glistened with the condensation dripping from above. The uneven ground was smooth. Eons of dissolved minerals had accreted into hardened puddles reminiscent of melted wax. The domed ceiling was spiked with stalactites. Bats shuffled restlessly in their shadows. He wondered how they had managed to find their way this deep into the mountain before the ice broke away and revealed the cave.

A light bloomed behind him and stretched his shadow across the floor.

"These aren't as old as the others," Rivale said.

Ladd glanced back to find her scrutinizing the carvings on the stalagmites. When he turned around again, he caught movement in his beam. A quick black blur. Near the ground. There and gone before he could clearly identify it. His skin crawled at the thought of a rat scurrying up his pant leg and nipping into the meat of his thigh. They were filthy, insatiable creatures. It might not be as effective as a flamethrower, but at least he had a flare gun in his pack. If nothing else, the sudden and blinding glare would serve to startle the vermin back into the godforsaken warrens in which they dwelled. He slowed to retrieve it from his pack and felt emboldened with his finger on the trigger, even though he knew he could only use it with the utmost caution for fear of violating the integrity of the site and destroying anything of potential anthropological significance.

"Put that thing away before you end up setting yourself on fire," Pascual said. "This may be little more than a peashooter, but it will definitely ruin a rat's day."

The wan light glinted from the barrel of the Smith & Wesson 22A semi-automatic target pistol in his fist.

"Where the hell did that come from?" Ladd asked.

"My backpack."

"You know what I mean."

"A lot of bad things can happen to an American traveling abroad. I never leave the country without it."

Ladd shook his head and followed his nose toward the rear of the cavern.

"I don't have to tell you, Ramsey, how much a genuine hominin fossil could fetch on the black market. Entire expeditions had been slaughtered for less."

Ladd conceded the point. He just hoped Pascual didn't accidentally shoot him in the back.

The camera flashed as Nelson captured the glyphs for Rivale, and then set about documenting the cave as a whole. Ladd was finally able to take in the magnitude of his surroundings. The cavern was the size of a small warehouse. Natural stone columns connected the ground to the fifteen-foot-high ceiling at random intervals. Petroglyphs covered every available surface. Most of the individual designs were no larger than an inch square. Rivale was right. They looked like the cuneiform on the ancient tablets he had seen, which only served to heighten the sense of surreality. How had a four thousand year old form of writing found its way onto the walls inside a frozen mountain a continent away and, by all accounts, a geological era apart?

Ladd walked around a column and directed his beam into a darkened corner. Dozens of tiny eyes flashed red before the rats fled with an indignant racket of squeals. He had been right about the source of the smell, just not the mechanism of demise. The brown bear was suspended from the ceiling and the walls by a series of ropes, which drew its arms and legs away from its body, spread-eagle. Its hide was stretched beside it from floor to ceiling to tan. The carcass still wore fur on its clawed paws like mittens and socks. Its diminished form seemed disproportionate to its savage head, from which dull eyes stared blankly past him. Its dry tongue protruded from the right side of its contorted jaws. Its neck had been torn open to such an extent that it appeared to be held in place by the spine alone. Connective tissue shimmered silver over its broad chest muscles. There was a massive gap where it had been absolved of its viscera. The sloppy wounds where the rats had helped themselves were readily distinguishable from the gouges where something much larger had stolen bites.

Someone had hunted this bear and dragged it in here. Very recently. And that someone could still be in there with them at this very moment.

"We should get out of here," Ladd whispered.

"Over here," Rivale called.

Ladd spun around at the sound of her voice. She was in the opposite rear corner, silhouetted by the glow of her flashlight, which she focused upon the ground.

"There has to be another entrance," Pascual said from behind him as Ladd crossed the cavern.

His guts tingled. Something was definitely wrong here. The sudden urge to sprint from the cavern nearly overwhelmed him.

He passed a dark orifice filled with shadows impervious to his light on his left. His beam barely penetrated the darkness.

Rivale nearly knocked him over in her hurry to retreat. She had shoved aside a heap of desiccated flowers, leaves, and grasses to reveal a foul puddle of concentrated urine and feces. The brownish-black logs were well-formed and undeniably human.

Someone was definitely living in here. Several people, most likely. One man couldn't haul, hang, and skin a bear. So where were they hiding? And better yet…why?

"I don't like the looks of this," Nelson said. "We shouldn't be in here."

"We can't risk the climb back down after nightfall," Rivale said.

"We can hole up in that cave up there and set off at first light."

"There's another option," Pascual said. He stood in the mouth of the tunnel that branched from the back wall, shining his light deeper into the mountain. "That bear had to weigh at least a thousand pounds. Whoever dragged it in here didn't scale the mountain like we did. There has to be an easier way out."

"We don't know who's in here with us or where they might be," Ladd said.

"You're letting your imagination get the better of you. There's no reason to suspect that whoever's here is hostile. It's probably just a nomadic Kyrgyz tribe riding out the winter. They'd probably even be willing to show us the way out of here."

"This doesn't feel right, Carlos. You saw the bear. It looked like someone had been gnawing the meat right off the bone."

Pascual waved off his concern and started into the stone passage. He was probably right, but Ladd couldn't dismiss his unease so quickly. He had tapped into his survival instincts, which screamed for him to get out of there before it was too late.

Ladd forced his legs to move and followed Pascual. Rivale and Nelson fell in behind him. The clatter of crampons and their haggard breathing echoed in the confines. Nelson flashed the camera repeatedly, more for light than for documentation's sake. The narrow walls were covered with writing. It would have taken lifetimes to carve so many symbols. Ladd hurried to catch up with Pascual as he exited the passage into another chamber. Were it possible, this one smelled worse than the last. The musty, sour aromas of body odor, ammonia, and festering meat made his eyes water.

His cleats made a crunching sound as he stepped from the bare stone onto a more forgiving substrate. He crouched and shined his light at the ground. Sand. He scooped up a handful and allowed it to cascade between his fingers. The grains were small and powdery, as though individually they had no substance at all, like the sand from a tropical beach or the most remote desert. Whatever the case, it definitely wasn't from around here. He again thought of the cuneiform and its Arabian origin as he stood and followed Pascual deeper into the mountain.

*   *   *

The tunnel opened into a chamber much smaller than the last, perhaps the size of a two-car garage, but the ceiling was much higher. As with all of the others, the walls were covered with the cryptic writing. A mound of sand filled the room, drifted against the far wall, as though a dune had been magically transported into this one cave.

Nelson flashed his camera. Ladd glimpsed what had to be thousands of bats suspended overhead between the stalactites. They wavered from side to side as though blown by a breeze only they could feel.

Their flashlight beams crisscrossed the cave like spotlights at a movie premier, showing them random pieces, but never the whole.

"There's another passage over here," Pascual said.

Ladd turned toward where Pacual stood in the opposite corner, silhouetted by his flashlight, which diffused into another pitch-black corridor.

"How in the world did all of this sand get in here?" Nelson whispered.

"I feel a faint breeze," Pascual called. His voice echoed from the orifice. "At least we know we're heading in the right direction."

Ladd skirted the edge of the dune. His reluctance to walk on it was irrational, he knew, and yet he simply couldn't bring himself to step on any more of it than absolutely necessary. There was something unnatural about it. Not the sand itself, per se, but the fact that it simply shouldn't be here. He felt a swell of relief when he ducked out of the room and into the tunnel.

"Amazing," Pascual said from somewhere ahead, his voice hollowed by the acoustics.

"What is it?"

"You have to see it to believe it."

Ladd wasn't in the mood. The feeling that he needed to get out of this mountain this very second nearly overwhelmed him.

The stone corridor opened into another domed cavern. Pascual stood in the center, directing his light at the walls as he slowly turned in circles. Another dark channel exited the far side.

Ladd followed the beam with his eyes. The walls weren't covered with writing. Hundreds of recesses had been meticulously carved into them instead, small arched shelves separated by a finger's width of granite. They were barely large enough to accommodate the skulls wedged inside them. More shadowed eye sockets than he could count stared directly at him.

"It's an ossuary," Ladd said.

"Of sorts. There aren't any other bones. Only the skulls." Pascual's voice positively trembled with excitement. "Notice anything interesting about them?"

Ladd directed his light at the nearest arch to his left and stumbled backward in surprise.

"Jesus."

"Tell me about it. I've never seen anything like them on a hominin. A Great Ape, maybe, but not on a proto-human."

"What in God's name do you think—?"

"Ramsey!" Rivale shouted from behind him. He spun toward the tunnel leading back to the room with the sand. "Ramsey!"

Something in her voice awakened the panic inside him. He took off at a sprint, made awkward by his crampons. Something was definitely wrong. Everything was wrong. They shouldn't be here. No one was ever meant to be here.

Ladd burst into the cavern to find Rivale kneeling beside Nelson on one of the dune's peaks, waving her hand, palm-down, over the sand. He hurried to her side. She glanced up at him, eyes wide.

"Hold your hand right here. Just like this," she said. "Can you feel it?"

Ladd removed his glove and waved his hand over the ground just as she had. The tip of a reed reminiscent of the stalk of a cattail stood several inches above the sand at a slight angle. Warm air caressed his palm when he passed over it.

"What is it?" he asked.

"I don't know. Nelson found it. And several more just like it."

"At least four more," Nelson said.

"There's something under here." Ladd brushed the sand away from the base of the thin reed, only to find that it extended deeper than he had suspected. The fine grains slid back into place. "What could possibly—?"

"Quit screwing around and just do it already," Pascual said. He shouldered Ladd aside and shoved scoops of sand away from the reed. "For someone in such a rush to get out of here, you're sure taking your sweet time about it."

Ladd glanced back toward the tunnel through which they had initially entered. Suddenly, the prospect of descending the sheer, icy face of Mt. Belukha wasn't nearly as intimidating, even blindly in the darkness and the blizzarding snow.

"Stop, Carlos."

"I can feel something down there."

"For Christ's sake, stop digging! Let's get out of here while we still—"

"What the hell is that? Someone. Give me some more light."

Rivale shined her beam into the bottom of the foot-deep hole as Pascual brushed away the grains that trickled back down the sides. He jerked his hand back and scrabbled away.

Ladd saw a prominent brow over eyelids dusted with sand, the ridge of a slender nose, a pair of lips pursed around the base of the reed.

"It's too late," he whispered.

The eyes snapped open at the sound of his voice.

TWO

Seattle, Washington
Thursday, October 11th
12:06 a.m. PST
(1:06 p.m. NOVST)

"It seems cruel to be doing this, especially in the middle of the night," Officer Elena Sturm said. She directed her Maglite into the rubble and appraised the treacherous descent through eyes so blue they appeared almost translucent. Her midnight-black hair was pulled into a short ponytail through the back of a ball cap with the department logo, her uniform impeccably pressed beneath her rain-beaded "Seattle PD" windbreaker.

"No cameras," Officer Dave Henley said. Her new partner, who wore his uniform a size too small to showcase his ripped physique, offered a smirk. "Last thing the mayor wants is to see this on the news. You know the kind of thrashing he'd take in the press. Besides, he wouldn't want any of these sewer rats crawling up here and spoiling his precious little soirée."

Still doesn't make it right, Sturm thought, but didn't share the sentiment with her partner, who was far too enthusiastic about their assignment for her tastes. She surveyed what was left of the Maritime Industrial Center, which had once been a thriving commercial fishing operation steeped in the rich seafaring tradition that had spawned the greatest city in the Pacific Northwest, which itself had given rise to the foundation of modern American society in the form of Microsoft and Starbucks. The entire commercial district bordering Salmon Bay, which glimmered in the moonlight a hundred yards to the west beyond the decrepit and crumbling piers, had been condemned and gated off behind a fifteen-foot chain link fence more than a year ago to make way for progress. Where once fisherman had hauled their catches directly from the ocean to these processing, packaging, canning, and shipping

factories, there would soon be upscale flats, trendy shopping and
dining establishments, and office space for the dozens of
burgeoning software enterprises the city hoped to entice to the
region. All that would remain of its heritage were the memories
captured in the bronze statues and placards that would line the
modern boardwalk rimming the bay, and the lone finished project,
the eighty-million-dollar Bertha Knight Landes Cultural Center, a
ninety-thousand square-foot affair of burnished brass, smoked
glass, and polished marble, which featured convention space
decorated with salvaged relics and photographs of a bygone era. Its
grand ribbon-cutting ceremony, a week from this Saturday night,
would play host to Seattle's elite, who, for two thousand dollars a
plate, could don their tuxedos and gowns for an evening of dancing
hosted by the Seattle Philharmonic and get an exclusive peek
behind the emerald curtain. The entire waterfront renewal project
was slated for completion in five years, but in the meantime, an
urban nightmare of ruin on an almost apocalyptic scale surrounded
this lone architectural jewel.

The perimeter fences were draped with tarps painted with an
artist's rendition of the "Future of Seattle," which depicted
stylized, futuristic high-rises of tinted glass and glinting steel,
nothing like the crumbling hulks that lay behind it. Tractors,
earthmovers, dump trucks, and a ten-story crane with a wrecking
ball lorded over buildings so old and dirty they appeared somehow
contagious. Trailer homes with the names of the various
construction companies stenciled onto their weathered façades
were stationed in parking lots of broken asphalt, from which waist-
high weeds proliferated. Smokestacks had long since grown cold
and stood like tombstones over the bodies that had once given
them fiery life. Roofs had fallen in sections, allowing the rain to
puddle inside and rot the wooden frames. Graffiti dominated soot-
stained red brickwork and concrete block walls. Broken glass and
trash littered the ground. The windows of the once proud factories
were either broken out or boarded over, and "Keep Out" signs
were posted on every flat surface. Mounds of fractured cement,
broken bricks, and cracked timber, heaped twenty feet high, rotted
where they had been felled while the process of hauling them away
moved at a snail's pace. It was no different than any other

abandoned industrial district, with the notable distinction that it reeked of fish guts.

"Fist time under?" Henley asked. Again with the smug grin.

Sturm nodded and returned her attention to the dark maw in the foundation of the demolished fish processing facility, where chunks of debris had been rolled aside to widen the makeshift opening.

"It's like a maze down there." Henley removed his cap and slicked back the water from his shaved scalp before donning it once more. "Until you've been under, you have no idea. These warehouses and factories were built more than a hundred years ago, back when things were made to last. Half of this basement stood up to the demolition, and most of these buildings along the waterfront are connected from when they used to share some kind of forced-air heating system. There have to be tens of thousands of square feet of tunnels and rooms for people to hide in down there."

Better get used to it, she thought. She'd be doing this each of the next ten nights, until after the fancy fundraiser dinner to celebrate the opening of the cultural center, named for the first female mayor of Seattle. Sturm imagined society's elite: drinking champagne, fluted glasses clinking, the clamor of superficial conversation, dapper tuxedos, glimmering jewels, shimmering gowns. Heaven forbid one of these poor homeless souls scurry out of the hell to which cruel life had damned them in hopes of scavenging the leftover pate and caviar.

"So, we doing this or what?" Henley asked.

"It's not going to collapse while we're in there, is it?" she asked as she ducked into the darkness. It was meant to sound flippant, but she heard the tone of worry in her own voice.

"I wouldn't wager a vital organ on it."

"You're supposed to say something a little more reassuring."

"How 'bout this? Keep your pepper spray handy. These rats don't like when you shine your light in their eyes."

Five steps in, Sturm had to drop to all fours and crawl. Concrete shards prodded her palms and bit into her knees. A stray lance of rusted rebar scraped her shoulder. Sometimes she absolutely hated this job. She had to remind herself that it was only temporary. Joining the force out of college had seemed like a good idea at the time. It paid well enough and she could work the third

shift, which left her free time during the day to pursue her Masters
Degree in Criminalistics from the University of Washington while
she earned the necessary practical law enforcement experience.
Now that she was within months of completing her internship at
the Washington State Patrol crime lab and she already had an
actual paying job lined up with the Crime Scene Response Team, a
partnership between the Crime Laboratory and Criminal
Investigation Divisions, she could finally see the light at the end of
the tunnel. Soon enough, she would be part of the CSRT, an elite
team of forensics experts who specialized in everything from
biochemistry to microanalysis and firearms to forgery, the cream
of the crop in the state of Washington, who were loaned out to
various law enforcement entities from the smallest rural sheriff's
department right up to the Federal Bureau of Investigation when
prompt resolution was of the essence. And then she could leave all
of this bureaucratic nonsense behind her.

It couldn't come soon enough, she thought as she wriggled
deeper into the darkness, which seemed immune to the glow of her
flashlight. If only her parents could see her now, the Queen of the
Ambrosia Apple Festival, crawling through a tunnel that reeked so
badly of piss and sweat that it overrode even the vile fishy aroma.
Had the loss of their orchard, after so many years of fighting
against the elements and infestations, the plummeting barrel prices,
and then finally the bank, not driven them to early graves, they
could have found themselves down here, among the lost souls she
now prepared to mercilessly roust.

Because it was her job.

"Not for much longer," she whispered. She reached the
terminus and maneuvered her body so that her feet were in front of
her in order to drop down into the sublevel.

Sturm eased deeper into the structure, sweeping her flashlight
beam slowly from side to side and across the brown puddles of
rainwater and urine on the cracked paving stones and bare earth.
The sheer tonnage of debris braced tenuously overhead on slanted
iron girders, warped wooden planks, and jagged sections of
concrete, through which the occasional pebble or stream of dirt
cascaded, weighed heavily on her mind. Bare bricks, exposed
wiring, and damp-rotted timber showed through the collapsed
sections of yellowed plaster on the walls. She passed leaning

doorways that barely offered enough space to squeeze into smaller rooms full of antique equipment with rusted pipes and cracked gauges. Empty liquor bottles had been smashed in the corners near piles of rumpled newspapers and threadbare blankets. Some of the walls were scored black with carbon where fires had been built, the smoke vented through natural channels in the rubble. The realization that people were actually living down here hit her like a fist to the gut.

So where were they all now and how would they react to her intrusion?

"They're like roaches," Henley said. "The moment you hit them with your light, they scuttle off and hide."

Sturm rounded on him.

"You refer to them as roaches or rats again, and I'll knock your teeth down your throat."

His face flushed red and the muscles in his jaw bulged. The weak aura of her flashlight beam left his eyes in shadow, but she could feel their glare like the lick flames.

She turned away before he could respond and headed deeper into the warren. He mumbled something from behind her about partners needing to have each other's backs. She again reminded herself that it was only a matter of time before she would be off the streets.

The smell intensified and she heard a whispering sound. She swung her beam toward the source as she passed through a crumbling brick orifice into the adjacent building. There was a heap of blankets and jackets against the wall to her right. They were ragged and dirty, and at first she thought they'd been abandoned, until she saw the filthy faces staring back at her.

Sturm froze. Her eyes met those of a little girl who couldn't have been more than eight or nine years old.

"All right, Morlocks," Henley bellowed. His voice reverberated in the confines. "Rise and shine. Gather your shit and hit the bricks. You have sixty seconds before I break out the pepper spray."

She watched in shock as more than a dozen men and women stood from the covers she had at first mistaken for refuse and shuffled off into the shadows. Her eyes tracked the young girl, who carried a naked plastic doll by the leg in one hand and rubbed sleep out of her lashes with the other, until she vanished through a dark channel in the wall, presumably to wander the streets until dawn or bed down on a park bench until she was again forced to move along.

Sturm stood in silence for a long moment before a smell she recognized far too well resolved from the comingling aromas of excrement and body odor.

"Keep moving or we'll be down here all night," Henley said.

"Give me a minute."

Sturm tilted her head, sniffed the air, then directed her flashlight toward the back corner to her left. She tromped over broken two-by-fours and cracked cement until she reached a mound of dirt and debris that had been swept up against the exposed bricks. Her approach disturbed the flies, which rose and swirled around her head in an insufferable buzzing cloud. Blackened flesh and gnawed bone showed through the furrows the rodents had carved to reach the source of the smell. She crouched and brushed away the detritus to reveal a face. The open mouth and eyes were packed with dirt, the facial wrinkles crisp with grime. The features were definitively female, the long gray hair tangled and knotted. Maggots squirmed through the flesh and bodily dissolution. She had to cover her mouth and nose against the powerful stench. Based on the level of decomposition, Sturm guessed the woman had been dead somewhere in the neighborhood of a week.

And these people had been living down here with her. In the same room. All this time.

Her heart ached at the realization that these men and women must have buried the woman. Had they done so out of respect, out of love, or simply to avoid being cast out of their home if the authorities ever found out?

"We find them like this from time to time," Henley said, his voice softer. Sturm glanced back at him and saw through the chink in his armor. "You have to steel yourself against it."

He turned and walked away. She heard a burst of static and his mumbled words as he called in their discovery.

A tear crept from the corner of her eye.

There was no way she could steel herself against something like…this.

No one should have to live like this. No one should have to end up down here, interred in an unmarked grave. Unwanted. Unremembered.

No one.

THREE

Altai Mountain Range
Siberia
2:26 p.m. NOVST
(1:26 a.m. PST)

Straps of yellow nylon flagged across the snow on the furious wind. Retired US Air Force Brigadier General Franklin Spears, now Chief Executive Officer of Phobos Biodefense, the global leader in threat assessment and countermeasure implementation for both the private sector and international government agencies, knelt and tugged on one of the straps until he encountered resistance, then started shoveling the snow away with his gloved hands. His men were mere shadows beside him through the sheeting ice crystals, which blew straight up the canyon on the gusting gales. Even the stands of pines clinging to the steep slopes offered precious little protection. The storm had been raging since before they even set out from Aktash, knowing full well what they would find. If they found anything at all. The last communication from his son's party had been more than six days ago now. Within forty-eight hours, he had assembled a rescue party and chartered a plane across the Pacific. Now, after nearly three days of searching, they had finally found sign of Nelson's passage.

The tent had been shredded and nearly buried under the accumulation. Had they arrived a day later, they might have walked right over it without knowing.

"Give me a hand with this!" he shouted.

Two of his men crouched beside him and helped pry the outer nylon and the inner polypropylene layers of the Arctic Oven tent from the snow to reveal a jumble of sleeping bags and camping gear. There was no sign of Nelson or the others. Their rucksacks were conspicuously absent.

"What's that?" the man to his right asked. Beneath their balaclavas, goggles, and fur-fringed hoods, it was impossible to tell one man from the next until he spoke. Rodney Poole, Phobos's chief Search and Detection Specialist, stripped off his gloves and chiseled at a frozen blotch on one of the Vaude Arctic sleeping bags. He melted it between his fingers and dabbed it on his tongue. His expression told Spears everything he needed to know.

"Over here!" Daniel Abrams, Spears's Threat Intelligence Solutions Specialist, called.

Spears could barely see the man's silhouette a dozen paces away through the blizzard. He rose and tromped across the crust to where Abrams dug at the snow. A blue hand, rimed with ice, stood above the ground as though crawling out of the grave. He threw himself down beside Abrams and frantically scooped aside mounds of powder and ice to expose the length of the arm, the shoulder, the back of the head and the torso. The jacket was crafted from animal hides stitched together with thick black twine like a medical examiner's sutures, the hood rimmed with what could only have been the fur of a husky. Tears of relief froze in Spears's lashes at the realization that this wasn't his son's body.

"Help me turn him over," Spears commanded. His son was still out there somewhere, quite possibly freezing to death at this very moment. They had no time to waste.

The frozen corpse made cracking sounds as they rolled it onto its back. The man's face was a block of ice, his eyes and mouth stuffed with snow. His broad face and high Asiatic cheekbones identified him as the native Kyrgyz guide his son's party had hired to lead them up Katun Valley to the foot of Mt. Belukha. What at first looked like a necklace of unrefined rubies poked out over the man's heavy-knit scarf, which Spears shoved out of the way. The crimson crystals weren't gemstones. He chipped away the blood until he could clearly see the wounds. They were sloppy and deep, the frozen edges demarcated by the ridges of teeth. Something had torn out this man's throat.

"What the hell could have done that?" Abrams said.

"Bear?" Cameron Bristow, a promising young field agent, said from behind them.

"A bear could have taken his whole damn neck in its mouth."

"You got a better idea?"

Spears jumped back to his feet.

"Keep looking!" he shouted.

He thought back to the last email he had received from his son, a single rushed paragraph sent almost as an afterthought to pacify an overprotective father.

After three days of waiting, it looks like the storm is finally breaking. We plan to climb the southwestern face at dawn. I can see you shaking your head from here. Quit worrying already, would you? You know me. I'm like Spider-Man up there.

Spears removed his field glasses from his rucksack and turned them upon the sheer face of the mountain. The blizzard made it nearly impossible to see, but he eventually found the dark orifice.

He prayed his son had made it that far, and that his party was merely holed up out of the elements, waiting for the storm to pass. It was the prayer of a desperate man, he knew. After six days, any food reserves would have been long since consumed and without their SubZero Mummy sleeping bags they would have been lucky to survive more than a single night.

Of course, that scenario was predicated upon the assumption that they had survived whatever attacked the camp.

Spears and his team needed to clear the area around the base camp as quickly as possible. Unless they found his son's remains nearby, they had a long and perilous climb ahead of them.

FOUR

Seattle, Washington
3:53 a.m. PST
(4:53 p.m. NOVST)

Elena Sturm leaned against the side of a brick building that had once been a shipping warehouse. From where she stood in the shadows, she watched the coroner's people drag the woman's body out of the hole in the rubble on a skiff. The rain made a dysrhythmic clapping sound on the body bag. There were no swirling cherries, no spotlights directed toward the orifice. No media crews jostled for the best shot of the men loading the remains into the van. Nary a single reporter hounded her for details. Not only had the woman lived and died in exile, but now they were sneaking off with her body like thieves in the night. As though her death meant no more than her life had.

Sturm felt a soul-deep sorrow as an ache in the marrow of her bones.

This was why she had nearly killed herself getting first through undergraduate, and then graduate school, why she worked these unholy hours so she could survive the unpaid internship with the Washington State Patrol, why she had wanted to be a criminalist in the first place. Everyone needed to be remembered. Everyone needed to have their story told.

Someone needed to speak for the dead.

She would always remember the look in her father's eyes when he told her they were losing the farm that had been in her family for more than a century, the tears that had shimmered in her mother's. How glassy they had looked when she buried them. The medical examiner had ruled her father's death a myocardial infarction, but no such simple explanation could describe how he had dropped dead in the orchard while trying to draw what little blood he could from the failing soil that would soon belong to an unsympathetic bank, which would rather let the acreage rot than allow a man to eke out his subsistence on it. Her mother had passed a year later at her aunt's house in Tacoma. Sturm didn't care what the official cause of death had been ruled. Her mother had wasted away from a broken heart and the lack of the will to persevere without her soulmate at her side. Meanwhile, their former homestead, where her great-grandfather had planted the first seeds, had gone feral and the house that had once contained only love and laughter had fallen into disrepair. The few apples that still grew were riddled with worms. Her parents were dead. And the only mark of their passing was a weather-beaten "Prime Acreage For Sale" sign staked at the edge of the property on the side of a road no one had any reason to drive.

It was a common tale and yet one that deserved to be told, regardless of whether or not anyone cared to listen. Not because of the callous government or the unfeeling bank. Not because of the injustice of it all, but because her parents had mattered.

If only to her.

The rear doors of the coroner's van slammed closed with the sound of twin gunshots that echoed across the forlorn waterfront, where once countless fishermen had earned their living from the sea. Before the advent of corporate fishing fleets, before day trading and the internet and men who made fortunes without producing tangible products or contributing to the welfare of society. She wondered how many of them, how many of their wives and children and grandchildren, now lived in the bowels beneath her feet. How many of them had she evicted from that warren so that none of the partygoers would have their fancy dinners ruined by the sight of that child with the one set of clothes and the filthy, naked doll?

The taillights of the van flared red. She watched as it bounced over the rutted earth toward where a lone officer held open the chain link fence at the sidewalk, in its bed, a nameless woman secreted away so that none of the politicos would have to give a second thought to her circumstances while dropping two grand on the plate of food that might have saved her life.

And then the van was gone.

Sturm sighed and lifted her face to the sky. The cold rain drummed on her closed eyelids and streamed down her cheeks.

She allowed it to wash over her until she could take it no more, but it wasn't enough to cleanse her. Not even close.

"You were the one who found the body," a deep voice said from directly behind her, startling her from her thoughts. It was a statement, not a question. She hadn't heard the man approach, not so much as the clap of a single footstep in a puddle or the squish of mud beneath transferred weight. She turned toward the source of the voice and found herself staring up into the face of a man she'd never seen before. The brim of his ball cap cast a shadow over his features. She could only see the outline of his granite jaw and the tip of his nose, but she could feel the weight of his unseen eyes appraising her. He was a good foot taller than she was, with broad shoulders that tested the strength of his navy blue windbreaker. She could only assume that the letters on the back of it matched those on the front of his hat.

"Since when does the FBI care about the death of a single indigent?" she asked.

"Officially, it doesn't. Not unless the mayor calls the governor, who in turn wakes up my SAC and demands that he send out the best agent he has." He gave a slight bow and she saw his sharp brown eyes, his dark bangs plastered to his forehead by the rain. "And voila...here I am. Special Agent Grey Porter, at your service."

She shook his proffered hand and introduced herself in return. So this was how the situation was going to play out. She suddenly felt sick to her stomach.

"You're here to make this inconvenient little problem go away."

"Quite the contrary, my dear. We're going to ID this woman with all due haste and make sure this kind of thing doesn't happen to anyone else so that the city can sleep easy at night."

"You mean so that no one gives a second thought to this taxpayer-funded deathtrap? A woman lost her life here. Those people living down there? They're human beings. Someone's children. Possibly spouses, parents—"

"Let's leave the squabbling to the politicians." Porter offered his most disarming smile. He couldn't have been out of his early thirties. "You and I still have a job to do."

"Tell me we aren't sweeping this under the rug."

"It's a politically sensitive situation, Layne." His use of the nickname only her father used infuriated her. "Sometimes things are simply outside of our control."

"Don't give me that crap." The words were out of her mouth before she knew they were coming. She visibly recoiled, but there was no taking them back now. She could only forge ahead. "If that had been the mayor's wife down there, the entire place would have been crawling with cops and reporters and you'd be able to hear the public outcry all the way from Vancouver."

He smiled. There was no condescension in it, only an element of what might have been sorrow. As quickly as it had appeared, it was gone.

"Look, there are two ways this can play out," he said. "She can end up in the city morgue, waiting endlessly for someone to come along and claim her remains, or we can do everything in our power to identify her and find someone who cares enough to give her the proper burial she deserves. Either way, it's already been decided way above either of our heads that she wasn't found here. Do you follow me?"

His eyes locked onto hers for so long that it made her uncomfortable. She was the first to look away.

"No one should have to die down there like that," she whispered.

"You do your job and no one else will."

Sturm was thankful for the rain, which masked the tears on her cheeks.

Not much longer now, she thought. And then maybe she could do something that might actually make a difference.

The weight of his hand settled upon her shoulder. When he spoke, his words were soft.

"You have to fight the battles you can win, Layne. Don't let them beat you. And don't let them change you. There will always be more battles."

She felt foolish for exposing her weakness to him, even worse for allowing him to console her. And in compromising her principles to play a game she wanted no part of, she felt a small portion of her soul die.

He removed his hand from her shoulder.

When she finally summoned the courage to turn around, he was gone.

Again, he hadn't made a sound.

FIVE

Altai Mountain Range
Siberia
8:12 p.m. NOVST
(7:12 a.m. PST)

The route up the mountain had been easy enough to follow, even under the darkness and the blizzard, thanks to the ice screws that had already been strategically placed for them. With every meter they ascended, Spears felt himself closing in on his son, which only served to amplify his dread. After scouring the region at the base and encountering no evidence of fallen climbers, he knew exactly what they would find in the cave.

His son and the rest of his party were dead.

He knew this on the instinctual level that only a father could. The blame was his to bear. When Nelson had announced the discovery of the skull fragments months ago…the look in his eyes, the excitement in his voice…Spears had finally understood that this was his son's life mission. Never in Nelson's largely pampered and unchallenged existence had he shown that kind of passion for anything. What kind of father would he be if he didn't do everything in his power to make his child's dreams come true? He had the resources and the connections. A few well-placed phone calls and the deal had been sealed. Perhaps the expeditionary team had been apprised of the conditions behind Nelson's appointment, but, as per the arrangement, Nelson had been none the wiser. The pure elation in his voice when he had called to share the news that he'd been selected to join the world's foremost experts on the expedition of a lifetime had been worth every penny. Not since his mother left them when he was barely ten years old had Spears heard his son that happy. And now Nelson was gone. There were no words to explain how he knew this. He just did. If he was going to have to carry the guilt with him for the rest of his life, then he needed to know why. What happened to his son up here on this mountain? That was the one question that would haunt him forever if he didn't learn the truth right here and now. And if he discovered that someone was to blame, he would spend his remaining days—and his not insignificant fortune—making sure that person was held accountable.

Once Spears and his men reached the cave, they donned their thermal/infrared night vision fusion goggles, which allowed them to clearly see the cavern around them and the heat signatures of any warm-blooded animals that crossed their path. Anything below eighty-one degrees Fahrenheit appeared in shades of black and midnight blue, while above that the scale ascended through lighter blues and purples to reds and oranges, and finally to the brilliant yellow of human body temperature. Everything above one-hundred-two degrees appeared solid white.

They found the first sign of Nelson's party near the back of the cave. A telltale diagonal spatter across a pyramid of skulls and the wall behind it. An arterial spurt. A puddle of blood was frozen on the stone floor and surrounded by sloppy smudges and palm prints. They followed a broad smear deep into a crevice, where it stopped at the mouth of a vertical shaft.

Spears unpacked his Colt IAR—a nine-pound, compact infantry automatic rifle—and slung the strap around his neck so that it hung against his chest.

"They dragged the body over here and just rolled it off the edge," Spears whispered.

"They?" Bristow said.

Spears nodded at the ground to his right, where a dozen partial, bloody footprints overlapped. They were faint, but the points of contact from the ball of the foot and the toes were distinct enough to conclude that the feet were bare. And definitely human.

"Cover me," Spears said.

He swung his legs down into the stone chute and started down the handholds. Every third rung, he glanced down to confirm there were no heat signatures waiting for him. It was a bottleneck, a prime spot for an ambush. As he descended, he tried to visualize what must have happened. To whom did the footprints belong, and why weren't they wearing shoes? Had the prints been made by whoever killed and dragged the body away, or by several people attempting to haul a wounded comrade to safety?

Spears found his answer at the bottom of the earthen tube. A starburst of blood marred the granite where the body impacted, spattering the ground and the walls. A diminishing smear led deeper into a large cavern that echoed with dripping water. Above him, the ceiling was fuchsia with bats hanging upside down and knifing between the stalactites. The fading footprints guided him to the center of the cavern, where they vanished altogether, leaving him only with the body's bloody trail, which was little more than a stroke from a nearly dry paintbrush.

His men clattered down the tube and hurried to catch up with him as quietly as they could. What little of their faces showed around their goggles in the ovular gap of their balaclavas glowed golden behind the deep blue cloud of their exhalations.

From the corner of his narrowed field of view, Spears saw the vague outline of what appeared to be the carcass of a bear, upon which several orange rats with flicking tails continued to feast. He didn't dare risk a better look for fear of losing the trail.

"There's more blood over here," Bristow whispered. "Whoever worked this guy over really did a number on him. Christ. There are even spatters on the stalactites."

"Bristow," Poole snapped. "A little restraint."

"Is there a body?" Spears asked, but he needn't have wasted his breath. Two more steps and the smears where the second set of remains had been dragged intersected his path at the opening of a crevice.

He pulled the IAR over his head, shouldered its short stock, and advanced in a shooter's stance. The passage narrowed to the point that he was forced to crouch. He moved slowly, watching for the first hint of body heat through the goggles as he neared the terminus. Stealthily placed footsteps joined his from behind. He detected the etchings on the walls from his peripheral vision, but refused to so much as glance away from his sights.

The tunnel opened into a larger room that felt at once disorienting. A mat of what at first looked like snow had drifted up against the far wall, and yet the air was stagnant and warm. There was no breeze to suggest access to the outside world. No, it wasn't snow. It was sand, clumped and crusted where it had aggregated with the blood. One section was positively black with it. How in the hell—?

Spears stopped dead in his tracks.

"I see them too," Poole whispered from behind him.

Spears waved his men around and to the left, while he moved to the right until they formed a half-circle around the dune.

Five dark blue plumes rose from various points in the sand like miniature smokestacks, barely warm enough to register in the thermal range. They rose in short bursts, then dissipated into the air. After another moment, they would rise again. They were rhythmic, although each cycled independent of the others.

Spears looked from Abrams to Poole to Bristow and back again, at the nearly identical clouds that bloomed through their masks. Something was down there. Buried in the sand. Something that was still breathing.

He imagined Nelson, buried alive. Unable to move. Terrified. Knowing with grim finality that he was going to die. What kind of monster would do such a thing to another human being? Rage boiled inside of him. Whoever was responsible for this would never again see the light of day.

"Get them out of there," Spears said through bared teeth.

He prayed his son was still alive down there, prayed for the first time in as long as he could remember.

A screeching sound from his right.

It was a sound he knew far too well. He had heard it in the cargo holds of aircraft carriers, in the rubble beneath bombed buildings where trapped men lay dying, in the tents that served as field morgues where the fallen were stacked like corded wood to be shipped back home.

He watched Abrams and Poole fall upon the sand and begin excavating the loose grains while Bristow covered their backs and the entrance to the cavern through which they had just passed for several beats before turning away and following the etched wall toward the sound. Another passage opened in the granite, at the far end of which he saw small orange shapes scurrying past the orifice and leaping up onto teeming columns of their ranks that reached all the way up out of sight. The riot of shrieks and squeals echoed down the tunnel, masking the sounds of digging behind him as he strode directly toward them, rifle at the ready.

The racket abruptly ceased when he reached the end of the passage. Hundreds of whiskered faces turned in his direction. They remained perfectly still, scrutinizing him as he walked toward them. The moment he entered the larger chamber, a shrill chorus of squeals erupted and they fled as one. A glowing orange flood poured outward from the center of the room and crashed against the arched walls. They scurried straight up what appeared to be thousands of alcoves, a massive honeycomb, and disappeared into the recesses. He felt them scurry over his boots and up his legs, but he didn't bat an eye. His sole focus was on the four bodies suspended by their ankles from the ceiling above a sticky, congealed pool of blood. He was only peripherally aware of the arcs of blood transecting the myriad alcoves and the grinning skulls leering down at him, of the tatters of fabric littering the floor, of the horrible stench of decomposition. The corpses had been hung so that their hands dangled several inches above the floor. What little skin remained was desiccated and leathery, the flesh stripped to the bone in sections. The buttocks and genitalia had been reduced to messes of macerated tissue. Only the hair remained to distinguish the four bodies, but it was enough. Spears would have recognized that unkempt blonde mane anywhere. He had spent the better part of the last decade fighting with his son to cut it.

His son.

Strung up by his heels.

Gutted and bled like a stag from a bough.

The implications struck him like a slap across the face. If these were the four members of the missing expedition, then—

"Fall back," he said in little more than a whisper. He wrenched his gaze from his son's remains and sprinted back down the passage. "Fall back!"

He heard a shout and the chatter of automatic gunfire.

All hell broke loose in a maelstrom of color.

*   *   *

Spears saw the white flashes of muzzle flare through the haze of dust at the end of the stone corridor. Shouts and screams were punctuated by the triple-tap clapping of the IARs. His own weapon seated against his shoulder, he tried to decipher the chaos as he burst into the chamber. Orange rats scurried at the periphery of the dune, squalling as they darted away from the melee. His men were discernible by their darker coloration, their body heat contained by their gear, save for the yellow ovals of their faces. The other bodies in the room stood apart, lithe gold forms with white cores in their skulls, chests, and groins. They darted away from the bullets with acrobatic skill: lunging, diving, ducking, crouching, moving with such speed and agility that they were mere streaks of light.

Spears heard the whir of a carbine and knew one of his men was in trouble.

Bristow shouted something unintelligible as he cast aside his clip and tried to load another.

A golden blur was upon him before Spears could even sight it down and pull the trigger. Bristow screamed and hit the ground on his backpack, his assailant on his chest, its arms rising and falling like striking adders. It buried its face in the crook of his neck, silencing his cries. A pulsing arc of flame-yellow spurted from Bristow's throat when the golden form jerked its head away and swiveled to face Spears.

He squeezed the trigger and the back of its head exploded like a firecracker, painting the wall behind it with spatters that quickly faded through the spectrum of colors.

"There're too many of them!" Abrams yelled. He swiveled to fire to his left and then back to his right in an effort to pin his attackers to the rear wall. Spears counted four more of them, but there was no way of knowing how many more of them there might be inside the mountain. "We can't hold them off forever in here!"

One of them was thrown backward, a white ribbon unspooling from its shoulder. It barely hit the ground before it was back on its feet again, cradling its arm.

Spears stumbled into a pit in the sand where one of them had been hiding and fell to his knees. He swept his rifle across the room to buy enough time to right himself. The bullets strafed the granite with a showcase of sparks. One of the bodies was lifted into the air. It struck the wall and collapsed to its chest. This one made no effort to rise.

A carbine whirred.

"Cover me!" Poole shouted.

He dropped to one knee in an effort to quickly change his clip, but they were on him before Spears could bring his rifle to bear on them.

Poole shrieked as he was driven into the sand with two of them on top of him.

Spears and Abrams fired as one. The air filled with blood in explosions of sunspots and snowflakes. The bodies thrashed and convulsed, dancing in the crossfire, before finally lying still.

"Jesus Christ!" Abrams shouted.

Spears whirled to his right. The lone remaining figure blew past in a blur. He fired a fusillade that peppered the wall behind it as the shape hurtled past him. It disappeared into the passage leading to his son's remains. By the time Spears reached the tunnel, only darkness waited.

Half of his team was dead. His son was dead. The hell if he was going to allow one of them to escape.

"They just came up out of the sand." Abrams's voice cracked when he spoke. "We were digging and all of a sudden…they just…just—"

Spears grabbed Abrams by the straps of his backpack and slammed him against the stone wall.

"Snap out of it, for God's sake! There's still one more out there!"

"And Lord only knows how many others."

Spears shoved him again, turned away, and started down the tunnel.

Fine. If he had to do this by himself, then so be it.

There was no sign of color in the domed cavern. The only source of movement was the hanging bodies, which slowly twirled and shivered back into place, undoubtedly disturbed by the gold shape that had charged through them on its way to the egress on the opposite side of the chamber. Spears blew past his son's corpse and jogged down the corridor, which constricted as it wound to the right down a steepening slope. He barely identified the pitfall in time to keep from plummeting into the stone chute.

He fired a trio of shots down into the darkness to buy himself the time and space to descend, then scurried down another series of smooth handholds. Twenty meters down, he turned from the wall and stepped into a cavern choked by odd geological formations.

The ceiling was barely five feet above his head and positively rippled with bats. The stalactites and stalagmites nearly met, as though he were in some great fanged mouth as it prepared to close. The echo of dripping condensation hinted at standing water ahead and to his right. He wound a circuitous route through what felt like a petrified forest, glancing from one side to the other, prepared to squeeze the trigger at the first sign of a heat signature.

Abrams made a sound like a clap of thunder when he dropped to the ground at the bottom of the ladder.

Spears didn't risk a glance back over his shoulder. With the speed his adversary had demonstrated, he needed to stay focused on what lay ahead of him. A fuchsia glow drew him forward. It expanded across the floor like an oil spill.

He splashed down into ankle-deep water so warm he could feel the heat through his boots. The ground grew slicker with each step until he was in past his knees. A gentle current tugged at his legs, but he couldn't tell exactly where the water flowed. The pool was maybe ten meters wide and appeared to become shallower to the sides. The pinkish glare skewed his perception of the surrounding darkness. When he eased out of the water onto the far bank, it took a moment for the aperture of the goggles to rationalize the faint spatters on the cavern floor. He couched and examined them as they cooled from midnight blue to black.

The question mark shape of the ball of a foot and the heel.

The smudges from the toes.

He followed the direction in which they led with his eyes, then lunged to his feet and into a full sprint, ducking and weaving through the stone slalom, unable to clearly see more than two strides ahead of him.

Splashing water behind him confirmed that he hadn't lost Abrams.

The roof lowered abruptly, grazing the top of his head and knocking him to his knees. He was going to have to crawl from here and hope the quarters didn't grow tighter. The footprints were no longer visible. His quarry knew these caves far better than he did. If he had guessed the direction of its flight wrong, it could potentially elude them forever.

A flash of gold in his peripheral vision to the right.

By the time he turned his head, it was gone.

He stared into a tunnel barely wider than the mouth of a fox's den. The heat signature had definitely come from inside there. Without a second thought, he shed his backpack and shimmied in after it, pushing his weapon across the ground ahead of him. If he didn't hurry, his adversary would have ample time to turn the tables on him. He dragged himself forward with his elbows and shoved off the walls with his toes as fast as he could until he finally crawled out into another cave.

The walls glittered with quartz. The jagged ceiling was so low that he couldn't stand fully erect. He eased onward more cautiously now, sweeping his rifle from left to right and back again, his finger tight on the trigger. Stone outcroppings created natural hiding places he was easily able to clear with his thermal vision.

Scraping sounds behind him announced Abrams's arrival. The nearly silent footsteps told him that Abrams had read the situation exactly as he had. They had their quarry cornered. There was nowhere left for it to run. Abrams would guard his rear in case it somehow got past him, but the dénouement was all his.

The rear wall drew contrast in shades of blue and black. For a second, he feared there might have been a tunnel he missed, until he saw the golden form cowering in a small recess at the foot of the wall, its hands over its face and its knees tucked protectively against its chest as though it could somehow hide behind them.

Spears pointed the barrel of his rifle directly at its head. He wanted to see the expression on its face when he pulled the trigger, when it knew with complete certainty that it was going to die. He wanted to memorize its expression—the terror, the comprehension—so that he would always have an image to replace the one frozen onto his son's lifeless face when it arose unbidden from his subconscious.

"Lower your hands," Spears growled through bared teeth. "I want you to see this coming."

It pressed itself harder against the wall, as though in an attempt to become one with the granite. Its slender legs trembled, the muscles rippling like the hind quarters of a beaten dog.

"Look at me, damn it!"

It tucked its face behind its shoulder and swatted blindly at him with one hand. Its palm was small, the fingers disproportionately long and capped with talons.

Abrams's hesitant footsteps scuffed behind him.

"Move your hands and look at me!"

Spears reached for its wrists and it kicked him solidly in the shin. He stepped to his right and it kicked him again. Another grab for its wrist and it jerked its arm away. It slashed at him again and he glimpsed the golden outline of its eyes, of its shivering irises.

It could obviously see him, too.

"Grab its arms," Spears said.

Abrams stepped around him and knelt in front of the creature. He grappled with its wrists until he finally secured his grip, wrenched them away from its head, and turned his face away so he wouldn't be spattered by the blowback. Spears screwed the barrel of his rifle into its right eye and clearly saw its face for the first time.

"Jesus," he whispered.

He dropped his weapon and sat down hard on the cold stone floor.

There were some lines never meant to be crossed.

"What are we supposed to do now?" Abrams whispered.

It rounded on him and bared a set of teeth far too large for its mouth.

"I…" Spears started, but the truth was that he simply didn't know.

The creature turned and snapped at him like a rabid dog, exposing long canines that tapered to sharp points.

SIX

Seattle, Washington
Sunday, October 14th
2:53 a.m. PST
(3:53 p.m. NOVST)

Sturm felt detached from her surroundings, as though she were a mere passenger trapped inside someone else's body. She had thought that after the first few nights of merciless rousting, the men, women, and children who dwelled in these dark warrens would see the futility of returning and find their way to one of the downtown shelters, and yet, night after night, they came back. It wasn't for a complete lack of options, she now understood, but because this was their home, decrepit and dangerous though it may be. Which made it all the more soul-crushing to have to weave through this maze, shining her light into their semi-conscious faces and telling them to hit the bricks. Where they went from here, she had no idea. She never saw them go and by the time she reached the surface under the cloud-shrouded moon, they had blended into the scenery as though possessing the power of invisibility, vanishing in plain sight. She felt as though a part of her died every time she came down here, and prayed that those who resided in this dank darkness were immune to that sensation, for otherwise by now they would surely be dead inside. The prospect of a world without hope brought a tear to her eye. For not the first time, she clutched her badge in her fist, the edges of the metal biting into her palm, and fought the urge to hurl it to the ground and stomp it flat like tinfoil, but there would always be others to take her place, others who would take pleasure in throwing these poor miscreants out into the moonlight by the scruffs of their necks and kicking them in their rear ends for good measure, just to get them walking toward a city unsympathetic to their plight, a city where people pretended not to see them for fear that their worst nightmares would be reflected back at them from hollow eyes devoid of life. All while slurping their six-dollar lattes and managing their Facebook profiles on their iPhones.

Sturm wondered where these people would go when the wharf reclamation project ratcheted into high gear and there were no underground tunnels left to call their own. And how long they would last without even a crumbling roof over their heads.

She imagined the young girl with the filthy face she had seen that first night down here. The girl must have dropped the doll, which had seemed so precious to her. Sturm had found it the following night, just laying there in the dirt. Her first thought had been to pick it up and try to return it to the girl, but she knew she would never track her down, no matter how hard she tried. So she had left it where it was, hoping that the little girl would be able to find it should she ever need it. And each time Sturm passed it, the doll reminded her that maybe the world wasn't quite as bad as she thought it was.

Red eyes flashed in her light from high up on the wall where a brazen rat watched her through a gap in the bricks. It showed no fear, only the whisker-twitching hunger of the kind of predator responsible for the infected bites she had seen on the bare hands and faces of those she drove ahead of her like cattle.

She hurled a chunk of concrete that chased it back into the wall with a squeal. It would come back, she knew, and with reinforcements. She tried not to ruminate over the fact that the mayor was less concerned about the disease-infested vermin than the homeless down here.

By now, she could navigate the warren blindfolded. There were still countless passages branching into fallen sublevels— accessible only by worming on one's chest—that she had yet to explore, but she could fly through the main corridors like a bee through a hive. Her vision had acclimated to the darkness to the degree that her flashlight was often more of a hindrance than a help. She knew through which crumbling orifices to crawl to pass from one building to the next, which forks to follow based on the texture of the ground underfoot, and which rooms to avoid by smell. She often heard the disembodied sound of someone softly crying, but never quite managed to isolate its source in the pitch black. She no longer flinched or covered her head when dirt and pebbles suddenly rained from the ruins above her or the ancient timber cracked with the sound of an M-80. A part of her almost felt as though the collapse of the ceiling would be a relief and wondered if that was the thought these people clung to as they bedded down to sleep under their blankets of newspapers and refuse.

That was one thing for which to be grateful. At least they hadn't encountered any more bodies, although Lord only knew how many more were down here, buried in the earth and concrete dust, their bones picked clean by the armies of rodents. The woman they had so unceremoniously whisked away a week ago was still filed away as a Jane Doe in a refrigerated drawer, waiting for someone who would never come to claim her body and memorialize it with a tombstone bearing a name that no one seemed to know. Sturm feared she would be the only one standing in the rain beside the open hole in a potter's field when they lowered her plain pine casket into the ground and dozed the mud back over her.

Not much longer now, she continued to assure herself, but the words lacked conviction. What she had seen down here had changed her. She couldn't fathom the possibility that she could move on with her life and just forget that a separate world existed right under her feet, a world apart, a world without hope.

Sturm tripped and fell forward. She barely caught herself on a rotting joist that speared her palm with splinters. She cursed and swung her light around to see a pair of boots, the leather eaten away, the laces long since deteriorated. They moved and the man who wore them rose from the shadows. She glimpsed a leathered face, stretched and wrinkled by the sea, lips so chapped the skin had peeled halfway down to the chin, and a pair of black eyes resigned to the fact that there would be no more sleep this night.

"I'm sorry," she whispered.

The man grunted and shuffled away from her. The other three shapeless forms she had mistaken for heaps of garbage, thanks to the black plastic bags they wore, followed him without a sound.

Sturm stood there, picking at the slivers in her hand, until their silhouettes merged with the darkness. Her shoulders shuddered and her legs trembled. She leaned against the wall and covered her face to hide her tears.

The two-way transceiver clipped to her shoulder crackled and Henley's voice echoed in the confines.

"You almost done back there? I'm exiting the processing plant now. I was thinking...maybe if we push it, we could get out of here in time to hit Denny's before we have to resume our regular patrol."

Sturm sniffed and wiped her nose with the back of her trembling hand. She tried to modulate the tremor in her voice when she pressed the button and spoke.

"I'm right behind you."

She stumbled onward, weaving through the rubble.

The disembodied sound of crying haunted her, echoing from both ahead of her and behind her in the corridor, from the rooms filled with broken machinery and garbage, from inside the walls where the rats nested in the dust, from the recesses above her in the demolished building.

And she realized that the sound was coming from her.

SEVEN

Seattle, Washington
11:53 p.m. PST

Spears leaned back into the leather embrace of the Lincoln Town Car's rear seat and stared out the window toward the eternal Pacific. The driver allowed time to pass in silence, and hadn't said so much as a single word since picking him up directly on the tarmac at Sea-Tac. Never once did his eyes stray to his passenger in the rear view mirror. He understood his job, and left Spears alone with his thoughts until called upon to speak. At this point, Spears was too exhausted to communicate with more than grunts and nods anyway. For the first time in his life, he truly felt his age. It was as though in accepting the loss of his son, he had relaxed his stranglehold on life's throat. There wasn't an inch of his body that didn't ache or hurt or throb, but the physical pain was nothing compared to the emotional. It felt like a fist squeezed his heart every time it beat, willing it to stop, while another twisted fingers into his guts. His mind played a flickering reel-to-reel of disjointed images, of his son as a boy interrupted by dark still-lifes of his carcass as a man, strung up by his heels like a slaughtered cow. He remembered how cold Nelson's skin had been, how its texture had been all wrong, as he slowly lowered his son to the floor and cradled him in his lap, stroking his desiccated hair, burying his face into the crook of his son's neck and braying in grief and anguish. Abrams had left him to his misery while he cut down the rest of Nelson's party and stacked their corpses off to the side of the cavern. By the time Spears had been able to pull himself away from the boy he had loved more than life itself, Poole and Bristow had been added to the pile, while on the other side of the chamber were the pale, naked carcasses of the monsters that had killed them. So great was his rage that he dropped his son's head from lap with the sound of clattering teeth, stormed over to where they lay, and fired his rifle at their remains until his clip ran dry. He remembered his war cry echoing into oblivion, the rifle falling from his hands, and collapsing to his knees in the spatters of cold blood and chunks of flesh until Abrams eventually roused him from his stupor.

"What do you want to do with it?"

Spears had looked across the room to where the creature slumped, hogtied with climbing ropes, against the far wall beneath the almost sentient gaze of its ancestors. It wore a mask of dried blood from the gash across its forehead where the blow from the butt of Abrams's rifle had knocked it unconscious. Its eyes blinked sporadically against the blood running through its eyebrows and the disorienting effects of the concussion it was no doubt experiencing. It breathed through the blood in its sinuses with a high-pitched wheezing sound. Each inspiration was an effort that required opening its mouth wide enough to display its long canines.

More than anything, Spears wanted to run across the cave and stomp its skull flat with his cleated boots, but even through his fury he recognized the potential of what he had. This was the species his son had set out to find, an evolutionary offshoot that had somehow managed to survive in complete isolation since before recorded history began; a species like man, and yet diametrically opposed. Here was a species that had adapted the ability to see in the dark, a species bred to kill without advanced weaponry, a species faster and more agile than its more cumbersome cousins. There were certain factions that would undoubtedly love to crack the secret of these traits, and agencies that would pay any price to rummage around in its DNA. There was a fortune contained inside its diminutive form, but money was inconsequential when it came to the future he envisioned, where battles were fought by soldiers given every possible advantage rather than being thrown to the wolves. He imagined men crawling through the dark caves of Afghanistan, tracking the terrorists where they hid, and ensuring that there would never be another cowardly attack on American soil. He had seen a ray of hope through this creature's amazing eyes where before there had been only despair. More importantly, he recognized that his son's life hadn't been in vain. It was through his sacrifice that the lives of countless Americans would be saved, soldiers and civilians alike.

Spears allowed his eyes to close and listened to the droning buzz of the tires on the wet asphalt.

They had navigated a series of passages that eventually led them down through the granite heart of Mt. Belukha to a tunnel barely large enough to crawl through. It opened to the outside world no more than two hundred meters from the remnants of his son's campsite. They had labored for more than two days to haul all ten corpses out of the mountain and to a point where they could be extracted by helicopter. Even then it had taken two trips to ferry their cargo back down to Aktash. The challenge hadn't necessarily been in transporting the sheer volume of corpses, but in the requisite discretion involved with handling a living monster they had no choice but to keep bound and gagged. It had already bitten Abrams on the trapezius muscle beside his neck with sufficient ferocity to require more than a dozen haphazard field sutures. Despite Spears's best efforts, the wound had continued to bleed clear up until the two of them had parted ways thirty-six hours ago now. Considering the almost watery consistency of the seepage, Spears theorized that the creature's saliva must contain some form of anticoagulant. He was anxious to test that theory when it eventually arrived at the Phobos corporate headquarters, where even now his men were working night and day to prepare the proper holding facility and equipping various labs for the prominent scientists they had managed to lure from private institutions around the globe.

Spears had arrived in Magadan, a port town in the Magadanskaya Oblast province on the Okhotskoye Sea, a half-day ahead of Abrams, who had traveled by ground with their cargo in the back of a non-descript panel truck. He had arranged for their trans-Pacific crossing with the captain of the *Pacific Scourge*—a seventy-meter fish-processing factory ship bound for Orcas Island in the San Juan Archipelago off the northwestern coast of Washington—who had eagerly agreed to keep the secrets of his new passengers, both the living and the dead, in exchange for a boatload of cash. The risks involved with chartering an international flight had simply been too great. Unloading a stack of bodies on the tarmac of an airport of any size would undoubtedly raise an eyebrow or two, but they could easily be transferred in unmarked containers from the ship to the bed of a truck on a remote island under the cover of night. Worst case scenario, it would cost him a couple grand to convince a customs agent to look the other way.

At this very moment, the *Scourge* was steaming through the Northeast Pacific Basin on its way to an industrial dock in a largely anonymous chain of islands. In the meantime, there were still preparations to be made. He needed to tend to the accommodations for the creature and then for the corpses, which would be logged into the cold storage facility that had damn well better be ready when he reached headquarters. Once everything was in place, he could begin making covert inquiries with his connections at the Department of Defense.

But first and foremost, he needed to make the arrangements to lay his son to rest.

Only then would he be able to focus on the task at hand.

Spears allowed a single tear to roll from the corner of his eye. He wiped it away and stared back out the window to the west, where somewhere out there, the future of modern warfare drew inexorably closer on the cold black sea.

EIGHT

Pacific Ocean
128 km West-Northwest of the Washington Coast
Monday, October 15th
12:02 a.m. PST

"I don't like this," Nate Dingman said. Even though Alvaro Ruiz was only an arm's reach away, he had to shout to be heard over the sheeting rain and the waves crashing against the bow. A curtain of seawater fired up over the gunwale, dousing his useless slicker. Shin-deep water raced across the deck, tugging at his rubber boots before funneling through the scuppers. He took a drag from the cigarette he held by the filter inside a plastic Pepsi bottle to keep it dry. "We both know there's something wrong with that guy."

He glanced back over his shoulder toward where the stranger they had mysteriously picked up in Magadan leaned over the rail and emptied his guts into the sea.

"Captain say we no ask questions." Ruiz's eyes ticked up toward the wheelhouse, where Dale Hargrove, the Master of the Ship, was silhouetted behind the rain-beaded glass by the lights from the bridge. "He say we to stay the hell away from him or we no get paid."

"Oh, he'll pay us all right. We haven't spent the last four months down there up to our eyeballs in guts for nothing. And if he wants us to keep our mouths shut, then he'd better give us a cut of whatever that guy's paying him. You know damn well that anything he's doing down there in the hold can't be legal."

"I no want nothing to do with it. Captain doing something illegal? I say fine. Just give me my money and get me off this boat."

Dingman shook his head and pulled one last lungful of smoke before a wave swept over the bow with a *boom* and he had to drop the bottle and grab onto the rail of the staircase leading up to their cramped quarters on the Shelterdeck. The stranger clung to the gunwale and barely managed to keep from being ripped from his feet. He appeared to lack even the strength to keep himself upright. Something was definitely wrong with him. He looked like he was more than just seasick. For all any of them knew, he could have one of those crazy African monkey-fucker diseases that eat a man alive from the inside out. Dingman wanted no part of it. Whatever the guy was paying the captain wasn't enough to justify getting all of them killed, even if he did decide to throw a couple bucks their way. And that was a *big* if. He couldn't help but notice that Hargrove avoided the guy like he had the plague, as though he knew something that the rest of them didn't. Not once had the captain—or any of them for that matter—gone down into the hold where a new padlock had been installed on the smallest of the three freezer units and everything in dry storage had been cleared out for the man, who generally stayed locked inside with whatever the hell he was smuggling, and Dingman was certain that that was exactly what he was doing. He'd heard about everything possible being smuggled out of the former Soviet Union, from arms to drugs to whores. After four months working shoulder-to-shoulder with nothing but hairy, sweaty men reeking of chum and covered with scales and entrails, the prospect of a little bit of Bolshevik tail was more than enticing. Of course, if they were carrying whatever had made that guy so sick…

"You no do nothing stupid," Ruiz said. His dark eyes locked on Dingman's beneath the cowl of his slicker. "We almost home now. We get money and we no look back."

He clapped Dingman on the shoulder and ducked back into the main corridor.

Ruiz was right, no doubt, but Dingman couldn't bring himself to clamber back up to the cabins or the mess, where the men who weren't agitated by the liquor were agitated by something else. You could wring the tension from the air. Every man was convinced that his wife or his girlfriend had been cheating on him the whole time he was away, that his children were now calling someone else daddy, that there would be a process server waiting on the dock to serve him with whatever warrant he had initially enlisted to avoid, or any of the millions of piddly-dick concerns that could turn an angry drunk into a violent brute. No way. He wasn't going back up there anytime soon. Not until the majority of them were passed out in a communal puddle of vomit. Besides, as much as he looked forward to putting back out to sea on this floating deathtrap eight months from now, perhaps there might be an opportunity to score enough cash on the side to make it so that he never had to set foot on this godforsaken vessel ever again.

He glanced at the man puking over the rail from the corner of his eye one last time before ducking into the ship and sliding across the wet floor to the steel stairs leading down into the hold. Whatever was down there, he wanted his rightful share.

Dingman rounded the landing and recoiled from the stench of rotting entrails. It was a scent he would never get used to, no matter how much time he spent down here. And no amount of astringent or scrubbing would ever be able to scour it away.

He passed the processing floor on the left, where tons of fish were dropped through the trapdoor on the bow to be gutted and scaled before being wheeled across the corridor to the packing room on the right where they were bundled and packaged for frozen storage. Both rooms were generally staffed twenty-four hours a day by three shifts of men who could barely be heard shouting over the clanging and grinding of machinery, but as their tour was complete and they were on their way home, the facilities were dark, unmanned, and about as clean as they would ever be.

A row of light bulbs in glass and aluminum cages guided him deeper into the bowels of the ship toward the engine room. He passed the main frozen holds to either side, their doors and temperature gauges rimed with frost as the interiors defrosted, before he reached the smaller unit with its shiny padlock. A quick tug confirmed it was locked. Across the hallway was dry storage, where their initial food supply had dwindled to the point that the cereal and potato flakes and flour and grains could be consolidated onto a few shelves.

He peered down the corridor, to where a forest of pipes pumped oil, fuel, and bilge throughout the vessel and a single engineer undoubtedly dozed at the console. There was no sign of movement. A glance over his shoulder confirmed that no one had followed him down from the main deck. He drew a deep breath and gave the handle a solid twist.

It turned easily in his hand.

He leaned his shoulder against the door and tried to slow his pounding heartbeat as he checked the hallway one last time, then ducked inside and silently closed the door behind him. The room was pitch-black. There were no porthole windows. The humid air was stale and reeked of sweat, sickness, and excrement. He involuntarily gagged and clapped his hand over his mouth. The smell was far worse than anything the processing floor had to offer under its worst conditions, and there had been times when he was knee-deep in guts. By the time he found the light switch on the wall, he wasn't certain he wanted to see what was in there anymore. He heard a shuffling sound, a metallic clang, and what he could have sworn was wet, heavy breathing.

There was someone in here with him.

For the briefest of moments, his nerves got the better of him and he debated just slipping back out into the corridor and making a break for it, but after several slow breaths, he mustered his courage and flipped the switch.

A lone bulb bloomed from the ceiling, casting a brass glare over the room, creating more shadows than it exposed. The wire racks along the wall to the left and against the port hull had been stripped bare, save for the haphazard mounds of the man's belongings: soiled clothes, an unzipped rucksack, a soft briefcase overflowing with printouts, a laptop computer connected to some sort of satellite communications setup, jugs of water, and empty packets of freeze dried rations. A rumpled arctic sleeping bag had been kicked to the side. A mop bucket sat in the corner, its sides spattered with dried blood and vomit. The mop was crusted in a congealed puddle beside it.

"Jesus Christ," Dingman whispered. What in the name of God was wrong with this guy?

At the sound of his voice, chaos erupted around the corner to his right, where the crates of food had once been stacked floor-to-ceiling and unloaded five units at a time. Banging, clanging, thrashing. He held his breath and waited, mentally preparing himself for whatever was back there to come charging right at him. He could positively feel the germs and diseases crawling on his skin. Whatever the man was paying the captain definitely wasn't worth this. He could keep the money and shove it straight up his ass for all Dingman cared. Right now, all he wanted was to get the hell out of there and pray he hadn't been infected by whatever sickness—

A whimpering sound from around the corner.

It sounded like… No, it couldn't be… Could it?

He was just about to turn around and head for the door when the whimpering metamorphosed into the sound of someone softly crying.

He stepped forward to the edge of the wall and peeked around the corner. There was an iron cage against the back wall, bracketed to the hull with shiny new bolts. It couldn't have been more than three feet tall, four feet wide, and roughly half that deep, like the kind of cage they used to transport tranquilized wild animals. A shape was slumped in the corner under a tattered blanket. Beside it rested a dented tin food tray smeared with blood. There were piles of feces in the opposite corner. The ammonia from the copious amounts of dried urine on the walls and the floor of the cage made his eyes water.

The shape shifted and he caught twin circular reflections from a pair of eyes.

The crying grew louder and more desperate. In one swift motion, the blanket was cast aside and the occupant of the cage hurled itself forward against the bars. Its small hands curled around the rusted iron. The skin was so pale it was almost translucent. He could see the veins in the wrists, leading up the slender arms to where the form leaned forward from the shadows and into the wan light. Its face was bruised and crusted with blood, and its pinkish irises positively shivered in terror. It released a sob that hit him in the pit of his stomach. It had been stripped, shaved, and caged like a beast. Smuggling drugs or weapons or whores was one thing, but this… The depths of human depravity knew no bounds.

Screw this! He was getting it out of there and he was going straight to the captain. If that son of a bitch knew what he was transporting down here, then he was going to have to answer to all of his men. This crew might have been comprised of individuals of questionable moral character, arguably more criminal than not, but none of them, to a man, would stand by and allow this kind of thing to happen right under their noses.

Its eyes locked on his and he felt sorrow beyond anything he had ever experienced.

Damn the consequences. This ended right here and now.

The cage door was secured by a keyed latch. He spun around and searched the shelves. He shook the contents of the backpack and the briefcase onto the floor, but the key wasn't there either.

It continued to weep, its tears shimmering on its pale cheeks.

"Where's the key?" Dingman snapped.

It cringed at the sound of his voice and scurried into the back corner of the cage. It buried itself in the blanket and continued to sob.

"Damn it!" He spun in a circle, searching the room for any sign of the key. "Where the hell—?"

He froze when he heard the hollow echo of footsteps in the hallway, one louder than the other, a staggering gait. Whoever was out there walked with a pronounced limp, as though he were injured...or sick.

Dingman instinctively dashed for the entryway and killed the light. The door opened outward, so there was no way of hiding behind it. If he waited until the approaching footsteps halted on the other side, he could throw his shoulder into it, stun the man on the other side, and make a break for it. He could probably make it to one of the stairwells in the engine room and disappear into the ship, but he risked the possibility that the man would be able to identify him, or worse, put a bullet between his shoulder blades while he ran. Neither option helped the occupant of the cage. His decision was made for him when the footsteps stopped a mere foot away and the handle of the door rattled.

He ducked back around the corner and pressed his back to the wall. The man wouldn't be able to see him until he was all the way in the storage room and within striking distance.

The cage rocked back and forth to his right, raising a deafening ruckus, as its prisoner repeatedly hurled itself against the bars.

A wash of light flooded across the floor when the hallway door opened.

Dingman held his breath and balled his hands into fists.

A shadow crossed through the light a heartbeat before the overhead bulb came on.

There was a shriek from the cage and the man slammed the door shut before anyone outside might hear.

"Enough!" the man shouted. "Someone's going to hear you, and then what are we supposed to—?"

Dingman lunged at the man the moment he stepped around the corner. He caught a glimpse of blood on the man's face, running from his nose and from the corners of his mouth, draining from the crimson sclera and the corners of his eyes. He squared his shoulder to the man's chest and drove him backward against the shelves. The aluminum rack broke away from the wall and the laptop careened to the floor with a crash. He felt warmth drip onto the back of his neck and trickle under his collar. The man grunted and rained blows down on Dingman's back as he tried to slip out of his grasp. The efforts were weak and uncoordinated. Dingman pivoted and lifted, cleaving the man from his feet and swinging him to the side. He slammed the man to the floor with a shoulder to the gut that knocked the wind out of him, and leapt up to his knees before the man could catch his breath. Two quick blows to the man's jaw and he was out cold.

The shadow in the cage ceased screaming and crawled closer to the bars. Its eyes were so wide that Dingman was reminded of a Precious Moments figurine, so innocent, so helpless.

He tried not the think about the potentially infected blood on his knuckles and spattered on his face as he rifled through the man's pockets, first in his wet jacket, then in his pants, where he found a ring of keys. One was offset from the others on a smaller ring of its own. He scrabbled across the floor and jammed the key into the lock. It slid into place with a click.

The man moaned behind him. He was coming around faster than Dingman expected.

He looked into those wide eyes as he turned the key in the lock. There was a flash of comprehension in its face and the corners of its lips curled into the ghost of a smile.

"What are you…doing?" the man sputtered through a mouthful of blood. "Don't—"

The lock disengaged with a resounding *snick* and the small gate sprung outward.

"No!" the man yelled.

Something changed in those innocent eyes. Gone were the fear and the innocence, replaced by something frightening, something feral, something almost…predatory. Its lips peeled back to reveal sharp teeth and a pair of fangs so long they nearly pierced the lower gums.

"Oh, shit."

"What have you done?" the man shouted. "Hurry! Close it! For Christ's sake, close the goddamn cage!"

The barred door flew open and struck Dingman in the face, knocking him backward.

It was upon him before he could even draw the breath to scream.

NINE

Pacific Ocean
106 km West-Northwest of the Washington Coast
9:49 p.m. PST

Russ Tarver secured the Zodiac to the stern of the *Pacific Scourge* and scaled the ladder up to the deck. The dark factory ship canted from side to side at the mercy of the waves. Three stories loomed over him, the upper platforms empty, the windows vacant. The pilothouse was capped with a satellite tower nearly the size of an oil derrick. A gust of wind pelted him with a mixture of sleet and raindrops the size of dimes, forcing him to duck his head and close his left eye. His bald head was already soaked beneath his stocking cap and rivulets of ice-water coursed through his thick black brows and beard. He heard footsteps clatter up the ladder behind him even over the scream of the wind and the deluge. Jerry Worrell caught up with him, his slicker seemingly made of fluid. His dark eyes and even darker beard were the only parts of him visible beneath his heavy-weight cowl.

"So what now?" Jerry asked. He had to shout to be heard over the clamor of the storm.

Russ brought his Motorola HT 1000 two-way radio to his chapped lips and called back to the ninety-eight-foot trawler *Dragnet*, which rose and fell on the rough sea fifty yards off the *Scourge's* starboard bow. The lights on its mast and in its wheelhouse were like twinkling stars through the torrent, its frame a skeletal carcass of outrigger booms and hydraulic winches against the seamless horizon. He focused on the dim trapezoidal windows as he spoke.

"We're on board the *Scourge*, but there's no sign of anyone. The whole ship's quiet as the grave."

"*Just duck your head inside and make sure there's no one in need of help,*" the captain and owner of the trawler, Ron Anders, said through the storm-induced static. "*Lord knows we don't have the time to screw around and the last thing we want is to make someone else's problems our own.*"

"Ain't that the truth. We're asking for trouble as it is."

"*I'll see if I can get close enough to give you some light.*"

Russ nodded and shoved the two-way back into his parka.

"What'd he say?" Jerry asked.

"You got ears."

"I can't hear a damn thing!"

"He said you better get out your flashlight. You're going in first."

"That ain't what he said."

"So it's what I said. Get moving. The sooner we're done, the sooner we're out of here." He pushed Jerry ahead of him toward the open doorway beside a two-story garage door, behind which he assumed the winch assemblies and the control console for the A-frame above him were housed. Lighting his own beam, he followed Jerry farther onto the craft.

The *Dragnet* had been on the home stretch back to Seattle when the captain had barely seen the *Scourge* in time to keep from ramming it. The dark vessel hadn't been emitting a sound on the sonar. She'd just been drifting through the shipping lane as though dead in the water, her engines silent, not a light on her deck. Several blats from the air horn and repeated attempts to hail her on the radio had fallen on deaf ears, but the unwritten maritime code prevented them from simply leaving her adrift in the Pacific.

All aboard the *Dragnet* were dog-tired from nearly half a year in the Bering Sea, where they'd been hauling net-loads of flounder and hake and selling them to the Russians for the third straight year. This year's take had put all of the others to shame. They already had one-point-eight million dollars in cash buried in the refrigerated hold under tons of pollock, mackerel, and Pacific cod, which would bring in another hundred and fifty thousand stateside. That was the money they would report as income to Uncle Sam in an even split between the five of them, while a flat million of the cash would go into Anders's pocket, leaving two hundred grand, tax-free, for each of the rest of them.

The one thing they could least afford to do was call attention to themselves. Their meager haul didn't justify five months' work, which would only arouse suspicion and raise questions they weren't prepared to answer. And if anyone found out about the cash, not only would it be subject to official scrutiny, but surely the IRS would start digging into their personal finances and find all of the discrepancies that would lead to the hundred grand each of them had squirreled away over the past three years. This here was the big score, the one that would make all of the grueling exertion worthwhile. Working a trawler wasn't like sitting on some sport boat with a dozen lines in the water. It was dangerous, physically demanding, twenty-four-hours-a-day manual labor: hauling in nets that weighed several tons, dripping with water colder than a witch's teat; shivering too hard to sleep; taping together broken, clawed fingers, blue from the subzero temperatures. He had earned this money as much as any man on the planet ever had, and no bureaucrat sitting in some cubicle with dry loafers and a seersucker suit was going to steal a dime of it from him.

They just needed to figure out if anyone on board this ghost ship was in need of assistance, and then they could be on their way again. He imagined the crew in their heated cabins, bedded down like pansies, waiting out the storm, or maybe the savage sea had scared them all so badly they had needed to be airlifted back to shore.

Russ chuckled at the thought as he followed Jerry across the dark threshold and into the central corridor of the main deck. The smell stopped him in his tracks. It reeked of an entire catch rotting in the hold after the refrigeration unit crapped out. Jerry must have smelled it, too. He stood stock-still, a silhouette against the diffuse glow of his flashlight beam.

Their breath hung in clouds around their heads.

"We got no business here," Jerry whispered. "All we got to do is tell Anders we didn't see nothing and get the hell off this boat."

Russ agreed wholeheartedly, but there was a part of him that needed to know. He stepped around Jerry and swung his beam in front of him. It reflected from puddles on the floor. Exposed wiring hung from severed conduits in the ceiling. An occasional blue spark fizzled and died. A bright light passed over him through the doorway behind him, stretching his shadow down the silent hallway, and then it was gone. It reappeared through each of the open doorways to his right, one at a time, as though some invisible phantom were flicking the overheads on and off in sequence. It was the spotlight from the *Dragnet*, he knew, sweeping across the side of the larger vessel and passing through the porthole windows.

"You're on your own," Jerry said. His receding footsteps slapped through the puddles on his way back into the rain. "We should have just left—"

His words were swallowed by the shrieking wind.

"*What's going on in there?*" Anders's voice crackled through the two-way. "*Surely you've found someone by now.*"

Russ dialed down the volume on the transceiver as he advanced into the ship. Water dripped to the floor with a metronomic *plip…plip*. The squeak of his wet soles echoed back at him from the darkness ahead. His pale column of light passed over a sign to the right that read "Machinery Shop." There was a handprint on the wall below it in what appeared to be some kind of oil. A quick glance into the interior confirmed that other than rows of work tables with toppled chairs, several sinks, and racks of tools, the room was empty. He turned to the left. The "Winch Housing" sign was bisected by a spatter of fluid that had dried in dark ribbons.

"*Answer me, Russ,*" the radio hissed. "*Tell me what you see.*"

The floor was smeared with crusted streaks, as though someone had dragged a filthy mop across it and never bothered to return.

Another blue snap above him rained golden sparks.

His beam crossed a sign to his right—"Galley"—and the closed steel hatch beside it, which looked like it had been sloppily painted finger-painted with mud. The matching door to his right was pitted and dented, the sign illegible beneath more of the dark fluid.

The smell intensified and he gagged, but he had to know.

He had to know.

"*Get your…out…there,*" Anders's voice wavered through the static. "*We…call it in…reach port.*"

It was like walking through a dream. His legs were numb, yet he could hear his footfalls from both ahead of him and from behind him at the same time. The tapping sound of his pulse in his head was indistinguishable from the patter of fluid dripping from above him, his harsh breath distorted as though he were breathing into a mask.

The next doorway to the left stood wide open just past a sign that read "Mess." An array of shattered dishes covered the floor beside overturned tables. His light reflected from aluminum plates and bowls, broken glasses, silverware and standing fluid. He had to clap his hand over his mouth and nose as he stepped inside and slowly moved his column of light from left to right.

"Anybody in here?" he tried to call, but it passed through his palm as a series of grunts.

He walked around the tables until he reached the back of the room. Glass from broken bottles twinkled at his feet. A sticky puddle crept across the ground like a shadow. The two porthole windows admitted precious little light. At first he thought they were opaque, and then he saw the bodies crumpled below them and realized that they were spattered with blood.

Russ gasped and stumbled back out of the mess. Even as he turned and ran down the hallway, his mind was still trying to rationalize what he had seen. Two men: one on his side, the other folded backward. Mouths agape, eyes wide, necks opened as though by a shovel. The doorways flew past to either side until he burst out into the storm. His first step onto the wet deck sent him sprawling. The back of his head ricocheted from the boat. He saw stars as he slipped and slid toward the stern.

Anders's voice barked at him from his jacket, but he couldn't make out the words.

Jerry was already in the Zodiac, cranking the outboard. Russ threw himself down the ladder and nearly capsized the raft.

"Jesus, man—" Jerry started, but Russ shoved him aside, yanked the motor to life, and guided them back toward the *Dragnet* through troughs that dropped violently beneath them and drenched them with spray.

Felix Juarez, a stocky Hispanic with jailhouse tattoos scaling his neck above his parka, popped up from belowdecks at the sound of the Zodiac's whine. He waved them over and helped haul the smaller craft back on board while Russ hurried inside and thundered up the stairs into the wheelhouse.

"What the hell's going on?" Anders snapped. The gray-haired captain whirled to face Russ, smoke from the cigar clenched between his yellowed teeth swirling around his coarse features. His forehead creased over his hazel eyes when he saw Russ's face.

"Get us out of here," Russ said.

"Tell me what you saw. Is everybody—?"

"Get us out of here!" Russ shouted. "Now!"

"What did you see? If anyone on that ship needs help, we're honor bound—"

"They're all fucking dead!" Russ shouted.

Anders looked into his wild eyes for a long moment, then simply nodded and turned back to the rain-sheeted glass.

Russ stomped down the stairs and headed toward the port rail, where he stood beneath the dripping net and stared between the outrigger booms toward the ebon shape of the factory ship. A shiver rippled up his spine. He didn't know what had happened on that ship, but he wanted no part of it. Damn the maritime code. There was no one left on that ship to save. Images of what he now understood to be blood assaulted him: streaked on the corridor floor, painted on the walls by unimaginable suffering, spattered on the windows in the mess, in front of which two nearly decapitated corpses had been left to rot.

The sooner they were far away from this ghost ship the better.

He heard a *thump* from the bow and turned in that direction as the engines roared, churning up flumes of water in their wake. One of the hatches to the lower hold flapped open and closed at the mercy of the wind.

The spotlight flashed across the starboard bow of the larger ship. He read the letters painted on the hull—"*Pacific Scourge; PNG-4189; Orcas Island, Washington*"—before the ship fell behind them into the roiling darkness once more, leaving him to wonder what in the name of God had befallen her crew.

TEN

Seattle, Washington
Tuesday, October 16th
1:53 a.m. PST

Russ tore the page out of the phone book and walked away from the desolate booth under the lone street lamp. The working harbor was as dark and deserted as it would ever be, which was exactly why they had slowed their pace and timed their arrival to coincide with the lull. Nearly all of the buildings and warehouses were dark, save for the harbor master's office and one pier nearly a mile to the north where a crane unloaded containers from a Handymax freighter with Japanese letters on the hull. He could hear the grinding of the crane, the resounding boom when it dropped its cargo in the storage lot, and the occasional shouted directions echoing across the bay. They were otherwise alone on the commercial fishing docks, where the trawlers, seiners, and sports boats were tethered to the piers in long, silent lines. The waves clapped against their hulls as they rose and fell in a gentle rhythm. Far to the south, the shoreline was pitch black, a conspicuous gap of nothingness along Salmon Bay, where he could vaguely discern the outlines of the demolished buildings of the old wharf against the backdrop of the lights of downtown, two worlds from different eras juxtaposed upon one another. From where he now stood, in the shadows under the overhang of the fish market, he could see his crewmates as shadows on the deck of the *Dragnet*, their bags slung over their shoulders as they prepared to disembark onto their home soil for the first time in nearly half a year. Their haul would keep in the hold for one more night. They'd be back in a matter of hours to transfer their cargo into refrigerated panel trucks, assuming the market prices for their catch were agreeable, but for tonight, they were going to sleep in their own beds, if only for a few precious hours.

But there was one thing he needed to do first.

Since he had been the one who had witnessed the carnage on the *Scourge*, the duty of making the call had fallen to him. He had done everything in his power to put the whole situation out of his mind, and yet nothing seemed to work. He couldn't even blink without seeing the black smears of blood framed in his flashlight beam on the walls and the floor, the two corpses sprawled in front of the windows painted with their pain. There was nothing they could do for whoever had been on that boat now. Russ and his men had too much to lose. The cash on the *Dragnet* aside, they had undoubtedly committed a felony by not calling in their discovery the moment they nearly broadsided the factory ship in the middle of the Pacific, but it was too late to change that now. Besides, why should they stick their necks out when the fate of the *Scourge* had already been decided? Their involvement changed nothing. They'd probably even spend the next year in and out of the offices of various lawyers and law enforcement agencies, answering the same questions over and over, all the while defending their innocence in a situation that had always been outside of their control, but there was still the unwritten code to uphold. Whether he wanted to or not, he owed the men on that infernal ghost ship the phone call he now had to make.

He unwrapped the disposable cell phone and threw the plastic packaging in an oil drum-wastebasket beside a scaling trough with entrails coiled through the holes in the drain covers. After a frustrating minute trying to figure out how to work the blasted phone he'd purchased down the street at the Shell station, he dialed the number from the torn page, crumpled it up, and dropped it in the trash. The phone rang in his ear.

He felt like a punk. The arrogant seaman who had once served aboard the *USS Nimitz*, who had seen a world he never knew existed from the deck of one of the most feared aircraft carriers ever put to sea, who had grabbed his groin in one hand and raised the middle finger of the other toward shores where the meek huddled in fear, curled up like a beaten dog inside of him. There was now only the prematurely aging man for whom self-preservation superseded all else and the hard life had pummeled into the kind of coward who was now poised to pawn the responsibility for the lives of those aboard the *Scourge* onto whoever picked up the phone when he dialed the number and pressed "Send."

When a drowsy female voice answered the Coast Guard's Maritime Emergency Hotline, he recited the line exactly as he had practiced.

"Write this down. Word for word." She tried to interrupt, but he just plowed ahead. "The Factory Ship *Pacific Scourge*, PNG-4189, is dead in the water at forty-nine-point-two-one north latitude and one-twenty-eight-point-two-six-three west longitude. I don't know what happened onboard, but there don't appear to be any survivors. How you handle it from here is your call. Did you get that?"

"Sir, there's no sign of an activated EPIRB distress beacon in that area. Please repeat the coordin—"

Russ terminated the call, ejected the battery, and hurled the cell phone out into the bay.

There. The deed was done. Now he could slink off into the night like the chump that he was. He'd just have to find a way to live with the man he'd become. Who was he kidding? With his share of the money in the hold, he'd be able to forget all about this mess in no time at all. He supposed men had sold their souls for far less.

His footsteps echoed on the hollow planks of the pier as he headed back toward the *Dragnet*. Already he was thinking about a hot shower in his own apartment and snuggling up into his dry, warm bed and putting all of this behind him where it belonged.

ELEVEN

Pacific Ocean
104 km West-Northwest of the Washington Coast
7:02 a.m. PST

The Bell UH-1 Iroquois helicopter raced across the Pacific. Its mechanized thunder echoed back from the cresting black waves. Special Agent Grey Porter listened to the pilot coordinating with the Coast Guard through the cans on his ears. He craned his neck in an effort to see the western horizon, where he could barely discern the skeletal outline of the *Scourge*. Two Coast Guard vessels circled it like sharks. Their crews had retreated to their boats as he had instructed, and now waited for the FBI and the contracted forensics specialists from the Washington State Patrol's Crime Scene Response Team to begin their investigation before towing the factory ship back to Seattle. Porter was certain the scene couldn't be half as bad as it had been described to him, but that didn't mean he wouldn't have his work cut out for him. Piracy on the high seas was on the rise. It was starting to feel like a return to the seventeenth century out here. While the Bureau wasn't called upon to investigate every instance, it was becoming more and more frequent. Murder on a vessel of this size with international ports-of-call generally meant trafficking of some kind, and whether in drugs, firearms, or human beings, it fell under Federal jurisdiction. Porter cared little about smuggling. The men and women from the CSRT, seated beside him and in the chopper behind him, were infinitely more qualified to deal with that. He was here because he was the best field operative the Violent Crimes Division had to offer. It was his job to identify the perpetrators and hunt them to the ends of the earth, if that was what it took to being them to justice.

And the clock started now.

"I can't get any lower than this," the pilot shouted through the cans.

Porter looked down at the long bow of the *Scourge*, a full fifty feet below them. The rotors were already whipping the ropes and rigging across the desk as though they were caught in a cyclone. Any lower and they might as well let a herd of wildebeests charge through the crime scene for all the damage they were doing.

"Just hold her steady," Porter said. He slipped out of his seatbelt and made his way to the open side door, where a crewman passed him a harness attached to a steel cable. The wind buffeted him with rain as he seated himself in the harness and approached the edge. He gave a curt nod to the man at the winch and stepped out over the nothingness.

The deck below him rose at a steady pace. He twirled in slow circles, affording him a full view of the bow. Waves broke over the gunwales and flooded across the deck. If there had been any evidence out there, it washed through the scuppers long ago. All of the windows of the upper decks were dark and lifeless. There was no indication that anyone had ever been aboard, as though the vessel had been put to sea unmanned and set to drift for eternity. Of course, he knew that wasn't the case. He'd already been informed of what he could expect to find inside.

He splashed down into ankle-deep water, shed the harness, and heard the cable zip upward behind him. The entire ship rocked at the mercy of the ocean. The engine was silent and still underfoot. Waves boomed against the hull. Rain clapped on every surface. He was soaked to the bone before he even reached the open doorway and stepped into the shadows.

The smell struck him with enough force to make him recoil.

He clicked on his flashlight and drew his Beretta 92FS Inox. Surely whoever was responsible for the slaughter was long gone, but there was no point in taking any chances. His beam passed over smears and spatters on the smooth walls, none of which were pitted with bullet holes, scored by ricochets, or showed any other indications of a prolonged siege. A thin stream sloshed from side to side on the floor in time with the canting ship.

Columns of pale light crossed the corridor from the doorways on the starboard side, highlighting the ribbons of water trickling from the seams on the walls and the bloodstains that had already dried to a brownish crust. He glanced through the each doorway as he passed, taking note of the condition and the presence or absence of bodies. There were two in the mess, as the Coast Guard had already documented. He paused in the stairwell at the end of the hallway. A flight led downward into the absolute darkness of the hold, while another led upward to the cabins and the wheelhouse. He could return to the hold later. There was probably nothing more significant than fish rotting in the thawing freezers down there anyway. First and foremost, he needed to figure out where the rest of the bodies were and what happened to the crew.

He glanced back and watched two of the forensics techs haul their cases into the mess before starting his ascent. His footsteps clanged on the iron stairs as climbed, his flashlight directed upward at a steep angle toward the landing above. The lurching ship tossed him alternately against the railing and the wall. There were no bloodstains on the walls here, only sporadic, ill-defined smudges on the rail. When he reached the landing, he peered out into the corridor. Narrow doorways lined both sides of the thin walkway every eight feet or so. Only a fraction of the minuscule crew cabins appeared as though they were currently in use. While the *Scourge* could house and employ nearly forty men, Porter had learned that a large percentage of them had been Russian nationals who'd been hired right off the docks for pennies on the dollar, leaving only the ten American seamen and the captain to make the return trip. He found one of them in his bunk with the side of his throat opened wide enough to see the faint white glimmer of his trachea. The wall above the man's shaved head was spattered with long arcs of blood.

Porter furrowed his brow.

It looked as though the man had been attacked by a wild animal while he slept. He hadn't even attempted to kick off the covers.

What in the name of God could have done such a thing? And worse, was it still skulking through the darkened rooms with them right now?

His entire perspective changed in a heartbeat. He hadn't considered the possibility that this ship could have been smuggling endangered species. Great cats fetched huge cash on the open market. For all he knew, there could be a dozen starving tigers with a taste for human blood stalking him at this very second. While he hadn't relished the idea of dealing with lawless pirates, he vastly preferred it to the scenario that now played out in his mind.

He ducked back out into the hallway and cautiously cleared the next three rooms before he encountered the fourth victim. Another man was dead in his bunk, savagely attacked while he slept. The same type of wound to the neck, the same arterial sprays on the wall, the same lack of defensive wounds. What kind of monster killed so quickly and violently, but didn't consume its prey?

Suddenly, the ship was alive with the sounds he hadn't paid attention to before. He heard every creak, every buckling rivet, every scream of the wind, every single raindrop, every thump of the rough waves.

He unholstered his transceiver and turned up the volume. They each carried one that had been set to a common frequency while they were still in the air.

"Porter here," he whispered. "I'm on the shelterdeck. We have a much bigger problem than we thought."

"*If you're referring to the nature of the wounds, we already know.*" He recognized the voice of the CSRT's lead investigator. Sondra Galiardi spoke in a clipped manner, as though she nipped off the tail end of each word. "*I take it you found more bodies.*"

"Two more up here. Killed in their sleep. Same MO. No sign of a struggle."

"*Any indication of what could have done this?*"

"I was hoping you might be able to tell me."

"*I won't have anything even remotely conclusive until we can create an odontological mold of the bite marks.*"

"Care to wager a guess before I stumble blindly into it on one of the upper decks?"

"*The teeth marks are distinct. Dentition could almost pass for human.*"

"No human could have done this."

"*I didn't say the marks were definitively human. I'm basing my observation exclusively on the shape of the maxillary ridge. That's the arch of the front teeth.*"

"Thanks, Sandra. You've been incredibly helpful."

Porter dialed down the volume before she could reply. If there was one thing he knew with complete certainty, it was that whatever attacked these men in their sleep hadn't been even remotely human.

He slowed at the end of the hallway and surveyed the stairwell leading up to the two remaining decks, then advanced upward into the darkness on the swaying steps. He cleared the landing and swept his beam into the silent corridor. This level was maybe half the size of the lower two, the doorways spaced farther apart to accommodate the larger cabins for the more important personnel. The officers' quarters to either side were empty, the beds unmade, the linens draped across the floor as though they had followed the abruptly awakened men across the room toward the door. He found the chef in the second room on the left, beside the head, sprawled prone on the floor. The hairy man was as wide as he was tall, his swollen bulge of a neck torn open like a punctured tire. His grease-stained white smock was a stark contrast to the puddle of black blood that had dried beneath him.

In all three instances, the attacker had gone straight for the carotid. The cessation of blood flow to the brain would have rendered them unconscious in a matter of seconds. They would have bled out in under two minutes.

He cleared the captain's cabin last. Everything appeared to be in place, save for the contents of the wardrobe, which must have tumbled out onto the ground when control of the vessel was handed over to the raging sea.

There were still six men unaccounted for. It was possible that they had sought refuge in the hold when the attack commenced, but, judging by the foul aroma that intensified with each step up the remaining staircase, he had a pretty good idea what he would find in the pilothouse.

He wasn't disappointed.

After performing a quick head count, he radioed down to the others.

"There are five more up here," he said. "They took their stand in the wheelhouse."

"*Then we're still missing one,*" Galiardi said.

"Assuming our initial information was correct."

"*Which means he could be our perp.*"

"Or another victim."

"*Then he either—*"

"Found a way off the ship," Porter interrupted, "or he's down in the hold."

He holstered his transceiver and took a mental snapshot of the room, taking note of the splintered bullet holes in the paneling around the doorframe, the arcs and spatters of blood on the walls and the bridge, the corpses pressed up against the wall beneath the bank of windows and tucked under the console as though they had run out of room to retreat and tried to become one with the walls. The watery horizon yawed wildly through glass beaded with blood on one side and rain on the other.

Porter inspected everything other than the faces of the men at his feet, then hurried out of the pilothouse toward the stairs. The crime scene unit would be able to tell him precisely what transpired in here soon enough. For now, he had more pressing concerns.

He needed to find out what was in the hold.

TWELVE

Seattle, Washington
7:28 a.m. PST

Russ Tarver made his way down the commercial pier, his third McMuffin in one hand, his second cup of coffee in the other. These were the simple pleasures for which he had longed during the endless months at sea. Never in his life had he felt as content as he did right now. Four hours of uninterrupted sleep in his own warm, dry bed, a belly full of food that didn't taste as though it had been rehydrated with bilge water, and hundreds of thousands of dollars waiting for him just fifty short yards away down the warped, weather-beaten planks. He smiled for the first time in so long that muscles unaccustomed to use ached in his cheeks.

He didn't once think about the ghost ship they had chanced upon out on the open sea. Calling it in to the Coast Guard had absolved him of whatever guilt he might have felt. Today was a new day, a day to start his life over again. The past was now his shadow, trailing at his heels as he embraced the bright future he deserved, that he had *earned*.

The sounds of morning were all around him: gulls squalling as they wheeled overhead; cranes and winches grinding; engines churning up flume; a chaos of competing voices on the PA systems mounted to the roofs of the harbor master's shack and the fish market; containers clanking; foghorns blaring. The air smelled of petrol, oil, and brine, with an undercurrent of fish guts and fishermen's sweat. He took all of it in and savored it. Captain Anders was going to be pissed that he was almost thirty minutes late, but he wasn't about to let anything spoil this most perfect of days.

Storm clouds hovered over the horizon where they fed the Pacific, promising rain in a matter of hours. The sun beating on the back of his neck reminded him that he no longer had to care. Never again would he be forced to haul nets in a freezing deluge. From here on out, when the weather wasn't to his liking, he could simply go inside the new double-wide he would soon be purchasing with cash. Nothing fancy, nothing to draw the scrutiny of the IRS. Just something he could slap down on a little chunk of land all his own, where he could ride out his days with the stacks of money he prepared to disinter from beneath tons of pollock, mackerel, and cod.

Russ paused at the end of the pier, fastened the suspenders of his rubber waders over his chest, and started down the slanted ramp toward the *Dragnet*.

He had half expected to find the captain standing on deck, shouting at him for being late when he arrived, but he was pleasantly surprised to find no one topside. Nothing could ruin his perfect day, after all. Two massive wheeled bins nearly the size of Dumpsters waited for him at the bottom of the ramp. He slipped on his stiff work gloves and shoved the first one across the gangplank to where another pair were already stationed and waiting to be filled. Neither of them appeared to have been used yet. Perhaps he wasn't the only one who had gotten a late start on this most gorgeous of mornings. Or maybe the captain was still haggling pennies on the price of their catch. That would be just like Anders, trying to squeeze blood from a turnip while they were already sitting on a fortune.

"So are we doing this thing or what?" he called as he thumped down the stairs into the hold. "There's a new F-150 out there calling my name."

He passed through the cramped room he had shared with the other sweaty men for too many consecutive months and ducked into the corridor leading to the climate-controlled units. The thudding of his footsteps on the metal floor beat a counterpoint to the hum of the generator that powered the coolers.

"Don't tell me you all waited for me to start unloading all this crap."

Russ stopped halfway down the hallway. Matching pressure-sealed doors to either side led into refrigerated units the size of single-car garages. Ahead, the engine room was a jungle gym of pipes and shadows. He jerked open the door on the left and was struck in the face with frigid air that reeked of innards. The room inside was so dark he could barely discern the mountain of fish. He closed the door and yanked open the one to his right. Same thing. Nothing and no one.

"Where the hell—?"

He stopped midsentence. His blood ran cold.

What if the others hadn't gone home when he had? What if they had simply divvied up the cash without him and absorbed his share? Had they merely left him a fraction of his earnings in fish as a joke?

His heart raced and his palms grew clammy.

It wasn't like he could go to the police if they screwed him over. What would he say? He'd been swindled out of his cut of the money they'd been attempting to secret from the government?

He tasted blood and realized he was biting his lip. His face reddened with anger and his fists curled so tightly that his knuckles cracked.

There was no way he would allow things to go down like this. Russ Tarver was not a man one ever wanted to cross, not while he still had a pulse.

His money had damn well better be there or he would find the others, wherever they tried to hide, and take back what was rightfully his. No. He would take all of it, so that they fully comprehended the severity of the mistake they had made.

Russ threw open the door to the freezer on his right and toggled the light switch. A single bulb bloomed under a frosted glass dome high on the rear wall. He debated retracting the room-size hatch that was the roof, which allowed them to dump entire nets full of fish into the unit from the deck above him, but there was just enough light for his purposes. He knew exactly what he was looking for and where they had stashed it. The cash had been bundled, bricked, and sealed inside newspaper wrapped in countless layers of cellophane. He didn't remember precisely how many bundles there were, but they had been a tight fit inside the meat locker freezer they had shoved into the back corner and buried under the mountain of mackerel and cod that nearly reached the ceiling. And it had goddamn better well still be there.

"There'll be hell to pay of you jacked me!" he shouted. "You hear me? I'll find you wherever you go!"

He stormed into the room and kicked his way into the stinking heap. A slimy avalanche of carcasses slid toward him and past his thighs. He reached into them and shoved them aside with both hands as though attempting to breast stroke. A mess of entrails wrapped around his wrist. He jerked his hand back and a long, slender reddish-brown cod with three tall dorsal fins and whiskers like a catfish came with it. There was a gaping hole in its gut, the edges ridged as though someone had taken a great big bite out of it and then thrown it back. He flung it behind him and wiped his glove on his bib. He reached into the mountain and found another one. And another. There had to be a good dozen of them, all of them missing chunks of their undersides were their hearts and organs should have been. The stringy bowels dangled from the holes where it looked like someone had bitten right through the ribs and scales.

What in the hell had gotten in here with their freaking catch? Surely they hadn't hauled them in here like that.

It didn't matter. Nothing mattered other than digging out that locker and making sure that—

Something warm and wet slithered down the back of his bare forearm. He glimpsed a smear of crimson on his skin from the corner of his eye. He jerked his arm out of the pile and looked where it had been. Jerry Worrell stared back at him from under the jumble of fish. His face was a bloody mask; his wide, sightless eyes shot through with vessels.

Russ grabbed him by the front of his flannel shirt and pulled him up out of the mess. Jerry's head lolled back so far it nearly fell off. Black blood the consistency of sour milk oozed from the massive wound on his throat.

"Son of a bitch," Russ whispered. "What the hell is going on...?"

His words trailed off when he saw the tangle of limbs down under the fish where Jerry had been. He recognized the captain's jacket, the dragon tattoo that spiraled around Juarez's bicep and coiled around his lacerated throat.

Memories of the ghost ship they'd encountered far out on the Pacific assaulted him. The blood on the walls, the men crumpled on the floor with their necks savagely opened. He remembered staring back at the *Scourge* from the deck of the *Dragnet* as they sped away from it.

He closed his eyes and his breath froze in his chest.

He remembered hearing something on the deck of the *Dragnet*, a noise that sounded almost as though someone had leapt down onto the boat from the factory ship, then the wind blowing the hatch open and closed with a loud *thump, thump—*

Thump.

Russ whirled around at the sound of the freezer door closing. He looked just in time to catch a blur of motion before the light snapped off with a sharp click.

"Who's there?" he shouted. "Turn the light back on!"

He heard the slapping sounds of wet carcasses flopping onto the metal floor.

"You'd better back the hell off right now or so help me—!"

The mound of fish around him shifted.

He slowly ducked and reached down to his left until he felt the coarse fabric of Anders's jacket. After a moment of blind fumbling, he found the pocket where the captain kept his Zippo lighter.

More sounds of slippery fish sliding against one another, like so many slithering snakes.

Russ yanked out the Zippo, snapped back the lid, and struck the flint wheel.

A golden flame erupted from the lighter.

It reflected back at him as twin circles from a pair of eyes.

He saw a flash of sharp teeth.

Felt the warmth of breath on his neck.

Then a sudden searing pain.

He rocked his head back and tried to scream, but heard only the wet sound of fluid spattering the ceiling.

The lighter fell from his hand and extinguished.

The darkness consumed him.

THIRTEEN

Pacific Ocean
104 km West-Northwest of the Washington Coast
7:40 a.m. PST

The digital camera flashed again and again, strobing her vision as though lightning repeatedly struck through the doorway behind her. The effect was disorienting, but it was imperative that they capture the entire area in painstaking detail, from the position and condition of the bodies to every minuscule smear, spatter, and drop of blood. She had just finished measuring and documenting the wounds to the men's throats, and was preparing to start mixing the fast-drying latex composite to pour into the gashes in order to begin the process of creating an odontologic cast of the mouth that had inflicted them when she heard the sound of footsteps pounding down the corridor. She looked up in time to see Special Agent Porter burst into the room.

"You're coming with me," he said. "Now."

She glanced over her right shoulder at one of the specialists, who was busy scraping dried blood into a variety of test tubes and petri dishes, then over her left to where Galiardi was supervising the collection of trace evidence with a tape roller, the blacklight search, and the fingerprinting of the remains and the surrounding area. None of them looked up from their designated tasks.

Porter whistled like he was calling a dog.

"Hop to it, Layne. I need someone who can handle a firearm."

Her anger rose as she set aside the latex mixture and wiped her gloved palms on her pants. She was still wearing her uniform blues and utility belt. She had received the call on her cell phone as she was pulling into her carport at her apartment complex, already imagining herself curling up in her bed for a few precious hours of sleep before heading back to the lab for another unpaid day of internship. There had been no time to change, no time to wash the stench of the underworld out of her hair and clothes if she was going to make it to the chopper in time. She had simply turned her car around and raced toward the State Patrol Lab, where she'd barely been able to inhale a scalding cup of coffee before the helicopter arrived. Her hands shook and her eyes burned from the lack of sleep, but these were minor inconveniences with which she'd learned to function.

"You." Porter pointed at the tech with the camera. "Give her your digital."

Sturm took it from him and shouldered past Porter into the hallway.

Her face was flushed red when she rounded on him.

"Don't you ever whistle for me like I'm some kind of—!"

"Save it, Layne. I need someone who can watch my back and give me a preliminary forensics analysis at the same time. You fit the bill."

"All of the others have field training in addition to—"

"You already have a gun on your hip and I don't have the time to argue."

He turned and strode away from her.

"Where are we going?"

He stopped at the darkened mouth of a stairwell and looked back at her.

"Down."

Porter directed his flashlight beam toward the hold, and, leading with his pistol, started his descent.

Sturm removed her Maglite from her utility belt and drew her sidearm. Holding them in tandem, she followed Porter down the metal stairs, their footsteps echoing like the beating of tin drums. Every other step, she turned back toward the upper level to ensure that their retreat remained unobstructed. She nearly backed into him at the bottom of the stairs, where he had paused to survey the pitch-black corridor. Water trickled down the staircase with a sound like a toddler urinating, into shin-deep standing fluid that smelled uncomfortably of bilge, brine, and motor oil. The cold bit through her clothes and straight into her skin. Her heartbeat accelerated and she felt the claustrophobic sensation of the walls closing in on her, a sensation with which she was becoming increasingly familiar. Her beam twitched in her trembling hand.

She blamed it on a combination of exhaustion and caffeine, and willed her hands to steady before Porter noticed, if he hadn't already.

The slick floor canted beneath them as they advanced into the hallway, their beams reflecting from the water, unable to penetrate its inky depths.

"Keep your eyes open," Porter whispered.

"You think that whatever attacked them is down here?"

Porter didn't answer. He veered to his left into some kind of processing room, sliding his feet as though walking on ice to keep from making the water splash. Sturm did the same as she cleared the room to her right, which smelled as if she were crawling into the slit gut of some massive fish. She exposed the shadows behind the heavy equipment and above the thigh-thick pipes that traversed the ceiling. Porter was already moving deeper into the hold when she exited the room.

They each opened one of the opposing freezer doors. The water pulled at their ankles as it rushed into the formerly sealed rooms. Both were empty, except for the reek of rotting fish that must have leeched into the rust-stained metal walls.

She was just about to open the second door on her right when Porter whispered behind her.

"There's a body in here."

She turned to see his silhouette framed in the doorway of what appeared to be a storage closet. Metal racks glinted from the walls past him. She peered in both directions down the corridor before backing into the room behind him.

"Keep an eye on the corridor while I clear the room."

He sloshed away from her while she worked her flashlight and pistol from left to right and back again, her finger taut on the trigger in anticipation of squeezing at the first hint of movement. She pictured the savage wounds on the necks of the victims upstairs and tried not to wonder what kind of creature had inflicted them. If something capable of overwhelming and butchering an entire crew of roughnecks was down here with them now, it was going to take more than her little department-issue nine-millimeter to bring it down.

"Jesus," Porter whispered.

"What?" Sturm asked, fighting the urge to turn and look.

"Switch with me. I'll watch your six. You tell me what you see."

Sturm cautiously backed past him and turned to face the room. She traded her gun for the camera and snapped off several shots, then slowed to evaluate the details with her own eyes. The contents of the shelves had fallen into the water. A molehill of rehydrated potato flakes filled the corner to her left, where the screen of a laptop computer broke the surface behind heaps of fabric, soggy boxes, and random detritus. The body floated facedown, arms spread at its sides, toes dragging on the floor with a grating sound. The man's neck was bloated like a pale white water wing, his hands swollen to the point that they looked ready to burst. She had to nudge him with her toe to turn him enough to see the gash across the anterior portion of his neck.

"There's one too many," Porter said.

"What do you mean?"

"The men. There are twelve bodies when there should only be eleven."

"It'll take time to identify them. Once we do, you can compare the names to the list of—"

"I already know which one doesn't belong."

"How can you possibly…?"

She lost her train of thought when she shined her beam to the right and discovered why Porter sounded so confident in his assertion. There was an iron cage bolted to the back wall, the door closed and latched. Water passed through the rusted bars like the tide sluicing between the legs of a pier. The corpse inside it had been shoved into the corner. She caught a glimpse of the face and had to look away.

The other men had all been killed in the exact same fashion: a brutal, yet surgical strike to the anterolateral neck to tear out the common carotid. The bloodletting would have been swift and fatal, almost clinical, if such a trait could be ascribed to an animal.

This man…this man's death was the complete opposite. It was a display of passion, of ferocity fueled by a blinding red rage.

"Talk to me, Layne. What do you see?"

She scoured the walls and the ceiling with her flashlight, which showcased the copious amounts of blood and spattered arcs she would have expected inside a slaughterhouse.

"The man in the cage was viciously worked over to inflict a high level of pain, unlike the others we've found so far." She lowered her beam to the cage. "Based on the proportions of the enclosure, I speculate we're dealing with a single animal, and it's definitely smaller than an adult great cat."

"Unless there are more cages down here."

"Correct."

"Keep going."

She finally mustered the nerve to bring the light to bear on the man in the cage. His face was disfigured with countless lacerations that stripped him of his humanity. It was as though his skull were merely coated with chunks of flesh haphazardly hurled from a distance. She could see his spine through his neck and his ribs through the tattered meat on his chest.

Again, she found herself assigning a human characteristic to whatever beast had done this.

"The attack appears almost…personal," she whispered.

"Great. A beast with a grudge," Porter said to himself. "It has to still be down here somewhere."

Sturm shivered at the thought.

"You're sure it wasn't on any of the upper decks," she said.

"I cleared them myself."

"And there's no way it could have gotten off the ship?"

"You're stalling, Layne."

He was right and she knew it.

"After you then." She readjusted her grip on her pistol and tried to slow her racing heart. "Lead on."

Porter spun without a word, returned to the hallway, and advanced slowly, his beam scouring every inch of the walls and the floor. Sturm guarded their rear, conscious of the tremble in her cone of light as she swept it from side to side. Despite their cautious progress, their splashing footsteps echoed up and down the corridor, masking every sound other than the groaning of the hull and their harsh breathing.

Neither of the remaining freezers held anything more than the stench of fish, which followed them down the dark passage like an apparition. The engine room was inhabited by long shadows that stretched away from their lights, cast by bilge, oil, and fuel pipes the size of tree trunks. All of the machinery was silent, the gauges flatlined, the computer terminals lifeless. Ribbons of water trickled from the ceiling, traced the lines of conduits, and pattered the standing water like a spring rain. Only their black reflections moved across the water.

"Could it be outside the ship on one of the catwalks?" Sturm whispered.

"There's a chopper circling it and two Coast guard vessels painting it with their spotlights. They would have seen it."

"It isn't down here. Is it possible that you missed—?"

"No," Porter snapped.

Their transceivers crackled at once. Galiardi's disembodied voice echoed in the stillness.

"There's something you need to see up here."

"Did you find it?" Porter asked. He whirled and sprinted back into the hallway before Galiardi could reply.

"No. But I think I know how it might have gotten off the ship."

Water flew from Sturm's knees as she ran to catch up with Porter. He was already vanishing onto the landing above her when she hit the stairs and climbed out of the water. Galiardi was waiting for them outside of the doorway to the mess when they reached her.

"How did the Coast Guard know this ship was here?" Galiardi asked. The tone of her voice hinted that she already knew the answer. "Who called it in?"

"It was an anonymous tip from a prepaid, disposable cell phone."

"And you weren't able to trace it."

It was a statement, not a question.

"Not for lack of trying," Porter said. "Why? What do you know?"

Galiardi raised a handheld blacklight and led them into the mess toward the bodies. She stopped near a smear of blood on the floor, looked back at them, and then knelt and shined the bluish glow across the floor. A telltale pattern appeared in the dried blood. It disappeared again when the light passed.

"Son of a bitch," Porter whispered.

It was the print from the bottom of a boot. Someone had stepped on the puddle of blood *after* it had dried. The impression of the damp tread was as clear as day under the ultraviolet light.

"Whoever came across this vessel boarded it," Sturm said.

"And if they got close enough to get onto this boat…." Galiardi said.

"Damn it!" Porter said. "We need to find that ship!"

II

Cruelty has a human heart,
And jealousy a human face.
Terror, the human form divine,
And secrecy, the human dress.

—William Blake

FOURTEEN

Seattle, Washington
Thursday, October 18th
3:53 a.m. PST

Two days later…

There was nothing left in the tank. Sturm felt as though she hadn't slept in weeks. Her hands shook and she could barely keep her eyes open. The sheer amount of caffeine was burning a hole through the lining of her stomach and her head ached like she'd taken a baseball bat upside the skull. The human body had been built for endurance, but she was seriously testing its threshold now. Between the full-time hours on the job and the added rigors of her internship at the CSRT, she was sleeping in hour-long spurts whenever and wherever she could steal the time. Her diet consisted of bitter fast food coffee to wash down the grease from the fried meat and powdered eggs, which coiled in her bowels like a stone serpent. She had taken to wearing sunglasses to hide the tears that spontaneously burst from her eyes, precursors to the breakdown she had begun to view as an inevitability. She was stretched too thin and she knew it, but she was so close to the finish line now…so close. In less than a month, she would be a full-fledged criminalist. There was already a job waiting for her. All she had to do now was survive the interim. It helped that one day slowly bled into the next, but it felt like waiting to bleed to death from a paper cut.

"You can do this," she whispered.

"What was that?" Henley asked. He slammed the driver's side door, stepped away from the cruiser into the weed-riddled lot, and stretched his arms over his head. When he yawned, Sturm had to fight the urge to strangle him.

"Nothing." She bit the inside of her lip and squeezed her hands into fists to feel the sting of her fingernails cutting into her palms. Anything to sharpen her senses and focus her mind on the task at hand. A task she dreaded more and more with each passing night. "Let's just get this over with."

"I hear ya. If we're quick enough, we can probably still catch the first fresh batch of the day at Krispy Kreme."

Sturm's stomach flopped at the thought. She turned away from her partner so he wouldn't see the green creep into her gills. Far to the north, she could see the outline of the *Pacific Scourge* at the southernmost edge of the commercial dock, where the Coast Guard had towed it. The *Scourge* now sat dark and silent behind a chain link cordon that prohibited access to the impound dock. She had spent the last two days scouring every surface in every room of that ghost ship with the CSRT team, for all the good it had done them. Whatever had butchered the crew hadn't left a single identifiable track, fiber, or hair sample, and they were no closer to finding the man who had notified the Coast Guard of its whereabouts than they'd been forty-eight hours ago. All they had to go on was a cast of teeth that didn't correspond to any known species. Based on the length of the canines and the protruding arrangement of the teeth, the mold reminded her of a silverback's jaws, only far sharper, and smaller and narrower, as though designed to fit into a human-size mouth, which was one of the assumptions under which they now had to work. Several sociopaths during the course of the last two decades had used dentures to inflict bite marks on their victims in hopes of creating physical evidence that couldn't be matched to them, so they couldn't rule out the possibility. Swabs of the wound sites had also revealed the presence of an amino acid complex nearly identical to the glycoprotein Draculin—the most powerful anticoagulant on the planet—found in the saliva of vampire bats. It thinned the blood by impeding the coagulation response and accelerated the speed with which the victim potentially bled out. As a unit, they were reluctant to commit to the theory of a killer or killers wearing false teeth capable of injecting large quantities of blood thinners, but for now, it seemed to be the most promising angle. There was still the question of motive, of course, and until they found one, they had no choice but to continue chasing their own tails.

And then there was the cage and the dilemma it presented. Was whatever had been imprisoned inside of it the reason everyone aboard had been killed? Were they dealing with the elaborately staged abduction of an animal of some great worth? Or was it the elephant in the room none of them wanted to acknowledge? Was it possible that the ship had been transporting an unclassified or biologically engineered species with ferocious jaws, anticoagulatory venom, and an insatiable appetite for blood? A creature capable of overwhelming eleven full-grown men and dispatching them with practiced ease? Had the second boat arrived to extract the killer for a clean getaway, or had it chanced upon the *Scourge* and simply served as a convenient means of escape for whomever or whatever had slaughtered the crew?

If they wanted answers, they needed to find the second boat.

Coast Guard choppers and ships continued to scour the Washington coast, but in diminishing numbers. Enough time had passed for a seafaring vessel of any size to have reached any port in North America or along the Eastern Asian seaboard from the point where they had found the *Scourge*.

She chuckled out loud and shook her head.

They had a killer with fangs that exsanguinated its victims through a bite on the neck. No wonder the other techs had taken to calling themselves vampire hunters.

"What are you laughing at?" Henley asked.

The expression on his face suggested that for the first time during their partnership, they were actually thinking the same thing.

She was losing it.

Sturm turned her attention back to the ruins that stretched away from them, down the incline toward placid Salmon Bay, and the dreaded nightly rousting.

She shouldered past him and approached the entrance to the subterranean warren.

"Are you coming or what?" she called back over her shoulder, and crawled into the vile, smothering darkness.

*   *   *

Sturm followed the same path she always took, ducking through holes in the crumbling walls, wending around support columns that creaked and released cascades of dust, and skirting mounds of refuse and excrement. She barely even noticed the smell anymore, which made her wonder if she ever truly rid herself of it or if she now wore it like a subtle, yet repulsive, perfume. The same sights passed to either side, the same shadows, the same overturned boxes, the same stretches of glinting shattered glass, the same puddles of stagnant rain water and urine. It wasn't until she was crossing from one building into the next that she realized something was different.

The doll.

The filthy, naked baby doll that the homeless girl had lost a week ago during their initial rousting was gone. She paused and offered a prayer up into the fallen rafters and chunks of brick and concrete.

Please don't let that little girl be back down here again.

A tear crept from the corner of her eye at the thought of an innocent child spending even a single night down here in this squalor, which positively stank of hopelessness and desperation.

She clung to the hope that the girl had simply returned to reclaim her sole precious possession and was now bedded down in one of the shelters on a small cot between her parents, and not shivering somewhere down here in this dark hell.

After she passed through the second building without encountering a single squatter, she called Henley on her transceiver.

"Have you come across anyone yet?"

"*No.*" His voice echoed in the stillness. "*They must have finally taken the hint.*"

Sturm stood there a moment longer, pondering his statement. Even after coming down here night after night, the denizens of these tunnels had always returned. Not because there was nowhere else to go, but because they thought of this place as their home. She briefly considered the possibility that these people had learned to expect them, and had simply vacated the premises long enough to watch them crawl through and were already slinking back down into the building behind them, but quickly dismissed that theory. Something had changed since she was last down here. She could feel it in the air, in the shadows all around her. These ruins weren't merely unoccupied. They were abandoned.

She shivered at the thought.

Where had everybody gone, and why had they deserted their home?

She struck off into the darkness again, guided by her woefully inadequate flashlight and the memories of the maze that she could now instinctively run like a lab rat. Where once men and women had huddled for warmth, there were now only heaps of damp newspapers and blankets. There were no sounds of shuffling footsteps; no wet, heavy breathing or coughing; no whispered warnings to the others hiding in the side rooms. She hadn't seen a single pair of rat eyes reflecting back at her. She was alone in this desolate basement, and yet, at the same time, the crawling sensation on the back of her neck insisted otherwise.

Sturm stopped and turned a slow circle. Despite the fact that her beam highlighted only rubble and there was no sign of movement, the feeling refused to abate.

She was too tired to be doing this. Everything would make more sense after a few hours of sleep, when she would be able to function with her full faculties, rather than on instinct alone. She hurried through the final building and emerged into the night to find Henley already waiting for her. It had begun to drizzle, but that was no surprise. In the Pacific Northwest, if it wasn't raining, it was about to rain.

"Did you see *anyone*?" she asked.

"Not a soul. It's quiet as the tomb down there." He stared at her for a long moment. "That's a good thing, Sturm. Maybe it means they aren't coming back and we can go back to doing our jobs again. I tell you, my girlfriend's getting tired of me coming home smelling like I've been passed out drunk in the gutter."

Sturm nodded and again looked far off to the north at the black carcass of the *Scourge*. She had felt the same way down there in the warrens as she had in the hold of that ship.

"Come on," Henley said, clapping her on the shoulder. "We cleared this place in record time. Let's take advantage of this opportunity to celebrate. What do you say? Donuts and coffee on me."

She allowed herself a meek smile and followed him around the side of the building, through chest-high weeds, around mounds of cracked bricks and mortar, and past bullet-dimpled signs to where they had parked the cruiser. The swelling raindrops drummed on the hood. Indigo lightning reflected from the rivulets of water on the windshield. She was reaching for the passenger side door when she glimpsed motion from the corner of her eye. When she turned, she saw a face staring at her though the chain link fence.

"I'll be right back," she said as Henley climbed into the car.

She walked through the weeds with her hands held palm-out at her sides in a non-threatening manner. The face disappeared. She was just about to head back to the car when it reappeared through a flap torn in the banner featuring the painting of the proposed waterfront development. The shamrock-green eyes were wide and wild, the brow and the nose caked with grime.

"You shouldn't go down there no more," the man said. His teeth were brown behind his chapped lips. "Tell me you din't feel it. Something down there that ain't s'posed to be."

"Where are all of the others?"

"Don't say you ain't been warned."

The man ducked out of sight. Sturm heard feet pounding on wet asphalt and sprinted to the fence. By the time she reached the gap and peered through the links, whoever had been there was gone.

FIFTEEN

Seattle, Washington
7:38 a.m. PST

"Tell him what you told me," the uniformed officer said. He had the physique and shaved body hair of a juicer and wore his uniform so tight that the seams appeared as though they might split with a deep inhalation.

"I already given my statement," a burly, gray-bearded man in flannel and denim, who looked more like a lumberjack than the harbor master, said. Rod Thompson had been a permanent fixture on the wharf since he returned from 'Nam nearly forty years ago with a gaffe for a hand. Even though he was in his mid-sixties and the tattoos on his arms had begun to fade and sag, he still looked like the kind of man who could go toe-to-toe with a heavyweight. Porter always remembered the man's eyes, which were gunmetal gray around the pupils. It was like being fixed in the sights of two unwavering pistols. But not today. The harbor master's eyes drifted across the dock without settling on any one thing. "I ain't going through it again."

"The just tell me how you found it on the way down there," Porter said. He cupped Thompson's elbow and guided him away from the fish market and down the pier. The majority of the berths were now empty, their former occupants dots on the distant horizon. Shrieking gulls eyed them from their perches on nearly every flat surface: the rails of the pier, the gunwales and masts of the moored ships, the roof lines of the buildings. Fishermen bustled past them from both directions, oblivious to, or perhaps unconcerned by, the presence of the police. Tourists snapped pictures of the waterfront with steaming Starbucks cups in hand, as thought they couldn't find the exact same brew on every street corner in their hometowns.

Porter and Thompson veered to the left and started down the slanted planks toward a trawler guarded by a uniformed officer who wore a pinched expression and pressed the back of his hand against his nose. Two steps later, Porter knew why.

"Yeah," Thompson said. "You smell that, dontcha. That's how come I found it. I been getting nothing but complaints 'bout that since yesterday."

"So you boarded the vessel?"

They approached the officer, who nodded and gratefully vacated his post. Porter could read the name *Dragnet* on the barnacle-crusted hull. The gunwales and the roof of the pilothouse were thick with gulls. The racket of those wheeling overhead made it nearly impossible to form a coherent thought.

"I tried hailing'em on the radio first. I didn't want to haveta walk all the way down here, get me? So I ended up down here anyway, long story short. I called out, but got no answer. So, yeah. I boarded her and wish to hell I hadn't."

"What did you see?"

Porter tried to usher the harbor master up the gangplank onto the trawler, but Thompson planted his feet and stared, white-faced, up at the ship.

"Mr. Thompson?" Porter said.

"I done seen it once, and that's enough for me. You'll find out what I seen soon enough."

"Did you touch anything or otherwise alter—?"

"Touch anything?" Thompson snorted a laugh. "You tell me if you see anything down there you feel like touching."

He shook his head and started back toward the pier without another word.

Porter slipped on a pair of non-latex gloves from the inside pocket of his sports coat and climbed up onto the ship. Were it possible, the stench intensified with each step. By the time he clomped across the deck, his eyes were watering and even breathing through his mouth was no longer helping. It felt like the godawful smell was seeping through his pores. He drew his flashlight at the open belowdecks door and climbed down stairs coated with white feathers and droppings.

The humid air was stifling, untouched by any kind of breeze. He retched and clasped his tie over his nose and mouth. A gull startled from the table at the bottom of the stairs. Its wings beat against his chest as it fought through him. His beam traced the wood-paneled walls, the fabric benches at the table that folded down into bunks, and the lone window, made opaque by salt condensation, high up on the back wall. There were feathers everywhere they could possible settle, especially on the floor, where dozens of fish carcasses had been plucked to the scales and bones.

His flashlight found the narrow corridor leading deeper into the hold. Desiccated fish crunched underfoot as he crept down the hallway toward an open freezer door, where a mound of festering mackerel, alive with green-eyed flies, had slid across the threshold. Neither the framework nor the door itself showed any indication of being pried or forced. It was nearly impossible to keep his eyes open when he stepped through the doorway into the mound of rotting fish. He tried not to think about the sludge he could feel seeping through his slacks and socks. This was one Brooks Brothers suit that wouldn't be taking up closet space anymore.

The dusting of white feathers contrasted the sheer number of flies, which whirled in his beam and drew large shadows across the rear wall like flakes of ash. The carcasses had been pecked and plucked, their skins and entrails peeled off and out. Near the back of the room, where the mountain was highest against the rust-streaked wall, he finally saw what he was looking for. A face leered out at him from beneath the long gray bodies. The man's eyes and lids had been pecked to the black sockets, the skin peeled in strips from his hairline. Only the cartilaginous nub of his nose remained above his bared teeth, made ferocious by the absence of his lips and cheeks. Flies crawled in and out of his mouth behind his clenched molars.

Porter dreaded what he knew he had to do next.

He shoved his way into the heap. The carcasses felt as though they disintegrated against his thighs and released a sludge the consistency of oatmeal, expelling a previously unimaginable reek that had been contained by the integrity of the scales. He carefully extricated the sickly gray fish from around the man's face, one at a time, and revealed a dark mat of hair, the tattered conches of his ears, his unshaved jaw line, the contours of his neck leading down into the collar of a flannel shirt.

"Well now," he said. "What do we have here?"

He shined his beam onto a dark swatch on the man's neck and shooed away the flies. The squirming of maggots in the wound made his skin crawl.

Porter snapped off one of his gloves, pulled his cell phone from the inside pocket of his jacket, and speed dialed his SAC.

"We were right," he said. "This is our mystery ship."

He listened for a moment, his eyes traveling around the freezer. He thought he saw a tattooed arm and the shoulder of a coat protruding from the fish.

"Yes, sir. I agree. We have a much bigger problem on our hands than we initially thought."

SIXTEEN

Seattle, Washington
8:52 a.m. PST

Franklin Spears hung up the phone and leaned back in his desk chair. He massaged his temples as he stared up at the bare white ceiling. Everything was spiraling out of control now. It was only a matter of time until the nature of his involvement was revealed. His source at the Department of Defense had hinted that there was only so much he could do to monitor the situation, let alone control it. The FBI had sunk its teeth into the investigation like a junkyard dog and was prepared to shake the hell out of it to see what came out. It was one thing when they were dealing with the deaths out on the open sea, but now that they feared whatever had killed the men on the *Scourge* was loose on the mainland, all bets were off. Spears had been forced to declare the fact that he had a man on the vessel, supervising the transportation of the lost exploration party's remains. It wouldn't have taken long for the investigation to lead to him, so it seemed prudent to be at least somewhat forthcoming from the start. It was better that way than giving them a reason to take a long look at the *other* cases he had unloaded and transferred alongside them into a panel truck. Only a few high-ranking officials at the Bureau even knew they existed, thanks to the favors he had called in from some of his old DoD buddies, who had ensured that the dead creatures they had packaged inside the hollow ribcages of butchered cow carcasses and sealed inside refrigerated crates, were discretely transferred to him, no questions asked. He had made no mention of the cage or what it had contained, but if victims started turning up in Seattle, he wouldn't be able to distance himself from the inevitable queries. And if the media got wind of the story, the DoD would roll over on him faster than he could blink, which left him with only one real course of action.

He needed to find his "special cargo" before anyone else did.

At least he finally had some idea where it might be. He could have a small team—himself included, of course—dispatched within a matter of hours. They had the advantage of knowing what they were looking for and a functional grasp of how to deal with it. The FBI was confident that it was hunting a genetically engineered animal. Those guys didn't have a clue. They could stare it dead in the eyes and not even know it.

Spears, on the other hand, had not only seen it with his own two eyes, he had learned much about it over the last few days. The bodies of the exploration party, including his son's, were currently in quarantine at a CDC facility downtown, where they would be cleared of infectious diseases before being released to the families for disposition. The others—the ones that only he and his inner circle knew about—were downstairs in his lab right now, where a team of scientists—paid handsomely for their discretion—was running batteries of tests he couldn't even begin to understand.

They had already mapped the creature's genome and compared it against that of *Homo sapiens* and *Homo neanderthalensis*. The DNA was a match in both cases to within a tenth of a percent. While they were still analyzing the chromosomes to determine exactly where the differences lie, they had discovered enough physical dissimilarities that Spears didn't care exactly which loci on which chromosomes caused them. That was for the eggheads to decipher. All he cared about was getting to know his enemy; finding its strengths and weaknesses and its points of vulnerability. A part of him wanted nothing more than to track down the escapee and make it suffer unendurable agony until it longed for the release of death, and then make it suffer some more. Those things had robbed him of his son, and for that reason his blood demanded that he erase their existence from the planet, like what should have happened millennia before. But he recognized the value of the knowledge contained within their miraculous bodies and how invaluable it was to the right parties.

Undoubtedly, their genetic code could unlock secrets that would turn the face of modern medicine on its ear, but he didn't care about that in the slightest. The world was already overpopulated enough without adding legions of the elderly and infirm to its burden. And the last thing they needed with war looming on the horizon was another couple billion Chinese. No, he recognized that these creatures were perfect killing machines. They had laid waste to his son's party and his men—men he had personally trained, if not to be invincible, then as close as a human being could come—with only their bare hands and teeth. The intrinsic value of unlocking their mutations lie in the military applications, and as a patriot, it was his duty to see his nation's defense strengthened in any way he possibly could.

And by any means necessary.

Wars were no longer fought on open fields where battle lines were clearly drawn. They were being fought in caves in the desert, where the cowards who directed their attacks at innocent civilians hid with the complicit knowledge of corrupt governments that simultaneously funded their activities and publicly denied their existence with smiles on their faces. Unlike the previous century, when wars were engaged with the sole intention of winning, the liberal media now hogtied the armed forces. American soldiers could only poke the hornet's nest and try to avoid the stingers of the clouds that emerged, when they had the power to incinerate it with a flamethrower and eliminate the danger once and for all. Truman never would have been able to decisively end World War II if CNN had been around to air the dropping of the atomic bombs. We now sent boys out into hostile territory with their hands tied behind their backs, to fight battles they weren't allowed to win, to die in sand that by all rights should have been melted to glass from afar decades ago. All while we permitted the enemy to operate on our soil with relative impunity, gathering arms and biological weapons capable of wiping out our cities, our entire infrastructure, while we no longer had the balls to do the same thing to them. And these were just unorganized sand people still living in the stone ages.

When the time came to engage the Chinese, they would wash over our shores like a tsunami and annihilate everything in their path. These weren't people who cared about human rights or global PR. China was amassing a force the likes of which this planet had never known, an army already believed to be half a billion strong, that could not just sustain the loss of a quarter million soldiers, but was ready and willing to do so. As Mao Tse-Tung once said, "We shall heal our wounds, collect our dead and continue fighting." It was a war we would not only lose, it would destroy the American way of life and eradicate the freedom for which Spears and his forefathers had willingly shed their blood and sacrificed their lives. Perhaps when the moment arrived, our puppet president would hesitate with his finger on the button, while the bleeding hearts decried the loss of lives and habitat and the effects of a nuclear strike on global warming, and the nation debated morality and God on television, but Hu Jintao would not. The attack would be sudden and unremitting, for he believed as Sun Tzu had more than two thousand years ago, "There has never been a protracted war from which a country has benefitted."

What was downstairs in Spears's lab right now was better than a nuclear bomb. It was a means of turning a war before the first shots were even fired, and ending one in such a way that the enemy would never rise again. Victory was obtained not when the last enemy fell, but when he no longer had the will to fight. The Japanese did not surrender because we wiped them out. They gave up because they were afraid, and these were people who flew missions with the sole intention of killing themselves, not a society prone to weakness. They ceded because we put the fear of God into them. We showed them in one decisive measure that we had the power and the resolve to annihilate each and every one of them and that we were willing to do whatever it took to win the war. We instilled fear in the fearless, and in so doing broke them like so many willful children. Fear was the most powerful weapon any army could wield, more powerful than an arsenal of warheads aimed at every population center. And fear was what former Brigadier General Franklin Spears would soon be able to provide for the country to which he had devoted his life, and for which his son, whether wittingly or not, had sacrificed his own.

The bodies in the lab were equipped with evolutionary enhancements that could turn even the meekest grunt into a killing machine capable of laying waste to an entire battalion with his bare hands. Their muscles were denser, more heavily concentrated with actin and myosin contractile proteins, which made them stronger than their human and Neanderthal contemporaries, and capable of reaching speeds previously undreamt of. That same muscular enhancement gave their jaws the tensile strength of a bear trap. They had predatory eyes adapted to complete darkness, like those of wolves, and blood thinners in their saliva that were potent enough to cause a man to bleed out inside his own body without shedding a single drop of blood. They were designed to be killers. He understood how the species had survived for as long as it had, but would never be able to comprehend why it had never become the dominant species. It should have wiped out its competition with little effort. But that was of no consequence now.

Spears allowed himself a smile as he imagined a single Green Beret with the creature's physical attributes crawling into a sandstone crevice in Afghanistan at sundown and emerging under the blood-red dawn with the bodies of a dozen Taliban tied to a rope like trout on a stringer. The image changed to that of a dozen marines standing shoulder-to-shoulder with the Great Wall at their backs as the ground trembled and the air shivered with the war cries of thousands of Chinese streaming across a battlefield soon to be littered with their corpses.

They stood at the precipice of a new era that would be defined by the bold actions of brave men.

The Spears Era, as he now thought of it.

There was only one thing standing in his way,

The missing cargo.

He needed to capture it before it fell into the wrong hands.

Preferably alive, but, in reality, that was no longer his concern.

Soon enough they would amass an army that would force America's enemies to tremble in fear.

SEVENTEEN

Seattle, Washington
10:12 p.m. PST

Sturm jerked her head up when it bounced from the passenger side window. She hadn't even felt herself dozing off. She surreptitiously wiped the corner of her mouth and glanced toward the driver's seat, where Henley stared straight ahead with a smirk on his face.

"Glad I could provide some amusement."

"I'll take it where I can get it."

He slowed the cruiser and eased it over the curb. Sturm hopped out, stomped at the pins and needles in her right foot, and crossed through the headlights to open the gate. Once the patrol car passed through, she closed it again and climbed back into her seat. Her head throbbed and the edges of her vision contracted in time with the pulse in her temples. She'd been burning the candle at both ends for too long. Between the overtime on her night job and the increased demand for her services at the CSRT with this new case, something had to give, and she feared it would be her body that relented first.

She popped a Sudafed and swallowed it dry. At least that ought to perk her up enough to get her through the next couple of hours underground, even if it left her shaky.

Henley pretended he didn't see as he guided the tires through the ruts toward the demolished buildings.

"Two more nights," he said. The words were meant to be reassuring, but all she felt was despair. "Two more nights and we can go back to holding up the counter at Denny's and waiting for domestic disturbance calls."

He parked the car, climbed out, and stretched his arms over his head as he did every night. Sturm fought the urge to claw out his eyes. Every little thing he did grated on her nerves, despite the fact that he was making an obvious effort to be patient with her situation. While she appreciated it, she didn't want any special treatment. She'd succeed on her own, without anyone going easy on her, like she always had.

"You think the mayor's going to invite us to his fancy shindig?" he asked. "You know, to reward us for making our city safe for the rich again?"

"We'll be lucky if he doesn't have us serving appetizers and champagne in uniform."

Henley chuckled. "I'm sure the thought's crossed his mind."

While he completed his stretching routine, Sturm looked to the north, where she could see the glow of the klieg lights directed at the *Dragnet*. She'd spent the entire day aboard that vile vessel, unloading festering fish one at a time, visually scouring each and every one of them for teeth marks and congealed blood from the victims. After being buried in carcasses and molested by flies for two straight days in that freezer, which had turned into a suffocating hotbox, the bodies of the victims had become like balloons filled with cottage cheese. Not that she got to work on them. While the paid portion of the team did all of the cool stuff, like performing tests on the wounds and the remaining blood and tissue, she had sorted through fish that had begun to decompose to such an extent that their scales fell off, their skin slid across the pungent meat and tore with the slightest pressure, and their eyes leaked a slimy sludge that reminded her of pus. Even after searching and removing every last mackerel, pollock, and cod, they hadn't found a single shred of evidence. There were no prints, no hairs, no fibers. Like aboard the *Scourge*, there hadn't been a single clue as to what or who had slain the men, other than the wounds on the necks of the corpses, which, at this point in the game, were all they had to go on.

They had made several casts of the jaws, which were being cross-referenced against every possible database and were now being tested by engineers using hydraulic clamps to estimate the force of the bites. The results of the tests performed on the saliva extracted from the wounds were a little more encouraging, but still couldn't point them in the direction of a viable biological suspect. Sequencing the DNA had been next to impossible as it was diluted with the blood of the victims and degraded by the acidic pH in the saliva to such a degree that they couldn't conclusively determine anything beyond the fact that it belonged to a higher order of mammal. The only thing they could state with authority was that the Draculin-like anticoagulatory protein complex was present in large quantities. Whether they were a component of the saliva or not, they had reached the victims' bloodstreams in sufficient concentrations that the men would have eventually bled out through the walls of their vessels, even if they hadn't exsanguinated first. There still wasn't enough information to formalize a working hypothesis. All they knew without a doubt was that it was only a matter of time before word leaked to the media and they had reporters crawling all over them. Thus far, they had been able to keep a lid on their investigation, and the mayor and various federal agencies had exerted their influence to control the flow of information, but they all knew they were on borrowed time. Their mandate was simple:

Track down whatever killed these men and do so in a hurry.

The problem they were all skirting around was that they had reason to believe that whatever it was was now on the mainland, which meant that it could be anywhere. And if it killed again before they were able to find it...

She shoved that thought aside and returned to the here and now. Henley was staring curiously at her as though waiting for an answer to a question she hadn't heard him pose.

"Let's get this show on the road," she said, and brushed past him toward the entrance to the demolished warehouse.

There was a long hesitation before she heard his footsteps on the weeds behind her.

*   *   *

They split up at the first fork, as was their routine. Sturm could still hear the scuffing sounds of Henley's passage on the other side of a crumbling brick wall, where rats gnawed at the exposed lumber. Soon enough, she wouldn't be able to hear him at all as he branched deeper into the ruins, stranding her alone in a heavy silence marred only by her heavy breathing, the groaning of the settling structure, and the slithering of sand and powdered cement through the rubble. She could still identify the spot on the dusty floor where the doll had once been. Part of her expected it to return one of these nights like the denizens of the darkness, and while she was relieved that it hadn't, it was a link to the young girl who had lost it, whom she feared she might never be able to exorcise from her thoughts.

She passed the first alcove without any sign of the people she had rousted so many times. Maybe they had finally moved on. Maybe they had settled into a shelter and were taking the first steps toward reclaiming their lives aboveground. Maybe something good had actually come from this most heinous of assignments.

Sturm clung to that hope as she crawled from one bleak building to the next. After so many hours in the hold of the *Dragnet*, these dank rooms no longer had the power to make her retch. Perspective. It was like walking through a meadow of wildflowers by comparison, which was why she was unprepared for what her beam settled upon through a tent formed by fallen timber, which braced chunks of concrete and bricks like an igloo.

Her light cast shadows from the pale white fingers of a hand that was partially clenched as though holding an invisible ball. A ribbon of blood wound around the wrist like a bracelet.

She leaned her head toward the transceiver affixed to her shoulder and pressed the button to transmit.

"Henley. You need to get over here."

"*You need backup?*"

"Just get over here. I'm about halfway through the canning factory."

He said something else, but the words drifted off into the darkness, unacknowledged, as she lowered herself to the ground and shined her flashlight under the cribbing. She followed the length of a flannel-clad arm to the shoulder and the side of the head. The man's dark hair was mussed and tangled, the side of his face smeared with grime and speckled with blood. She nearly had to climb in on top of him to see his face. His tattered lips framed his open mouth, the front teeth chipped. His nose was visibly broken and his wide green eyes stared up into the rubble. She recognized them immediately from the night before. This was the man with whom she had spoken through the fence, the man who had warned her—

Sturm gasped and scrambled away from the body.

The neck.

The man's neck had been torn open in the exact same fashion as the crew of the *Dragnet*.

Her back met the decomposing plaster wall and she let out a shriek. She clumsily drew her sidearm and pointed it into the hole, where her flashlight beam trembled from side to side, animating the lifeless fingers as though they pawed at the air.

She willed her hands to still and took several slow, measured breaths. When the initial shock waned and she gathered her wits, she tapped into her training as a criminalist and evaluated the scene with the necessary detachment. The patina of dust and dirt on the ground was disturbed where she had crawled into the rubble. It was a mistake, but not necessarily a critical one. She could still see the markings where the body had been dragged down the corridor from the direction of the third building, to her right. The smears of blood on the smooth bricks were dry and brown, reminiscent of strokes by a damp paint brush. There were no arterial spurts or spatters, nor did a cursory inspection reveal there to be any on the walls. The man hadn't been killed here, but rather dragged to this particular point from wherever he had been slain.

Sturm crouched and scrutinized the dust. There were hundreds of footprints trampled one on top of the other, surely some of them her own, rendering the individual tracks indistinct. Perhaps they would be able to isolate some clear prints when they discovered where the man had been killed, but, for now, her priority was to preserve the integrity of the scene for proper evaluation. She had already fouled a large portion of the area immediately around her, but her initial reaction wasn't an uncommon one. She'd take her lumps when the crime scene response team arrived. At least she had recognized what she had found quickly enough to avoid doing irreparable damage.

She swung around and shined her light into Henley's face at the sound of his approach.

"Stay right there," she snapped. "Don't move."

He stopped dead in his tracks to her left and raised a hand across his brow to shield his eyes from the glare.

"What's going on?" He started to move forward again, but she halted him with her palm before he could get any closer. "Jesus. What is that? A hand?"

"Call it in."

"That wasn't here last night, was it?"

"Just call it in, for Christ's sake!"

Without moving her feet, she lowered herself to her haunches and shined her beam into the recess. The man's body stretched away from her. He had been dragged feet-first into the hole, with his arms trailing behind him. His well-worn boots stood at forty-five-degree angles to the floor. Between them, she saw the mouth of a dark tunnel leading deeper into the building, beyond her light's reach.

EIGHTEEN

Seattle, Washington
11:16 p.m. PST

"You're certain he was killed all the way over here?" Porter said.

"Unless someone else was," Galiardi said.

"That's a cheery thought."

"We haven't received the results from the blood test comparisons, but I'm comfortable working under the assumption that the man was killed here, dragged across the field and down into the building through what's left of that window over there."

Porter looked across the field of weeds, where the trampled path through the vegetation was still apparent. He could barely see the collapsed frame of what had once been a ground floor window and was now little more than a slit that didn't look large enough for him to squirm through on his belly. The lights from those working inside barely illuminated the window with the strength of a candle's glow, despite the sheer wattage spotlighting the chamber where they had found the man's remains. Outside was a different story. Two police cruisers had been pulled around to the side of the old market and parked side-by-side with the high beams directed at its northern brick façade at such an angle that they were nearly invisible from the street. Galiardi had pitched a fit at not being able to erect the sodium halide domes by which she was accustomed to working, but she had been rebuked every bit as firmly as he had. This investigation was to be conducted with the utmost discretion, and wrapped up with all due haste. There was to be no contact with the media whatsoever. His SAC had gone so far as to say that if he caught even of whiff of the story on the news, he'd make sure Porter ended up working the reservations out of the South Dakota field office. It was an idle threat, Porter knew, but that didn't change the nature of the assignment. There was to be no negative publicity surrounding the waterfront renovation project. Too much money had already been invested for largely lackluster results, and even more would still have to be raised. Taxpayer money. And taxpayers meant voters. None of the parties involved with the project—be it the mayor, the governor, or the congressmen who backed the initiative—could allow themselves to be attached to a public relations fiasco of such titanic proportions. If rumors that a body—let alone a second—had been discovered leaked to the press, this ship would sink in a hurry. As it was, the powers-that-be had yet to be informed of the prospect that whatever had slaughtered the men aboard the *Scourge* and the *Dragnet* might be loose on the mainland. They needed concrete proof of that before they opened that can of worms, which Porter supposed they now had. He'd deal with that soon enough. For now, they would treat this as the simple death of an indigent and go from there. Let the mayor make the call about where the body had been found. Or if it had been found at all. No one seemed too concerned about the niggling little details surrounding the murder of a man they suspected no one would ever miss. Or care about, for that matter.

Porter turned his attention back to the scene before him and returned his focus from the politics to the job at hand. The crime scene investigators already had a good half-hour jump on him, and appeared to have made the most of that time. They had already marked the point where the victim had scaled the fence and dropped down into the mid with two small, numbered pink flags. The impressions matched the victim's boots perfectly. The line of trampled vegetation between that point and where Porter now stood had yet to spring back into place. Each of the man's footfalls was marked by another pink flag. The distance between them, the deep toe divots and lack of heel contact, suggested that the man had hit the ground and broken into a sprint. He had been overcome near the base of the brick wall, where the disturbed detritus indicated that he had been attacked while trying to scurry through a crumbled section of brickwork into the building's basement. A starburst of black blood marred the dirt and weeds. Arterial spurts painted the ancient bricks. The standing puddle where he had fallen was diluted with rainwater, which continued to drip from the eave above with a metronomic plopping sound. The streaks on the ground and the flattened weeds diminished as they neared the ruins where the body had been discovered.

They were approaching the investigation was though they had two distinct scenes: the first where the man was killed; the second, where he was found. Uniformed officers scoured the vacant lot across the street for any sign of where the victim had come from and what had caused his frenetic flight. Half of the CSRT unit was underground, the other half here around Porter. Galiardi moved back and forth between the two, supervising and coordinating. The man's fingerprints had already been loaded into the system in hopes of ascertaining his identity through the IAFIS database. Of course, unless he had a criminal record or a history of government employment, they were going to have to wait on his dental records, assuming that a homeless man had even maintained his oral hygiene regimen and that someone had missed him enough to forward those records to the authorities. Unfortunately, he didn't imagine anyone was going to go out of their way to get an ID on this guy. Even if they did, he had to wonder if that information would ever see the light of day or if the man who had nearly been decapitated would wind up in a pauper's grave under an anonymous placard.

There was one positive, if he were truly searching for one.

At least whatever had killed all of the men aboard the two vessels hadn't gone far.

"Tell me something—anything—that might help us figure out what we're dealing with here."

Galiardi rounded on him, face flushed, teeth bared, ready to explode, but paused and took a moment to collect herself before speaking.

"Let me show you something," she finally said, beckoning him into the field with a sweep of her hand.

She was obviously taking their lack of progress personally. He was going to have to watch his phrasing. Right now, she and her team were just about the only allies he had in the cover-up he could positively feel coming.

"Look right here." She crouched and directed her penlight at a clump of ferns that had been squashed flat, the stems bent and broken. "And over here." She turned her beam on a crushed patch of wild grass. "And here." Again, another flattened fern.

"What am I looking at?"

"Our killer's footprints. Or, more precisely, the lack thereof." She stood and sighed. "As far as we can tell, every single one of his—or its—footfalls were deliberately placed where they wouldn't leave prints. Sure, we can tell exactly where it stepped, but there's no way of pulling an impression from a clump of grass."

"You can't possibly be implying that every one of its tracks landed right on a patch of thick grass to mask its passage."

"That's exactly what I'm telling you."

"So while this thing is running in pursuit of this man, it had the presence of mind to avoid leaving a single print—"

His cell phone chirped under his jacket. He held up a finger to indicate he needed a minute and removed the phone from his pocket.

"Scary thought, isn't it?" Galiardi said.

He turned away from her and distanced himself from anyone who might overhear his conversation.

"Porter," he said.

His SAC spoke for nearly two full minutes without taking a breath that Porter could exploit to interrupt or attempt to clarify what was being said. His orders were punctuated with a quick click and then dead air. He stared down at the darkened screen on his phone for a long moment before tucking it back inside his jacket.

He didn't like this development.

Not one little bit.

A pair of headlights flashed at the curb on the other side of the chain link barricade.

"That was fast," he said out loud as he walked toward the nearest gate.

As if things weren't interesting enough already.

NINETEEN

Seattle, Washington
Friday, October 19ʰ
2:42 a.m. PST

Sturm looked into the man's shamrock-green eyes clear up until the point that they ran the zipper up between them. They had strapped the body bag to a backboard in order to carry it out of the underground maze since there was no way a gurney would fit. The whole experience had been maddening and surreal. Since she was still on her patrol job, she'd been unable to participate in the collection and documentation of evidence. She'd been forced to stand back with her hands in her pockets and watch the same CSRT unit she'd worked shoulder-to-shoulder with for so many months doing the things she knew she should be doing. Never in her life had she felt so ineffectual. And now that the body was gone, the cameras no longer flashed, and the physical crime scene had been cordoned off and closed down, she was expected to go right back to work, clearing the warrens of whatever derelicts might somehow still be sleeping down here.

She stared down at the chalk outline of the body and the dark smears of blood and was reminded of a child coloring outside the lines.

"I guess we'll be missing the early bird specials," Henley said from behind her.

She nearly jumped at the sound of his voice. She hadn't heard him enter the room.

"What are we supposed to do now?" It took conscious effort to raise her stare from the ground to meet his.

"I can tell you what we *don't* have to do now." He smiled. "I just got word that we won't be doing any paperwork on this one."

She shook her head and looked back at the ground. The blood was a testament to the fact that a human being had died here, even if no one else chose to acknowledge it.

"Come on," Henley said. "Let's just cruise through this so we can get out of here. I'm ready to put this night behind me."

He struck off in the opposite direction, his footsteps fading until she was again alone in her own head. She realized her hand had fallen to the grip of her service pistol, her thumb primed under the snap of the holster. Maybe Henley had no idea what was potentially down there with them, but she did. She knew all too well what the monster that had done this was capable of. If it was still down here, she and her partner were in grave danger. She couldn't believe that any of the agencies that had been involved from the start, that had seen the carnage on the *Scourge* and the *Dragnet*, would simply abandon the scene of the crime while whatever had killed so many was still on the loose.

Then it hit her.

They wouldn't.

Not while there was a chance they had the monster cornered.

They were emptying the site as inconspicuously as possible, and then they were going to come in after it. The entire waterfront was probably already surrounded. They had probably formed a perimeter and were even now in the process of tightening the net. And yet she and Henley were still down here, isolated in the darkness under tons of debris. What role were they expected to play, especially considering that neither of them had been briefed about the operation and Henley was completely oblivious?

"Son of a bitch," she whispered.

They were bait.

Two beat cops crawling around beneath condemned ruins? Any number of accidents could befall them, and could be justified easily enough. Were their lives worth less to the city they faithfully served than its investment in a goddamn real estate development?

Sturm heard a skritching sound ahead of her.

She drew her pistol and assumed a shooter's stance.

Again, all she could hear was the settling of the building around and above her. It was undoubtedly just a rat, or maybe nothing at all. She was so tired that she couldn't trust her senses, let alone her judgment.

She held her breath and listened. The movement of air through the rubble made the building sound as though it were breathing.

Another scraping sound, like nails across concrete.

Then silence.

The sound had definitely come from directly ahead of her, beyond the recess where the body had been mere minutes ago, somewhere out of sight behind the canted timber and mounds of bricks.

She crouched and shined her beam past the bloodstains into a small gap in the rubble barely wide enough for her to wiggle through. Maybe just wide enough—

Movement at the edge of her beam's reach. A blur of bluish-white. The skritching sound.

She hadn't gotten a good look at it, but she'd seen enough to know that it wasn't a rat.

"Henley," she whispered into her transceiver. "Henley."

She feared speaking any louder.

The weight of the silence pressed down on her to the point that she felt the rubble might collapse and bury her alive. She was spooking herself, she knew. There could be any number of animals back there, seeking refuge in the dank caverns. She hadn't seen whatever it was well enough to convince herself that she had seen anything at all. Had it just been the movement of her light across a chunk of concrete?

Cautiously, she lowered herself to the ground and eased forward on her knees and elbows, holding her flashlight against the side of her Beretta. The mouth of the small tunnel yawned before her. She could see maybe a dozen feet into the orifice, to the point where the tunnel terminated against a section of brickwork still held together by mortar, furry with some kind of fungus or mold. Motes of dust sparkled like glitter in her column of light. She tried not to think about the man's dried blood flaking off onto her uniform as she squirmed right up to the point where her arms entered the hole and her shoulders wedged against the sides.

Decision time.

She watched for any sign of movement, any change in the air current to disturb the settling dust.

Nothing.

She should just back out and get the hell out of there. Let the FBI and whoever else was out there handle this operation—whatever it was—on their own. Screw them if they wanted to use her to draw out whatever might be down here. If they wanted this thing, they could come down here and get it—

A scraping sound. Mere feet ahead of her and around the bend to her right. Just out of sight.

The sparkling motes billowed to the left.

There was definitely something back there, something much bigger than a rat.

She leaned her head against her shoulder and pressed the button on her handset with her cheek.

"Henley." She had barely spoken loud enough to hear it herself. He was probably already nearing the exit to the outside world from the adjacent building. Still, she waited for a response that never came. "Damn it."

Sturm couldn't even turn her head far enough to glance back over her shoulder to make sure there was nothing creeping up behind her. In her current position, she was a sitting duck. Time to either press on or cut her losses. She drew a deep breath to steady her nerves, gritted her teeth, and squirmed deeper. The tunnel tapered as she went. By the time she reached the bend, her arms were pinned in front of her. She rolled onto her side so she could see to the right. The scratching sounds became frantic. She swung her beam toward the source in time to catch a fleeting glimpse of the bottom of a dirty, bare foot, a swatch of pasty white skin, and what she could have sworn were the stiff legs of a naked, grime-coated baby doll clutched in a small, filthy hand.

TWENTY

Seattle, Washington
3:11 a.m. PST

Spears crouched in the high weeds that had grown up against the weathered wall of one of the construction company's trailers and watched the two uniformed officers face off beside their cruiser through his thermal vision goggles. The woman was animated, repeatedly gesturing back toward the ruins with both hands, while the man patted the air between them in what was meant to be a calming gesture. After several minutes, he raised his face to the sky, threw up his arms in exasperation, and plopped down into the driver's seat. The woman stared at the rubble for a long moment before she finally walked around the rear of the Crown Victoria and eased into the passenger seat. Spears studied the surrounding area, praying for even the slightest hint of thermal color or movement, until the cruiser backed away from the building and bumped across the overgrown lot. Once the fence was again closed and the patrol car was nothing but a distant red glow of brake lights, he gave the signal for his men to converge.

The four of them had been stationed within the construction zone at the four points of the compass, hoping that the bait would draw their prey out into the open. It had been a long shot for sure, especially after the scene had been swarming with officers, but it had been a shot worth taking. The sooner they took this thing down, the better. They couldn't risk arousing any more suspicion than they already had. As it was, Spears had been forced to tip his hand to his connections at the DoD in order to clear out the area so he and his men would be able to hunt. He hadn't disclosed all of the details about the nature of their discovery in Siberia, but he had given them enough to whet their appetites for more, at least enough for them to order the FBI out of there, if only temporarily. The agent on the scene had been a challenge to shove out of the way.

He already knew far too much, and the expression on his face and the tone of his voice hinted at his suspicion of Spears's involvement. The agent's SAC had remained firm and the agent had reluctantly vacated the premises rather than risk the consequences. The look in his eyes when he left hadn't been one of acquiescence, though. Spears recognized the spark of determination and knew the agent wasn't about to let this one go. He would be back, but Spears fully intended to have this business wrapped up long before then.

He ducked low and dashed across the field toward the cluster of demolished buildings in the center. Flashes of midnight-blue and fuchsia emerged from his peripheral vision. Security Specialist Judd Ritter advanced on the middle building from where he had been hiding by the street to the left, while Lyle Barnaby dashed across the field from behind the decrepit pier. Paul Cranston would be rushing the ruins from the north, on the far side of the rubble from Spears. They were faceless grunts who had yet to distinguish themselves in his service, but since his most trusted men were no longer available to him, this was their opportunity to step up. All they had to do was access the subterranean level and rendezvous in the basement of the cannery. If they managed to survive long enough to do so, anyway.

Their mission was simple: Take the enemy. Alive if possible, dead if necessary, and complete their extraction by dawn. Swoop in and out and leave no one the wiser.

A strobe of lightning reflected from the ornate cultural center on the far side of the lot, then returned it to darkness. The whole idea of it mocked the culture it had unceremoniously displaced. He remembered when the wharves that had birthed this city, these very piers that had fallen into disrepair long ago, had pulsed with the lifeblood of the Pacific Northwest. And now this bloody heritage center would stand over its remains like a tombstone. He could only imagine that his father, who had slaved on these docks his entire life, from before sunrise until long after sunset, would claw his way out of his grave to spit in the mayor's eye if he could.

Thoughts of his father steered him back to memories of his son. He had to force down the rage in order to focus on his mission. If left with no other option, he would revel in the prospect of kicking in the beast's skull.

He zeroed in on what was left of the basement window and pulled up just short. The ledge was still crusted with the dead man's blood, but the rain would wash it away soon enough. It had already begun to sprinkle and the distant grumble of thunder promised a deluge. He knelt and peered through the window into the basement.

No color.

No motion.

He quickly ducked his head and slithered through. The second he hit the ground, he popped back up to his feet, pinned the Colt IAR against his shoulder, and advanced into the darkness.

*   *   *

Porter lay flat on the wet ground, shrouded by ferns, peering through binoculars over the crest of a low hill in the vacant lot across the street from the development. His position wasn't ideal for surveillance, but concealment had been his primary concern. He'd driven away like a good little boy when he'd been dismissed by this character who hadn't even bothered to introduce himself, then cruised around the block, parked on the far side of the lot, and crawled on his belly across trash and broken glass and through puddles and refuse to reach his current location. He had arrived just in time to see the police car turn out onto the main road, and then the black-clad men with their thermal vision goggles and automatic rifles rush the buildings.

Now that all four of them were inside, he had a decision to make.

What was he going to do about it?

His directive had been clear and concise: Get lost. This operation was being handled far above his pay grade. The problem was the level of secrecy involved, and he didn't like being cut out of his own loop. Whoever had leaned on his SAC obviously had some serious clout, enough to steamroll his investigation and unleash what appeared to be a team of mercenaries onto his crime scene, which led him to only one logical conclusion.

Whoever was pulling the strings knew exactly what had killed the crews of the *Scourge* and the *Dragnet*, and had recognized the significance of the indigent's death tonight. Hence, this unit had been dispatched under a black flag to resolve the problem before those of them investigating it were able to put the pieces together. So if he ever wanted to learn the truth, he was going to have to do so tonight.

He watched what little he could see of the construction zone for several more minutes before he finally returned the field glasses to his jacket and started toward the street.

*   *   *

Spears advanced slowly through passageways with crumbling walls and a ceiling that felt as though it could come right down on his head at any second. Through the broken brickwork and the hollowed plaster, he saw only dark tunnels leading deeper under the rubble. This was far worse than he had expected. Their prey could have squirmed through any of the holes and wedged itself somewhere they would never be able to reach. He thought of the caverns inside Mt. Belukha and how the creatures had buried themselves under the dirt. Were it not for the thermal vision goggles that had detected their breath rising from the reeds, they would have unknowingly walked right over them. If this one lone predator chose to hide from them in that same manner, they might never find it.

He followed the barrel of his rifle, which he swept slowly from one side of the hallway to the other. His men whispered through the com-link in his ear as they cleared each chamber, but Spears knew that their quarry held every advantage. Down here in the darkness and the close confines, it had the home field advantage. Each step brought Spears nearer the realization that unless this monster broke cover to come after them, their only chance was to blindly stumble upon it.

Water had begun to drip through the rubble overhead and plinked into the stagnant puddles on the floor. The storm must have finally commenced. With so much debris above him, he hadn't heard a single peal of thunder.

He ducked through a passage in a brick wall and entered the adjacent building. The acoustics changed and he heard the soft echoes of footfalls other than his own. He stepped to his right and across the threshold into a small room, the back half of which had

been demolished. There were broken bottles beside heaps of damp
and rotting newspapers on one side and piles of feces on the other.
The entire room stank of ammonia and despair, a stench he equated
to death. He peeked around the corner and watched the barrel of an
automatic rifle round the bend in the hallway, followed by the
blue, violet, and amber glow of one of his men.

Spears whispered into the microphone strapped to his throat
and stepped out into the hallway. Ritter nodded to him and turned
back to the corridor that would lead them deeper into the building.
Spears took the lead, and together they pressed onward into the
dark warrens. The doorways to either side, at least those that were
still patent, opened upon little more than rubble and garbage. It
was obvious where the rats and the Morlocks made their homes.
The piles of shredded blankets, moldy cardboard, and mildewed
sheets positively stank of body odor and desperation. The reek of
piss made it nearly impossible to breathe. He wondered how
anyone could possibly live like this. Already he could feel the fluid
settling in his lungs and the tickle of a cough in his throat. He
feared no amount of showering would rid him of its taint.

The hallway led to a large central chamber of sorts, the eastern
half of which was amassed rubble from the cracked stone floor to
the collapsed ceiling. A groan and the gunshot sound of cracking
wood overhead reminded him of the necessity for speed. Two
doors interrupted the western wall, through which he could see
broken conveyors and equipment that looked positively medieval
in design draped with dust, lorded over by pyramidal columns of
rubble that barely supported the floor above. They could
undoubtedly bring the whole works down on them with a loud
shout.

Spears smiled at his presence of mind. He'd had the foresight
to equip their rifles with suppressors.

They were nearly to the uneven, brick-edged hole in the wall
that served as the passageway into the adjoining building when he
caught a glimpse of color and the faintest hint of motion from the
corner of his vision.

He turned to his left and sighted down the barrel of his IAR. A
triangular orifice framed a tunnel that breathed dust. The canted
timber that formed the roof appeared petrified; the slanted concrete
of the wall quilled with rusted rebar. It couldn't have been much

larger than the kind of ribbed culverts he had crawled through in his youth.

"Report," he whispered into the wireless com-link. He studied the stillness for any sign of what had drawn his eye.

"*Barnaby,*" his man said through the earpiece. "*There's no direct route from the west. I had to detour to the north. I'm closing on your position now.*"

"Cranston?" Spears whispered.

A tiny sphere of venous blue streaked downward and struck the concrete dust in front of him with a *plat*.

"Cranston?"

The dust on the floor was black and crusted into a miniature stalagmite. He followed the trajectory upward until he was staring at the ceiling. A rapidly fading blue puddle clung to the decayed wooden slats. As he watched, a droplet swelled, shivered, and then plummeted to the ground.

"Damn it," Spears whispered.

Ritter's breathing grew harsh behind him.

Spears sighted down the dark tunnel and eased closer. The dust was slick and muddy underfoot, with just the faintest tint of cobalt blue. The coppery scent of blood pierced the miasma of vile aromas that stalked the ruins as he climbed a mound of rubble and leaned toward the mouth of the tunnel. Its dusty breath smelled of carrion.

A lone blue globule dripped from the low ceiling a half-dozen feet in. It turned black before it hit the ground.

Footsteps behind him announced Barnaby's arrival. Neither of his remaining men needed to say a word. They knew the score. Cranston had been overcome pretty much right where Spears stood now. The once hot arterial blood that had spattered the ceiling was already cooling below the threshold of the goggles, the puddles underfoot chilled by the earth. And they all knew damn well what had happened to Cranston from there.

And they hadn't heard a sound.

"Ritter. You follow me. Barnaby. Stand guard here. Nothing gets past you from either side. Understand?"

Spears pulled the trigger and released a fusillade of bullets that was no louder than thumping the side of an empty two-liter bottle.

Sparks flew where they ricocheted from the concrete. They impacted with what sounded like timber.

He scurried in right behind them, pulling himself along with his elbows and his knees, his rifle ahead of him. Cranston's blood soaked through his clothing. It was cool against his skin, but it stoked the heat in his core. Despite the darkness, his vision throbbed with red. His prey couldn't be too far ahead of him. Once he found it, he was going to make that demon wish it had never clawed its way out of its mother's wretched womb.

Ritter's scraping and scratching sounds trailed him into the constricting tube. The air grew colder and damper by the second. The carrion smell intensified in the stillness. His barrel clattered from something hard. He corrected his course to the right. The ground grew steeper as he crawled, the swatches of blood making purchase tenuous at best. Ritter cursed behind him and a cascade of pebbles tumbled down the slope.

He felt the stirring of the air and heard the change in intonation before he crawled out from the tunnel and sensed the ceiling rise above him, as though a great weight had been lifted from his shoulders.

The only color was provided by a heap off to his left against a jagged mound of concrete. A cold blue radiance burned in its center mass. The night vision allowed him to see the outline of the boots, the shape of the hunched back, the crown of the head. The aperture of the goggles stood from Cranston's forehead like a narwhal's horn.

Spears stood to his full height and turned slowly in a circle.

"Mother of God," he whispered.

He was in a domed chamber no larger than his master bathroom, but he felt as though he were inside a bee hive. The rubble surrounding him was honeycombed with black tunnels that led off in dozens of different directions.

From this one point, his prey could potentially travel throughout the ruins, from building to building.

It could be anywhere by now.

TWENTY-ONE

Seattle, Washington
5:27 a.m. PST

Porter crouched in the cab of an earthmover two hundred yards from where the men had parked their Humvee and studied the exterior of the building through his binoculars. If the men caught a reflection from his lenses when they emerged, they could easily mistake it for the cracked window of the dirty yellow Caterpillar. They had been underground for more than two hours already. Hunting, he assumed. But it was only a matter of time before the workers arrived to grade the area around the cultural center and lay slate paving stones in time for the ribbon-cutting ceremony still scheduled for Saturday night. There were massive rolls of chain link and hundreds of silver posts that would be erected around the ruins themselves, while the fencing would be torn down from in front of the center itself to allow it to be viewed in all its splendor from the main thoroughfare. Never mind the fact that people had died here. It was all about raising the necessary capital to kick this project into high gear. He wondered how much of that capital was being invested into the men crawling through the rubble down there.

He glanced through the rear window at the eastern horizon. The merest hint of pink stained the bellies of the clouds. The men down there would emerge soon. They would want to be long gone by the time the sun rose. Already, the occasional set of headlights cruised past and tires buzzed on the wet asphalt of the main road.

Movement at the base of the building drew his eye, a mere shifting of the shadows. The first man crawled out of the ruins, then turned around and reached back through the darkened orifice from which he had just emerged. He struggled with something heavy before crawling backward, dragging its weight along with him. A second man clambered from the hole while the first turned and scanned the surrounding area through his night vision apparatus.

Porter instinctively dropped down under the steering wheel and pressed himself to the dirty floor. Even if they were utilizing thermal imaging, they wouldn't be able to detect him through the cold steel-reinforced door. He waited nearly two full minutes before climbing back up onto the seat and risking a peek through the binoculars.

The men were already across the weeded lot and to their car. One man opened the rear door and stepped back. The other two, who carried a massive black vinyl or plastic bag between them, hefted it into the back of the Hummer and slammed the tailgate closed.

Porter ducked again. Undoubtedly, they would scan the lot once more to make sure that no one had seen them and get the hell out of there before anyone did.

By the time Porter raised his head, the rectangular brake lights were jostling down over the curb onto the main road. They flared long enough for one of the men to hop out and close the gate behind them before fading from view. He waited several minutes longer, listening for the sound of the Hummer's engine to return. Once he was confident that they weren't coming back, he shouldered the door open and dropped down to the ground.

Gulls squalled from the decrepit pier to the west. Several wheeled against the sky above where the men had parked; the tips of their wing feathers painted crimson by the rising sun. Containers banged and thumped far to the north, where the commercial dock sleepily came to life with the sounds of grinding gears, thrumming motors, and the air horns of the mighty Handimax container ships.

He followed the Hummer's tracks to the deep impressions where its tires had sunken into the mud. The men's footprints were clearly defined and impossible to miss. He could tell where they had stood, the prints deep and smeared where they had labored with the weight of the bag's contents. Crouching, he fished his flashlight from his jacket pocket and shined it across the ground. A smattering of scarlet reflected from a golden clump of trampled grass. He dabbed his fingertip onto one of the drops and rubbed it into the pad of his thumb until it dried and coagulated.

Blood. As he had expected.

Four men had gone in, but only three had come out. At least, three had walked to the Hummer. A fourth had been in the large plastic or vinyl bag, either the remaining member of their entourage, or whatever they had tracked down underground. He favored the former. Surely if they'd found their prey there would have been another bag to load into the trunk.

So what had happened to their man? How had he been killed? Porter could only speculate, but regardless, this confirmed the fact that these men knew exactly what was down there.

And that was precisely what he needed to find out. It was still his job to track down whoever or whatever was responsible for the deaths of so many, and to make sure that it wasn't able to kill again. Even if he had to go toe-to-toe with his SAC. Or any other self-serving government official.

Porter wiped his fingers on the wet grass and rose to his feet. The waves to the west sparkled like jewels. A soft breeze brought with it the smells of gasoline, brine, and whatever carcasses had rolled up onto the shore to rot during the night.

He returned his flashlight to his jacket and removed the handheld GPS tracking device. The unit was no larger than a cell phone; its transmitter the size of a cockroach. A green beacon radiated concentric circles from the center of the screen. The map of shifting streets beneath it showed him where the Hummer was now and in which direction it was traveling. He had planted the magnetized tracking device on the inside of the wheel well where no one would ever find it and then packed mud on top of it. Wherever they went, he would find them.

The time had come to go on the offensive.

Damn the consequences.

*   *   *

He passed the compound once, discretely, then found a place to park three blocks to the north and one block to the east, behind the loading dock of an interstate trucking company. Single-engine planes buzzed low overhead against the ceiling of wispy clouds. There was a commercial airport about ten miles to the east, the kind of small-scale operation that serviced hobbyists, shippers, and jump-flights up and down the Pacific coast. He had watched air shows there as a kid, from folding chairs in the back of his father's pickup truck, back when there was still the hope of turning this area into a commercial hub that serviced Canada and beyond. Everything around here was zoned industrial. Most of the buildings looked as though their better days were so far behind them that blowing asbestos into the rafters would be considered modernization. While still in obvious use, there were boarded and taped windows, and weeds had grown up through the cracks in the faded asphalt parking lots. The warehouses seemed to sag and the Dumpsters in the alleys were rusted and overflowing with garbage that had to be several weeks old. Everything looked as though it was in dire need of an arsonist's touch.

Everything, that is, except for the complex he had driven for nearly an hour past the wharves to find.

The twenty-foot chain link fence that lined the roadway positively shined. The coils of concertina wire on top of it looked sharp enough to disembowel anyone foolish enough to attempt to scale it. Security cameras covered every inch of the perimeter, directed past a culvert reminiscent of a moat at the base of the fence and toward the street, fifteen feet away. A guard shack stood at the edge of the lone point of entry. Any car that passed through found itself in a trap, facing yet another gate and a thorough search by uniformed security personnel with German shepherds and long poles with mirrors to search under the vehicles. Only when the car was thoroughly vetted would it be allowed to pass through the second gate and into a circular drive that wound around a small hill covered with a rainbow of perennials and a flagpole flying the Stars and Stripes. The main building looked like an ordinary office building: a six-story box of gray bricks and smoked glass. Parking lots dotted with luxury sedans and SUVs he would never be able to afford on his salary reached around the sides of the building, behind which dozens of identical concrete and aluminum warehouses stretched as far as the eye could see. The property was enormous, easily thirty or forty acres, and wherever the Humvee might have gone, he couldn't see it from the street. All he knew was that it was back in there somewhere, and, for now, that was enough. He had identified his opposition.

This changed everything.

Porter stopped in a convenience store with bars over windows so thick with grime he couldn't read the sun-bleached promotional posters taped to them from the inside and bought a cup of coffee that tasted like it had been precipitated to a sludge of grounds and then reheated. He whistled to himself as he walked down the street, pausing only long enough to sip from the steaming Styrofoam cup. When he neared the compound, he did so on the opposite side of the street and from behind a row of tractor-trailers that hadn't been moved in so long that their windshield wipers were buried in leaves and trash had drifted up against their tires. He found a suitable wash of shadows under a massive oak tree and behind a half-dead privet hedge, which afforded him a decent view of the guard shack and the main building through a snarl of skeletal branches. He adjusted the focus on his binoculars and read the inconspicuous sign stationed near the entrance, opposite the security post like the menu in a drive-thru.

"Phobos," he whispered. "What in the world is a private defense contractor doing sneaking around under those condemned buildings?"

That wasn't the foremost question on his mind, though. Of more importance was the nature of Phobos's involvement. These weren't featherweights he was dealing with here. These were professional, military-trained mercenaries who were leased to governments and major corporations all over the globe to provide security when their militaries and private armies alone weren't sufficient. These were the best and the brightest, men who only crawled out from under their rocks when a fortune was in the offing, the kind of money that only a select few domestic entities could provide. Not the paltry sums that could be secreted from the city's coffers. There were other interests in play here, and for the life of him, Porter couldn't even wager a guess as to whom. If preserving the timetable of the waterfront renovation project was the primary concern, then they wouldn't be worried about their funding if they had enough cash sitting around to hire a private army.

No. Those pieces didn't fit together.

Phobos's involvement had to be personal in nature. It had applied a ton of pressure onto people unaccustomed to being leveraged in order to buy its presumably elite team some quality time alone in the ruins.

Porter had to figure out that reason. It was the key to his entire investigation. He could feel it.

Uncover Phobos's motivation, and he would learn what was responsible for the violent murders. And every bit as importantly, who was ultimately behind it.

And he was running out of time to do so.

In less than thirty-six hours, if he couldn't find a way to stop it or convince the mayor to postpone his soiree, there would be hundreds of men and women clad in tuxedos and evening gowns dancing the night away within two hundred yards of a monster capable of butchering them all.

TWENTY-TWO

Seattle, Washington
8:00 a.m. PST

Spears stood beside Cranston's body and rested his hand on the soldier's cold forearm. His team of scientists had removed it from the bag and placed it supine on a stainless steel autopsy table with deep gutters along the sides. They formed a line at the back of the room in white lab coats and smocks, with plastic shields over their faces, their hands clasped in front of them, waiting patiently for Spears to do whatever it was he was going to do. Even he didn't know at this point. All he could do was grind his teeth and stare through the scarlet film that had descended over his vision.

Cranston's lifeless brown eyes looked through him as though he wasn't even there. Death hadn't released him from the suffering he must have endured during his final moments. The pain was etched into his face: in the tight lines at the corners of his eyes; in his taut lips, which stretched back from his bared, blood-crusted teeth; in the savage wound on the side of his neck that opened wide into an agonized red scream that exposed tendons and severed muscles.

The face he saw on the corpse wasn't that of a man he hardly knew, but that of his son.

His enemy had bested him yet again.

"Sir," one of the pathologists said, cautiously placing a hand on his shoulder. "We really need to begin while the remains are still...fresh."

A stress tick tugged at the corner of Spears's mouth. He turned and looked the pathologist dead in the eyes. The much smaller man squirmed under the intensity of his gaze like a worm on a hook, but held his ground. Spears growled, spun to his right, and heaved a tray draped with sterile instruments across the room. They clattered to the floor and skittered up against the wall. Spears stood there,

shoulders heaving, fists clenched, and then whirled without a word
and stormed out of the room.

"Sir?" the pathologist called from behind him.

Spears stopped just outside the cold room, his back to the man,
and waited.

"What would you like is to do with the body when we're
finished."

The screeching of his grinding teeth marred the tense silence
while he formulated his reply.

"Incinerate it."

"Yes, sir."

Spears's footsteps echoed down the hallway ahead of him over
the subdued sound of tearing fabric as the scientists commenced
their task. He passed the pressurized doorways to the labs that
housed tissue samples and cultures, scanning electron microscopes
and all sorts of equipment he had signed the checks for without
caring about or understanding their functions, and the room with
the refrigerated drawers where the bullet-riddled corpses of the
Siberian monsters now dwelled. He managed to contain the scream
building in his chest until the elevator doors closed, then bellowed
at the top of his lungs. By the time the sliding doors opened into
his office, which monopolized nearly the entire sixth floor, he was
physically and emotionally spent. He shuffled around his desk,
stood with his back to the room, and surveyed the industrial
wasteland below him through the smoked glass. On a clear day, he
could see the distant cone of Mt. Rainier, but today, dark clouds
boiled on the horizon, stabbing each other with forks of lightning,
mirroring the turmoil inside of him.

The phone on his antique maple desk, which was rumored to
have once been used by *the* General George S. Patton, buzzed
once, then again. He sat down in the chair and pressed the speaker
button.

"Yes," he answered, making no effort to hide his irritation.

"Sir," a man's voice said. "I have what you asked for."

Spears pressed the release button for the magnetic lock under
his desk drawer and unlocked the door with a thud.

Ritter walked into the office and strode directly toward the
desk. He set a rubber-banded tube that looked like a roll of old,
yellowed wrapping paper on the blotter. Spears slid the computer

monitor and the keyboard to one side and the framed picture of Nelson and him on the deck of a sport boat, smiles on their faces, a marlin held high between them, to the other. He unrolled the blueprints and turned them around so he could better see them. The pages were cracked and stained, the architect's work fading as the chalky blue powder dissociated from the crisp paper. Ritter leaned over the desk without asking permission, and tapped his finger on the center of the middle of the three buildings.

"That's the conveyor chute right there," he said. "You can see where the chutes run through all three of the levels. The problem is that with the aboveground floors demolished, we have no idea where those chutes run now, or even if they're still patent. Which I sincerely doubt."

"Things were built to last back then," Spears said. "You saw how well the basements held up to the demolition."

"True. But even hardened steel can't stand up to thousands of tons of rubble being dropped right onto it."

"For now, we have to assume that every branch is still viable until proven otherwise. How many are we looking at?"

"It appears as though there were four separate packaging or canning units on each of the three floors. The fish were unloaded from the boats and processed in the building to the north. From there, they were sent through one of two chutes on each level, for a total of six from the first building to the second. Additional tubes led from each of the canning units to the floor beneath it, then, ultimately, to a central conveyor. That's where we found Cranston last night. From there, everything was funneled into the basement, where the cans were sorted by hand, boxed, and carted into the shipping and warehousing facility to the south. And over here? You can see that a single conveyor led from each floor of the middle building into the warehouse for disposal of the rejects."

"So we're potentially dealing with more than twenty separate tunnels through the ruins."

"Assuming they weren't flattened when the building was leveled."

"If they had been, our target wouldn't have been able to get away, would it?"

"No, sir."

Spears studied each of the pages, one by one, memorizing each of the levels before shoving the pages away. If any of those chutes had remained patent during the collapse, the blueprints would be all but useless to them. They could lead to only God knew where.

"If I many, sir..." Ritter cleared his throat. "Why don't we just napalm the place and be done with it?"

"Ask the goddamn mayor and the governor."

"Sir?"

"There's no problem here, soldier. We'll handle everything tonight. By tomorrow morning, this situation will be resolved."

"Yes, sir."

"We still have preparations to make."

Spears spun his chair around until it again faced the window and the coming storm.

Ritter turned and started for the door.

"One second," Spears said, watching the low-lying clouds roll over the rooftops like smoke. He smiled. "There's something...special...I need you to track down for me."

*   *   *

Four blocks away, Porter sat in his Crown Vic, scrolling through the deposition of one former Brigadier General Franklin Spears on his dashboard computer monitor. The president of Phobos had confirmed that he had bought a place for one of his men on the *Scourge* at the last second. This man, an honorably discharged Marine lieutenant named Daniel Abrams, had been responsible for supervising the transportation of the bodies of a failed Siberian expedition back to the United States. Neither Abrams nor the cargo had been noted anywhere on the ship's manifest. Spears believed that the hurried arrangement was the cause of the oversight, but Porter wasn't so easily fooled. It had been a cash transaction that the captain of the *Scourge* had never intended to declare. This accounted for the additional man found dead on the ship, if not the crates of corpses that Porter hadn't seen on the ship either at sea or after docking. Another cash transaction, or perhaps an arrangement of a more political nature, must have taken care of the discrete transfer. The remains were in the process of being returned to their families, however, a fact that was corroborated by the CDC, who still had them quarantined.

He opened the file he had on Daniel Abrams and stared at the man's face on the screen. They had stumbled upon the man's body in the hold, he was certain of it. This was the man that had been stuffed into the cage and torn apart, the one whose disfigurement, Porter had speculated at the time, had been inflicted for personal or emotional reasons.

Maybe it was a reach, but his instincts insisted otherwise. Whatever had been in that cage…whatever was hiding down there in the ruins right now…this man he was looking at had been transporting it across the Pacific inside that cage, which meant that not only had Spears seen it, he had been responsible for trying to smuggle it into the country.

So what was it? Had it killed Spears's son and his expedition party long before any of this started?

All of the evidence pointed to the involvement of Phobos, and, specifically, to its founder on an intimately personal level. Not only did Spears know exactly what they were up against, he had placed himself in a position to resolve the problem without any oversight and with the utmost secrecy.

Porter accessed the FBI file on Spears. The details were sparse, the majority classified, but there was still a picture. He stared into the face of the man who had evicted him from his own crime scene last night.

There was no doubt this was personal for Spears.

And now it was personal for Porter, as well.

Spears may have the entire government in his pocket, but Porter refused to be coerced or intimidated. This was his investigation and he would see it through to its ultimate resolution. Regardless of the cost.

He looked long and hard into the cold, calculating eyes of the older man on the monitor.

"Make no mistake," he said. "You're mine, motherfucker."

TWENTY-THREE

Seattle, Washington
10:06 a.m. PST

Maybe she was losing her mind. Henley made no secret of his opinions on the matter. He hadn't believed her when she told him what she'd seen down there in the tunnel. They had argued to the point that he'd finally thrown up his arms in futility and driven them back to the station without even glancing over at her from behind the wheel. Perhaps he was right. Everything did look different under the light of day. She'd never been so exhausted. Her eyes stung from the lack of sleep and her mind felt sluggish, as though the neural synapses fired through molasses. Maybe the two had conspired against her and she hadn't really seen anything at all, let alone what she thought she had. But she was certain of it. If she closed her eyes, she could still clearly recall the blur of nearly translucent white skin, the filthy bare foot, and the very same baby doll she had seen night after night elsewhere in the maze before it disappeared. And damned if she wasn't going to prove it, if only to herself, which was why she now stood outside the construction zone, her fingers laced through the chain link fence, watching as the workers attacked the project on two fronts.

One group hastily erected a new fence around the perimeter of the cultural center, sealing it off from the ruins around it, while the other planted paving stones and laid sod. There was a semi parked in the side lot, its open trailer revealing table and chair legs and what looked like the framework for several portable gazebo-type tents. And none of the people appeared to have the slightest clue as to what had transpired beneath their feet mere hours ago. They worked in flannel or bare-backed, with work gloves and without, laughing, laboring, often lounging, as though there was nothing wrong with the world, as though the rain had washed away the evils of the previous night.

Sturm had tried to sleep to no avail, the thoughts in her head ricocheting against each other like billiard balls. She had showered, changed into a clean uniform, and waited for a call from the CSRT that never came. She should have taken advantage of the opportunity to rest, if not to sleep, and yet here she was, a full pot of coffee later, hands shaking, preparing to do the most idiotic thing she could possibly imagine.

She waited until there was no one between her and her goal, then hurried through the gate and made a beeline for the southern access point to the underground warrens. If anyone saw her, they paid her no mind. When she reached the building, she glanced back one final time to make sure she hadn't attracted unwanted attention, then scurried into the small hole.

Day instantaneously became night. She had expected to find thin columns of light piercing the rubble overhead, but the darkness was complete. As it had been every other time she's been down here. She clicked on her flashlight, shined it deeper into the darkness, and started the trek she had learned by rote. Even though she and Henley always parted ways, she could sense his absence. Her breathing grew fast and shallow. She unsnapped her holster and drew her pistol just far enough to clench the grip in her fist. Her light trembled as she swept it from one side of the corridor to the other, across the scarred walls and into rooms where she expected to see something streaking toward her at any second. She wished some brave homeless people had returned during the night. Any human presence around her would have been comforting. As it was, her skin prickled as though beneath the scrutiny of unseen eyes and her breath was too loud in her own ears. Even her softly placed footsteps sounded like the clop of horseshoes.

What was she doing down here? Nobody knew where she was. If anything happened to her, no one would hear her cries for help and it would be hours before anyone noticed she was missing at roll call, let alone decided to come looking for her.

It was too late to turn around now, even if she wanted to. She had already crossed into the second building, and if there was something hiding in the rubble, it undoubtedly already knew she was here. She gave up all pretense and drew her weapon, bracing it on her left forearm for stability and holding the flashlight backhanded. With as badly as she was shaking, she couldn't have knocked a tin can from a fence post at five feet. She had to pause to steady her nerves before pressing onward.

She could hear the attenuated sounds of the workers banging and clanging topside as though from a great distance. The ground shivered ever so slightly underfoot with their exertions and dirt cascaded from the fallen roof. She passed the point where they had found the homeless man's body and was nearly to the third building when she noticed a riot of footprints in the dust to the side of the main path. She traced them with her beam to the right, to the base of a pile of cracked concrete that led upward to a black gap in the rubble. From this angle, her light barely penetrated the orifice.

The concrete dust on the ground at her feet was beaded and crusted with blood. She shined the beam to either side of her, and then toward the ceiling. The spatters on the timber were still fresh enough that the swollen droplets still glistened. With all of the people that had been down here last night, there's no way they would have missed this. Something had happened after they left.

She remembered feeling as though she were being used as bait, that someone had been out there, waiting to converge on her position from the darkness. But who were they and whose blood was this? There was far too much blood for whoever was attacked to have survived. She thought of the figure she had seen, the one carrying the doll. Was that who had been slain? Had she blown her only opportunity to save that person's life?

There was only one way to find out.

She climbed up the fractured concrete and shined her light into the dark tunnel. There were brownish smears of blood all over the ground and droplets dried to the slanted ceiling. She smelled death and knew what she would find at the other end.

Sturm drew a deep breath, glanced behind her to make sure that no one had crept up on her, and then plunged into the hole.

*   *   *

The walls of the narrow tunnel closed in on her. For a moment, she feared she might get stuck or lost or any number of horrible things might happen to her. She started to hyperventilate. The terror kicked in and she crawled madly, banging her head, scraping her hands and knees. She felt the ceiling lift from on top of her head and tumbled out onto the ground in a small domed chamber. Tears rolled down her cheeks and she nearly sobbed with relief. She stood and turned her beam upon the walls in an effort to gather her bearings. A large metal chute was crumpled against the wall to her left. She could tell where it had once connected to the rear wall and the ceiling by the mouths of the smaller tubes. Rollers from a conveyor belt were scattered across the floor. The gears that had once driven the contraption were smashed and partially buried under debris to her right. The ground beside them was black with blood, as though whoever had been attacked at the other end of the tunnel had crawled in here to finish bleeding out. She had expected to find the body based on the intensity of the smell, but there was so little air circulation in this small chamber that it trapped the horrible stench, hoarding it for the green-eyed flies that spun lazily around her.

She stepped to the side of the room to preserve whatever footprints might be in the middle and eased around the circumference until she could better see. There were no spatters; only a wide black amoeba that confirmed her theory. The dust was disturbed, but not in such a way that she could tell how the victim had been positioned. She saw boot prints beside it, and the broad smears where the corpse had been dragged back toward the tunnel from which she had emerged.

Why had whatever happened down here not been reported?

She was just about to call it in herself, but thought better of it. Since she was off-duty, there was no way she would be able to justify why she was in there. And something about the whole scenario felt wrong. The way the crime scene unit had been rushed from the site...the way she and Henley had been left down here alone after the homeless man had been murdered...the riot of footprints that had led her here...the whole thing reeked of a cover up in high places. If that was the case, then was there anyone out there who she could actually trust? And if they had truly been willing to use her as bait last night, would they even care?

Maybe Henley would be willing to listen to her, but he had no more authority than she did. And he definitely wasn't the kind of guy to go out on a limb to help anyone. There was Galiardi, or any number of her colleagues at the CSRT, but they had already demonstrated their susceptibility to the application of pressure from above. Who else would possibly…

Special Agent Porter.

She had seen that look in his eyes numerous times, that look that said he couldn't be bullied, the relentless look of a hunter. He had been on both of the ghost ships. He'd been down here investigating every one of the deaths. If there was anyone who would not only believe her, but be willing to do something about it—

A faint whimpering sound.

Sturm held her breath and listened. At first she heard nothing and assumed the noise must have come from one of the metal tunnels branching from the room as it buckled under the weight of the rubble, until she heard it again. There was no denying it. It sounded almost like someone crying.

She raised her beam to the ceiling and looked into each of the smaller tunnels. The acoustics made it impossible to tell exactly where the whimpering originated. It sounded like it was coming from all around her at once. She turned a complete circle. There had to be a dozen separate branches leading in as many different directions. She stuck her head into each of them and listened as hard as she could.

The sound grew softer and softer until she could barely hear it at all.

She found the right branch on the fifth try. The hollow, haunting sound echoed as though from far away. It was the most pathetic, heart-wrenching noise she had ever heard. She had to kick off the wall to pull herself over the lip and into the metal tunnel. The stench of dead fish intensified as she shimmied on her belly, barely able to gain any traction. The tube sloped upward toward tar-thick darkness that choked her light back to the lens.

*   *   *

Sturm had no idea how long she'd been crawling. Minutes? Hours? It felt like an eternity. Time seemed to lose all meaning down here in the smothering blackness. The sound had ceased. The resultant silence contained an urgency that spurred her to move faster. Eventually, her beam limned the trapezoidal shape of the partially

flattened opening of the duct. Dust motes swirled beyond the
orifice.

She crawled over the edge and tumbled to the floor from
higher up than she had anticipated, dropping her flashlight in the
process. The bulb died with the impact. After a moment of running
her palms across ground that felt like a combination of fine-grained
cement and coarse gravel, she found it and shook it back to life.
The small bulb produced a weak, brassy glow no brighter than a
candle's flame. It immediately started to fade. She barely had time
to survey her surroundings before the light extinguished again. A
slanted iron girder, roughly six feet overhead at its pinnacle,
supported slatted wood that must have once served as the floor of
the level above her. The substrate beneath her appeared to be a
combination of dirt, broken bricks, powdered concrete, and
condensed salt carried through the gaps in the rubble by the breeze
from the sea and the rain. It was mounded in the corner to the left
as though fashioned into a nest by some burrowing animal or other.
Another small tunnel opened on the opposite side from the one
through which she had entered.

She listened to the darkness for the sound that had summoned
her here, but all she could hear were the faint stirrings of the
construction somewhere out there and the even fainter sound of the
wind whistling through the debris.

And then she heard the whimpering sound again.

Closer.

She was nearly right on top of it.

Sturm turned her beam upon the ground, flashing it quickly
from side to side. Her heart pounded in her chest and she could
barely breathe. The sound had been distinct. There was no doubt in
her mind that she had heard—

A child.

She could barely see the profile of the child's face in the rear
corner, eyes pinched tightly shut, tears glistening on plump cheeks.
The whole face was covered with what appeared to be a dry,
cracked crust of mud. The form was ambiguous, but Sturm sensed
it was female. The little girl had buried herself in the dirt and grit
as well as she could, leaving only the side of her face, her
shoulders, and one bare hip above the mound. The crown of the
doll's head breached the dirt where the crook of her elbow was

buried. The little girl shivered again and let out a whimper that pierced Sturm right through the chest. Never in her life had she seen something so terrible, so heartbreaking.

Sturm knelt beside the girl and carefully brushed the dirt from the top of her head, revealing an oblong cranium with a scalp so smooth it could have been recently shaved. More tears streamed from those closed eyes and she whimpered again.

"It's all right," Sturm whispered, stroking the grime from the girl's slender neck and upper arm. "I've got you. Everything is going to be all right."

The girl flinched as Sturm freed her pale arm, then the doll she remembered like it had been her own. Every inch of skin that Sturm uncovered was naked and pale to the point that she could see the bluish network of veins beneath it, even in the weak glow of her flashlight.

Sturm slipped off her uniform shirt and draped it over the girl's torso while she continued to brush off her legs. Her flesh was cold to the touch and stippled with goosebumps despite the complete lack of visible body hair. She couldn't have been more than ten or eleven years old.

The girl started to openly weep, her shoulders heaving with uncontrollable sobs. Sturm felt her own cheeks dampen with tears.

Who could have done this to a child? What kind of monster strips a little girl and abandons her in this kind of hell? The thought struck her a physical blow. Jesus Christ in heaven. Had someone raped her?

Sturm set her light aside, scooped the girl up from the dirt, and cradled her in her lap. In the fading brass glare, she looked upon the girl's features. What she had mistaken for mud was unequivocally blood. The girl wore it from her forehead all the way down to her neck, save for the pale ribbons cut by her tears. Her lips protruded from beneath her broad nose; features distinctly African in origin that belied her pale skin. She looked for the source of the blood. Any visible cuts or open fractures. Maybe it was just the light, but she couldn't see so much as a bruise.

"I'll get you out of here," Sturm whispered. "We'll make sure that whoever hurt you never has the opportunity to do so again."

She brushed her hand across the girl's prominent, hairless brow.

The tiny bulb flickered and died.

Sturm swore she saw the girl's eyes snap open and the circular reflection of the beam in large pink irises. The eyes widened in surprise before they disappeared into the darkness.

She continued to stroke the girl's forehead, her cheeks, around her eyes, whispering soothingly the whole time.

The girl snuggled into her chest, shivering and curling her fingers into fists in Sturm's undershirt. Her fingernails were so sharp that Sturm felt them pierce the skin on her ribs.

The girl continued to cry with a sound worse than anything Sturm had heard in her entire life. She felt the sorrow and the pain deep in her bones, in her heart, in her soul.

"It's going to be okay," Sturm said.

The girl stiffened against her and jerked her head away from Sturm's hand.

"We'll get you out of here, honey. We'll find our way out of these tunnels and—"

The girl leapt from her lap. Sturm couldn't see her in the pitch black, but she could hear her breathing, maybe three feet away, close to the ground, her breath coming in rapid, open-mouthed bursts.

"Don't be afraid. I'm not going to hurt you."

Sturm shifted forward onto her hands and knees and slowly crawled forward. The girl scrabbled to the side, making scraping sounds on the dirt.

"Everything's going to be all right. We'll get you back to your mommy and—"

Sturm nearly yelped when her knee pressed down on the hard plastic hand of the doll. She pried it out from beneath her and held it out in front of her, as though the girl could really see her offering.

The doll was snatched from her hand. She felt the movement of air and heard a scurrying sound cross the room. The clamor of nails on concrete. Then only silence.

Sturm swept her hand across the dirt until she found her flashlight, then shook it back to life. In the waning glow, she watched a cloud of stirred dust settle to the ground.

The girl was gone.

TWENTY-FOUR

Seattle, Washington
11:53 a.m. PST

"You're telling me there's a naked little girl crawling around down there under all that rubble," Porter said. He stared at the officer standing before him, at her filthy uniform shirt that hung open over her stained undershirt, at the torn knees of her dirty pants and her shoes that were so covered with dust it was impossible to tell they had even been polished black, at her tangled hair and her face so covered with dirt that the whites of her eyes stood out like beacons. There were obvious tear tracks on her cheeks and her hands shook with the kind of nervous energy only junkies knew. He recognized the signs of sleep deprivation without having to look too hard and knew it was only a matter of time before whatever reserves she had drawn upon failed her. "Okay. So what do you want me to do about it?"

With those blue eyes, so pale they appeared almost unnatural, she seemed to stare at him and through him at the same time. When her call had been routed from his office to his cell phone, he had been tempted to let it go to voicemail. After hearing what she had to say, he wished he had. But she had said the magic words that had made it impossible for him to do anything other than honor her request. *I can't think of anyone else I can trust.* So he had agreed to meet her in person and evaluate the details before he made any kind of firm commitment. He'd found her waiting on the curb half an hour later, looking like she'd been dragged through the sewers by a herd of stampeding bison, and he'd known right then and there that he was about to so whatever she wanted him to do.

"You believe me?" she said. "I thought for sure...I mean, I was certain you wouldn't..."

"I kind of thought we'd grab some coffee or something on our first date, but skulking around under condemned ruins will work, too."

"What?" Her face flushed red beneath the coat of grime. "This isn't a—"

He offered his most disarming smile and a wink. She merely stared at him for a long moment before the corner of her mouth curled into a smirk.

"Do you enjoy pushing people's buttons or are you simply helpless against the urge?"

"Depends on the person, I suppose." He glanced at his watch. Spears and his men wouldn't make their move until sometime after dark, which left him with plenty of time to kill. Perhaps this wasn't a bad situation at all. It would give him a chance to not only familiarize himself with the maze down there, but it would afford him the opportunity to potentially discover whatever was hiding down there before Spears did and disappeared with it under the cover of darkness. Besides, if Sturm was right and there was really a little girl under there, she was in worse danger than she had been when she was in the clutches of whoever might have taken her down there. If that was even what had happened. There was something about the appearance of this child that just didn't sit right with him. The place had been crawling with police officers last night. Why had she not come running for help? And with some unknown creature killing people in those warrens with her... "So are you going to show me where you found this little girl or what?"

*   *   *

The damn tunnel was so tight he could barely squeeze his shoulders through. Had he not left his jacket in the car, he might have found himself wedged in there and unable to follow her at all. He had already ripped the seams of his button-down and his deltoids felt as though they were being flayed to the bone. He pondered Spears and his men and wondered how they expected to move through here with enough speed to be able to not only scour the area in one night, but procure their quarry as well. They had to have something else in mind, but, for the life of him, he couldn't seem to figure out what it was.

Sturm dropped out of sight ahead of him. A heartbeat later, he heard her hit the ground and scramble to her feet. He had no choice but to try to catch himself with his arms when he followed her over the edge and fell down into the dirt. She stood in the middle of the room with his backup flashlight, shining it into the corner where he assumed she had found the sleeping child. He sat on his haunches and played his beam across the ground. It didn't take long to find Sturm's footprints, but they were the only ones he could see. He directed his beam at the wall and worked his way clockwise across it until he highlighted another tunnel on the opposite side.

"I followed her through there," Sturm said, "but I never caught up with her."

"Where are her footprints?"

"What?"

"Her footprints, Layne. There's not a single print in here other than yours."

"You think I'm making her up? Do you really believe—?"

He held up his hand.

"I didn't say that." He furrowed his brow as he tried to remember something Galiardi had said the night before. *As far as we can tell, every single one of his—or its—footfalls were deliberately placed where they wouldn't leave prints.* "I want to ask you a question, but I don't want you to take it the wrong way. Did you get a good look at this little girl?"

"What are you really asking me?"

"You said your flashlight was dying and you were barely able to see well enough to find your way in here before it gave out on you…"

"It was a girl, Agent Porter. A ten or eleven year old little girl. She was completely naked, so there wasn't a whole lot that she was able to hide from me."

"Tell me again what she looked like."

"I already told—"

"Humor me, Layne."

She closed her eyes as though to better view the image in her head and then apparently thought better of it and opened them again before they decided to stay closed of their own accord.

"Caucasian female. Four-foot-six to four-foot-eight. Weight approximately—"

"Skip the cop talk and tell me what you *saw*."

Sturm turned away from him when she spoke and allowed her light to wander through the rubble.

"Her skull was misshapen. It tapered back from her forehead, almost like one of those helmets you see the competitive bicycle racers wearing. Her scalp was smooth. Not just shaved, but bald. Every part of her was bald. Even her forearms and legs."

"Did you see her hands or her feet?"

"No. Or if so, I don't remember noticing anything distinct about them."

"Her face?"

"It was covered with so much dried blood that it was impossible to see any distinguishing characteristics." She paused. Porter waited her out. "Other than the structure of the bones. Her forehead was ridged at the brow, almost Mongoloid. Her nose was broad, and...I don't know...flat. And her lips jutted forward, like she'd bitten into an orange slice that was too big for her mouth and somehow closed her lips over it."

"Tell me about her eyes again."

"They reflected the light. You know, like you see when your headlights hit a deer on the side of the road."

"What about the color?"

"I didn't get a clear look. And the light was already fading—"

"Quit hedging your bets and tell me."

"They looked pink. Pinkish-red. But that had to be because of the light." She shook her head. "I make her sound like a mutant or something, but I'm telling you, she was just a little girl. A kid, for Christ's sake. A poor abused child. Lost and alone."

Porter focused on the image her words had conjured in his mind, which was anything other than that of a normal little girl, but he hadn't seen her and Sturm looked like she hadn't slept in days, so could he really trust the accuracy of her account? He imagined a child with teeth so large her mouth could hardly contain them and reflective eyes that suggested a degree of night vision. The lack of footprints. The fact that she had remained hidden when the police had converged with their bright lights and flashing cameras. This child's appearance and behavior both fell outside of the norm, but she couldn't possibly be capable of doing what he was thinking now. Could she? A child overcoming and slaughtering an entire crew of grown men? Of tearing out their throats and finding her way across the Pacific Ocean on her own? It seemed impossible, and yet there was no denying that there was something down here, something that was of the utmost importance to a private defense contractor and whatever government agency was greasing the wheels on its behalf to keep the entire police force and the FBI out of their way.

"Look at this," Sturm said. She knelt near the western wall and glanced back at him. "This was done recently."

Porter walked across the dirt and leaned over her shoulder so he could see. Her beam was focused on a section of fallen flooring from the level that had once been eight feet above them. The warped slats were broken on both ends, but still held together in a segment the size of a square of sidewalk by a pair of support posts. The wood had been carved down to the pale pine grain by what appeared to be the tip of a nail or other small, sharp implement. The edges of the etchings were still rimmed with sawdust and chips of wood. There were hundreds of individual characters, none of them more than an inch high, in at least a dozen horizontal lines. Or were they oriented vertically? He couldn't tell. It was obvious that someone had spent a great deal of time carving them, though. He'd never seen anything like it. The characters almost reminded him of a cross between an archaic form of Chinese and the kind of primitive petroglyphs the Indians left scattered across the Southwest, only less elaborate and with straighter lines that tapered downward like arrowheads.

Sturm pulled her cell phone from her pocket and took several quick snapshots of the characters with the built-in camera.

"We need to keep moving," he finally said.

She nodded her agreement and led him toward the other tunnel he had seen upon entering. He realized he had drawn his pistol and had to wonder, if his growing suspicions were correct, would he be able to look into the eyes of a little girl and pull the trigger?

TWENTY-FIVE

Seattle, Washington
12:48 p.m. PST

Sturm knew what Porter was thinking, but it couldn't be possible. Could it? She'd been alone in there with that little girl and nothing had happened to her. She couldn't imagine that poor child who had curled up in her lap and cried into her chest doing anything terrible to anyone. The sounds she had made …so full of fear and hopelessness…those weren't the kinds of noises that a monster made. Were they? No. She was certain of it. But the more she truly thought about it, the more the seeds of doubt began to take root. Physically, the girl had been no different than any other child. Well, there was the odd shape of her head, so unlike any person she'd ever seen before, and the teeth, of course. While she hadn't seen them per se, the girl's mouth had appeared barely able to accommodate them. Now that she stepped back and looked at the girl objectively, her facial structure was markedly simian, her jaws protruding like those of a great ape. She remembered the wounds on the necks of the men aboard the *Scourge* and the casts she had made from them. Was it possible that those long, sharp teeth she had originally envisioned in the mouth of a silverback could fit into the skull of such a small child? And, if so, and if this lone girl was responsible for so much death, why hadn't she attacked Sturm when she had the chance?

She was still lost in thought when a horrible stench assaulted her from somewhere ahead.

"You smell that?" Porter whispered from behind her. They were in the fourth branch of their systematic exploration of the network of tunnels, and regardless of how narrow their passage had become, he had somehow managed to stay right on her heels, his flashlight casting her shifting shadow ahead of her to where it met with the amber fan of her own beam. "You'd better be ready."

He didn't have to tell her. She was well acquainted with the smell of death by now and understood that every tunnel they cleared brought them closer to encountering whatever lurked down here, whether a seemingly innocent child or not. She cleared her mind of all thoughts of the coincidence and the timing of the little girl's appearance, of the speed with which she had struck to snatch the doll from her hand, and the eerie, almost predatory sentience that had reflected the light from those pink eyes, and focused on the darkness ahead of her, which seemed to constrict her beam to a useless aura that barely stained the mote-filled, suffocating air.

The tunnel gave onto a larger room. The walls had fallen and what remained of the ceiling was tented by aged timber that barely supported the weight of the rubble above them. Her rapid breathing echoed in the confines as she rose to a crouch and scrutinized the room down her pistol sights. Even this far underground and this deep in the ruins, the flies had somehow found their way into the rear corner, where the swarm buzzed angrily at their intrusion. Their swirling ranks cast shadows on the wall, like snowflakes in a car's high beams, above a mound of furry, festering carcasses. They teemed on the coarse gray hair and the long pink tails of at least twenty rats, their gray tongues protruded between their hooked, yellow teeth.

Sturm buried her mouth and nose in the crook of her left elbow, but the scent somehow found its way through and took up residence in her sinuses. She tried to breathe shallowly through her mouth. She was still five feet from the heap of rodents when she noticed the distinct ridges of teeth marks on their sides. It looked as though something had held them like ears of corn, by the head and the tail, and bitten right through their flanks. The viscera were gone, leaving behind cavities rimmed by the lower ribs and the hip bones. The fore and hind quarters were held together by little more than the spines, the skeletal musculature, and strips of greasy fat and fur.

Porter eased around her and added his light to hers. The rats' eyes and the exposed connective tissue were still moist enough to glisten. They stared at the carcasses in silence until Porter finally turned away and moved toward the opposite side of the room. Sturm backed away and pointed her beam at the ceiling. There were more symbols scratched into the cribbing overhead. She snapped several photographs with her camera and nearly bumped into Porter when she turned to catch up with him. His light was directed at the ground, where the dirt had turned to mud in a wet circle around several well-formed piles of feces that roiled with black flies. It almost looked as though someone had scattered dirt on top of the mess. The stool was still moist, and so dark in color it resembled tar. Sturm's mind raced back through her schooling to one of her many pathology classes. Bile generally dictated the color of stool, but it could be altered by any number of dietary and pathological causes. Most notably, black feces suggested a gastrointestinal bleed. This stool was positively rich with blood.

"It exsanguinated its human victims but didn't consume them," Porter said. "And yet it ate the rats without bleeding them first." He shined his light across the walls, searching for another exit from the room that didn't appear to exist. He focused his beam on the ground near the excrement and fingered something on the dirt. "What does that tell us?"

Sturm didn't know what to think, so she let the question hang in the air until he eventually nodded to himself and crawled back toward the lone tunnel.

"We're done here," he said, and ducked into the metal chute.

Sturm looked back at the ground where he'd been kneeling by the dark urine-mud. At the very edge, she saw what had drawn his attention. There were faint teardrop-shaped grooves in the dirt, as though some clawed animal had attempted to kick the dirt behind it to cover its spoor. She crawled closer and held her palm over them. The marks had to have come from something not much larger than her hand, something roughly the size of a large dog's paw...or a child's foot.

"You coming or what?" he called back to her, his voice made tinny by the tube.

"Yeah," she whispered. "I'm right behind you."

She felt a sinking sensation in her stomach as she crossed the small chamber and crawled into the hole behind him, the waning aura of his light already far ahead of her.

*   *   *

They found several more pieces of wood carved with the strange symbols over the course of the next couple of hours, but no other signs of whatever was living down here. No tracks. No carcasses. No urine or excrement. Nothing. It was as though the chamber in which she had found the child had been set up as a den of sorts, and another established as a depository for refuse. It was arguably a human behavior model, for animals tended to have no qualms about living in close proximity to their waste.

Time seemed to fly past and stand still at the same time, separate from the outside world, which existed only as an abstraction there in the smothering darkness. Sturm had no idea how long they'd been searching and had become so disoriented by the twists and turns in the network of tunnels that when the smell reached her, she was convinced that it had to be a figment of her imagination. Until Porter stopped in front of her and tilted his face upward to savor a deep inhalation.

She smelled the sea. The unmistakable aroma of brine riding a cool breeze sweetened by ozone and a coming storm. She breathed deeply and allowed the fresh air to cleanse her from the inside out.

"Careful ahead," Porter said. She watched his silhouette cautiously lean forward, flatten to the ground, and then slither out of sight. When she reached the point where he had disappeared, he shined his light up at her from below. "It's about four feet down. Watch out for the lip of the opening."

The tunnel ended abruptly in front of her where debris had smashed down through the tube into the levels below her. Porter crouched at the base of a mound of rubble, his head nearly touching the rounded brick ceiling above him. She glanced back up and saw where the tunnel continued deeper into the ruins. The ragged metal edge tore her uniform shirt as she eased herself down onto the sharp pile of broken bricks and crawled to where Porter waited in a passage that was nothing like the others, which had all been metal chutes designed to transport fish in various states of processing from one location in the building to the next. This tunnel had a time-smoothed, paving stone floor with a central channel crusted with salt and dead algae. The walls were cribbed with ancient timber and lined with bricks to which desiccated strands of seaweed clung.

"Bootlegger's tunnel," Porter said. "They're all up and down the coast, especially under downtown. A whole underground network developed during Prohibition, but you won't find any of them on the maps. These sneaky bastards were moving more than just mackerel back in the day."

"Thank heaven for criminals," Sturm said.

She inhaled the clean air and felt just the faintest hint of its movement on her sweat-dampened face.

"Probably how that thing got in here in the first place," he said. "This is going to make it much harder to contain. Especially if there are more tunnels like this one that won't show up on any blueprints."

"What do you mean by '*contain*'?"

"We can't just let this thing live down here forever, can we?"

"What if it's not a *thing*? What if it's...?"

She couldn't bring herself to vocalize the words.

"You'd better start thinking of it as a thing, Layne. A lot of people are dead. There's no way this *thing* is getting out of these ruins alive. Make no mistake about that. No one's going to allow that to happen. You know that neither you nor I can allow that to happen either. We have our jobs to do."

He turned and walked in a crouch to the northwest, if she hadn't lost all sense of direction. It wasn't long before she heard shrieking gulls and grumbling waves. The walls grew damp with condensation and the channel underfoot filled with water. The light from the outside world announced itself as a pale gray glow ahead. It grew steadily brighter as they approached until it resolved into a design of golden dots. The rusted grate was covered with seaweed and detritus from the other side. It opened easily enough when Porter put his shoulder into it, the rusted hinges screaming in protest. They crawled out under an elevated wooden pier that had collapsed down into the ocean, where its remains now colonized barnacles and green slime. When they finally picked their way through the wooden wreckage and scrambled up the rocky slope to the shore, they were maybe a hundred yards from the rear verandah of the Cultural Center, maybe an eighth of a mile north of the demolished warehouses. The active harbor where the *Dragnet* had been moored was barely a mile up the coast.

Porter stared past the Bertha Knight Landes Center, where the workers still labored around the property. Sod nearly surrounded the building and the tables were already being set up under the tents on the new paving stones. The transformation had been far quicker than she had thought possible.

It felt like they had been underground for days, and yet the sun had hardly dipped toward the Pacific.

"What are we supposed to do now?" Sturm asked.

Porter continued to stare in the opposite direction, as though looking for something he couldn't quite see.

"You know what we need to do, Layne."

"What exactly are you suggesting?"

Porter sighed and struck off toward the construction frenzy.

Sturm wanted to make him say it. That way he would be forced to vocalize what he proposed, but saying the words out loud changed nothing. They had no choice in the matter. They were going to have to go back down there and make sure that no one else suffered the fate that befell the green-eyed man the night before.

They were going to have to kill the monster hiding in the guise of an innocent little girl.

TWENTY-SIX

Seattle, Washington
1:36 p.m. PST

Ritter stood at attention just inside the doorway to Spears's office, his stare fixed somewhere out the window over Spears's head. He'd been waiting patiently, a bill of lading clasped in his right hand.

"Yes, sir," Spears said into the telephone. "You can trust that the situation will be resolved tonight."

Spears rolled his eyes and sighed while the voice on the other end droned on.

"Yes, sir. I just need your assurance that we will have the location all to ourselves. I don't believe either of us would welcome any unnecessary distractions…or attention."

The voice on the other end was high-pitched and whiny. The last word of every sentence seemed to have an upward lilt that made it sound like everything the man said was a question rather than a statement. If there was one thing that Franklin Spears despised, it was dealing with politicians, especially ones so low on the totem pole, who somehow perpetuated the illusion that they wielded the might of demigods. Under other circumstances, he would have taken great pleasure in telling this man exactly what he thought of his pseudo-authority and just how easy it would be to get to his family, no matter when or where, but he needed the city's cooperation for one more night. And then this glorified Rotarian could go suck on an exhaust pipe for all Spears cared. He hated kowtowing to these people, and took such displeasure from it that he vowed to exact a measure of revenge with more than his single vote somewhere down the road after being placed in the position of having to kiss the ass of a man who probably hadn't done an honest day's work in his entire life, let alone sacrificed for his country.

"Thank you, sir." It took every last ounce of his restraint to keep from slamming the phone on the cradle. He closed his eyes, massaged his temples, and gestured for Ritter to approach. "Everything in place?"

"Yes, sir," Ritter said, proffering the yellow copy of the bill. "We took delivery less than twenty-five minutes ago in building cee-one-three."

Spears snatched the receipt from Ritter's hand and quickly scanned it.

"That was the mayor on the phone. He just wanted to make sure that our little problem would be squared away before his fancy shindig tomorrow night."

"He still has no idea what's down there, does he?"

"The only thing on his mind is puckering up to the legion of sycophants. I don't even think he's spared a thought for the homeless people this thing is feeding on. He just wants to pump those fools for the money to finish the waterfront project so he can get himself reelected."

"Maybe we should take him on a guided tour down there, then," Ritter said, a smile tugging at the corner of his mouth.

"Believe me, there's nothing I would enjoy more." Spears tucked the bill into his desk drawer and rose from his desk. "Have you assembled our team?"

"As you requested, sir. They're waiting for us in Hanger Three."

"Good work, soldier."

"I should tell you, sir, they're a little confused as to why you didn't put this thing down when you had the chance."

"I won't tolerate insubordination."

"Nor will you get any, sir. I just figured you should know. You can't blame them for wondering if taking this thing down is worth more to you than their lives. What with these things having killed your son and all." He lowered his voice. "They *have* seen the remains in the lab, after all."

"I was under the impression that I hired men, not little old ladies who like to gossip. They think my only interests are personal? That somehow that's going to make me reckless, or worse, soft?"

"All I'm suggesting, sir, is that perhaps a little enticement might make such petty concerns disappear."

Spears ground his teeth and curled his hands into fists.

"So that's what this boils down to, is it?" Spears shoved past him toward the door. "Fine. Fifty thousand for its head. A hundred if it's taken alive. And you'd better believe that if I hear anything else along these lines, there'll be a permanent retirement ceremony. Understood?"

He didn't wait for Ritter's acknowledgement. He entered the elevator and pressed his thumb onto the security scanner so he could descend to the labs on the access-restricted sublevels.

"I have to make a quick stop first," he said through the closing doors. "The team will just have to wait."

Fuck Ritter and fuck his men. He was already paying them like kings. There was no way in hell he was going to give any of them a reward for doing their jobs. They were either loyal or they were disposable. Period. And the method of their dismissal was solely at his discretion. But any man who chose to try to leverage Spears for extra money not only wouldn't work in this business again, he'd be lucky to find employment as a drug mule for the cartels.

The door opened and Spears stepped out into the sterile white hallway. The air was cold and smelled of disinfectant and something that reminded him of burning hair.

Damn straight this was personal. He didn't care who thought what. But that didn't mean he couldn't still do what needed to be done. They were not only going to change how wars were waged, they were going to return the United States of America, the country to which he had devoted his entire life, to its former glory.

And there was no greater mission—nor one more personal—than that.

He walked directly down the corridor to the lab and burst through the door.

*   *   *

"It's quite amazing, really," Dr. Amon Trofino said. His copper skin and green eyes were framed by the mask over his mouth and nose and the sterile cap over his dark hair. He wore a plastic shield and a full isolation suit over the whole getup. He gestured to the forty-inch LCD touch-screen monitor and the digital skeleton that pirouetted in slow circles on an invisible axis.

"What exactly am I looking at here?" Spears asked. The suit felt uncomfortably light for something that supposedly offered complete virological protection. He was used to wearing the kind of heavy body armor that could stop a fusillade of bullets, not this overpriced composite fabric. It didn't help that he had neither the time nor the patience to wait for the doctor to cut to the chase. He needed to know every detail about his prey before he briefed his men, and he needed to know right now. After last night's colossal failure, this was now a one-shot deal. They couldn't afford to blow it again.

"This is a digital reconstruction of a helical CT scan. In essence, the thin, multiplanar slices were used to build a precise anatomical image from the inside out. Then we stripped away the soft tissue and musculature, which left us with this fully articulated skeleton and the complete vasculature system you see now."

"Which one is this?"

"The largest one. The one we call Alpha. All of the others demonstrate the exact same traits, though."

Spears stared holes through the doctor. When Trofino's eyes met his, the man's smile faltered. He cleared his throat and got right down to business. He avoided looking directly at Spears's face again.

"As you can see, the bones themselves appear disproportionately wide. That's a consequence of the widening medullary canals that run through them, due in large measure to the increased demand for blood flow and the corresponding expansion of the vessels that supply it. This reaction is typical of Thalassemia, an inherited form of anemia that requires frequent blood transfusions to compensate for the body's inability to produce the necessary amounts of hemoglobin and red blood cells. What you see here, however..." Trofino tapped the screen and it zoomed in on one of the upper arm bones, the right humerus. "This here is atypical of the disease. With Thalassemia, you would expect to find thinning of the bone cortex—that's the outer layer that provides stability and resists fracture—but in this case, you'll notice that the cortices are actually *thicker* than normal. And note the distinctly white coloration. That's not just dense bone. That's mineral deposition. And not just any mineral. That's iron. The bones are infused with so much iron that we dulled the blade on the Stryker saw trying to core a sample."

"Are you telling me that their bones are somehow plated with iron? Like armor?"

"It would take a serious blow from an ax to break one, I'd imagine. We hope to commence with that level of testing soon, pending your approval." He tapped the screen again and the image zoomed out to the twirling skeleton again. "And that's not the half of it. Look at the skull." He touched the cranium and the head drew into sharp focus. "The calvarium—the forehead from the brow to the hairline—demonstrates marked thickening. Again, as you would see with Thalassemia. Only instead of the pathological obliteration of bone, there's increased density, as you can see. The same kind of iron deposits I showed you on the humerus. And right here…" He turned the skull on its axis so that it stared directly out at them and pointed first to the forehead, and then beneath each eye in turn. "…and here and here, you should see the frontal and maxillary sinuses. They appear dark on a normal person's scan because they contain air, but these show a distinct lack of pneumatization, which means they aren't hollow. The proliferation of marrow in the frontal and facial bones has obviously triggered hypertrophy, causing the bone to grow to fill those gaps. As a consequence, the bones, by nature, have to shift, causing the malar eminences—the most anterior portions of the cheek bones—to exert pressure on the developing teeth, forcing them not only downward, but forward and together, which is why it looks like they can hardly fit their jaws in their mouths."

"That's all very fascinating," Spears said, drawing on the last of his patience before he ended up squeezing the doctor's throat in his bare hands, "but that still doesn't tell me what makes these things tick. Where are their weak points? How can I predict how they'll react in different situations? All of this is excellent work. I'm sure it will help us develop this project down the road, but right now I need to figure out how to ensure the success of tonight's operation."

"You're going to deliver it to me alive, right? You assured me—"

"That I would make every conceivable effort to take this thing alive."

"A living specimen would potentially save us *years* of research and trial and error. We could move forward with testing in—"

"We've had this discussion already, doctor."

Trofino opened his mouth to argue, but closed it when he saw the expression on Spears's face. The color slowly drained from his cheeks as he regained his composure.

"We're dealing with an extremely intelligent proto-human race that managed to remain undiscovered for countless millennia, even in this age when we've laid bare nearly every inch of the earth with satellites. This is a species not dissimilar to our own in cognitive functioning, but one whose physiology more closely resembles that of a Neanderthal. Pound for pound, its bones and muscles are far stronger than ours. This is a species that recognized the necessity for population control as a means of both survival and detection avoidance. This is a predator the likes of which we never imagined existed." He paused. "Let me show you something."

He toggled the image on the screen so that the bones vanished, leaving only a tangled web of arteries, veins, and internal organs.

"As I've said repeatedly, this specimen presents with all of the hallmark traits of Thalassemia. This is a condition nearly exclusively confined to a small Mediterranean population with its distant origins in Central Asia, from which they emigrated during the Seima-Turbino Phenomenon more than two thousand years ago. The exact same region where these creatures were found. Modern treatment consists of regular blood transfusions to provide the requisite hemoglobin and red blood cells, and even then, the bone cortices continue to grow thinner and thinner until they develop osteoporosis so severe that the bones become brittle and break. What you see here is the complete opposite. These things have figured out a way to not only counteract their physical mutations, but to use them to their advantage.So how have they been able to achieve this? They certainly didn't have our medical knowledge, nor did they have the tools necessary to transfuse blood." He tapped the bizarre image at center mass. "Look first at the stomach itself and the venous network surrounding it. See how their mucosal linings are bright white? That's from iron uptake. It's the same throughout the digestive tract. So what does that tell us? Iron, as I'm sure you know, is an integral component of blood, which we obtain primarily from red meat. An iron deficiency is one of the primary causes of anemia. From this image, we can infer that this creature has *consumed* copious quantities of blood, which caused trace amounts of iron to accumulate throughout its system over time. This isn't a trivial amount of iron, either. We're talking about accumulation you could scrape from the vessels with a knife. And where does the blood go once it's been enriched with nutrients from the GI tract? It goes right to the liver to be filtered of impurities and toxins." He widened the view on the monitor and tapped the liver. It was so white it looked like a solid triangle of metal, the filamentous veins leaving it like rays from the sun. "This much iron in the system would have killed a human being long before reaching these concentrations. These things have an uncanny metabolism, which incorporates the iron into the tissues instead of eliminating it as waste, and somehow manages to stave off the toxic effects. For us, a hundredth of the concentration you're looking at here would signify a condition known as hereditary haemochromatosis, which limits life expectancy to forty years at the most. For these creatures? This is an evolutionary adaptation perfectly suited to their physiology, which, as you can tell, is markedly different than ours, despite the outward similarities. These things have adopted a means of transfusion that bypasses traditional vascular routes and allows them to absorb the red and white blood cells they need through their digestive tracts without compromising the integrity of the cell membranes."

Trofino turned away from the screen and made an effort to look Spears in the eyes before settling on a spot somewhere over his right shoulder.

"So what does that mean?" the doctor said. He sighed and rubbed his bloodshot eyes. "This is a creature that has survived for tens of thousands of years at the top of the food chain. It bleeds its prey for sustenance using elaborate proteins that thin the victim's blood. It has the strength of two men combined. It can see in the dark and has teeth that would make a lion jealous. And it has the biological compulsion to consume blood at a rate I would speculate rivals its need for water. This is the definition of an apex predator;

a killing machine whose population is controlled only by the availability of prey, not by any form of societal constraint. You're looking at a species that's been honing the ability to kill, stoking its ferocious instincts, since long before our ancestors even dropped down from the trees. You want to know what you're up against? This is the most perfect predator that's stalked the earth since the time of the dinosaurs."

"We've already demonstrated we can kill them, doctor."

"You're missing my point. Maybe you'll be able to take this one individual down, but certainly not without casualties. The larger concern here is what if you don't? What if this creature has learned from your previous encounters, as it has historically demonstrated it has the ability to do? The problem is…what if it escapes? What if you chase this thing out of the ruins and end up turning it loose on the city at large? You could wind up being responsible for countless deaths—"

Spears seized him by the front of his isolation suit and slammed him against the wall.

"It won't escape!"

"Like last night?" Trofino said. His lower lip trembled when he spoke.

"You have something to say to me? Then say it."

"Any ecological niche can only accommodate a small number of predatory species, let alone the sudden arrival of a new apex species. Even if we're able to isolate the traits we're looking for and somehow incorporate them into the DNA of a group of soldiers, we risk including the mutation that can only be satisfied by the constant consumption of blood. What if we turn an elite fighting force into this kind of monster? We'd be creating a predator we could never control, one that would not only attack the enemy, but all of humanity. We could ultimately be responsible for our own genocide."

Spears bounced Trofino off the wall. The doctor dropped to his knees at Spears's feet.

"Then you'd better not let that happen, doctor."

"That's my point," Trofino said in little more than a whisper. "Without a living specimen on which to run the batteries of tests we require, we might not be able to figure out how to control the mutations in a human host."

Spears bit his lip hard enough to draw blood. This definitely complicated matters, but the risk would undoubtedly be worth the reward.

"Then you'll have it, doctor," Spears said through bared teeth that glistened crimson.

He turned and strode out of the room without another word.

*   *   *

His men were assembled in the hanger when he arrived. The mercenary spark in their eyes told him that Ritter had already shared the details of his incentive arrangement, which he now had to amend.

"We need to take this thing alive, gentlemen. A kill in this scenario would be considered failure."

The room echoed with their grumblings, but Spears waited it out, his eyes traveling across each of their faces in turn.

"A quarter of a million dollars to each of you when this thing is secured in the lab."

Suddenly, he had their complete and undivided attention once more.

"I trust you're all familiar with the contents of the crates behind you," Spears said. He leaned over a table where the enlarged satellite image of the ruins had been overlaid with a film of cellulose acetate onto which the building blueprints had been copied. He tapped the picture as he spoke. "The plan is simple. We infiltrate the buildings at these four points. Here, here, here, and...here. We lead with the flashbangs to clear the immediate vicinity, then we discharge the contents of those crates and get the hell back out of there and take up the positions I've clearly marked on this picture: one of you at each egress, one more on each corner of the building complex. We hold that perimeter and make sure that it doesn't get past us when it tries to flee the rubble."

He could see the question in their eyes.

"I said to take it alive. I never said it had to be in one piece." Spears smiled, eliciting the same response from his men. "Now get cracking. We still have preparations to make and not much time to make them."

TWENTY-SEVEN

Seattle, Washington
3:23 p.m. PST

"This is some truly amazing stuff, Officer Sturm! Truly amazing!" the voice on the other end of the line blurted the moment she answered her cell phone. "Tell me where you found it. No, wait. Tell me everything. From the start. Omit nothing. This has to be one of the most exciting days of my—"

"Slow down, Dr. Perriera," Sturm interrupted. "I take it you recognized the symbols. Were you able to decipher any of them?"

When she and Porter split up after leaving the ruins, she had contacted one of her old undergraduate professors, who had referred her to Dr. Eduard Perriera. The professor of Ancient Mesopotamian Studies had sounded put out and only mildly intrigued, but had asked her to send along her pictures anyway. She hadn't expected to hear back from him so soon, let alone with this level of excitement in his voice.

Sturm had been on her way home to try to catch a few hours of sleep while waiting for Porter to call her and make arrangements for the coming night when her ring tone had startled her so badly she nearly swerved into oncoming traffic. She must have started to doze off at the wheel. She turned right into the parking lot of a grocery store with a Starbucks inside of it and another free-standing drive-thru unit less than a hundred yards away, found a parking place off on her own, and waited for Perriera to continue.

"Not all of them. The writing is definitely a permutation of ancient Sumerian cuneiform, but some of the characters are like nothing I've ever seen before. I was able to identify maybe a half-dozen words or phrases. I'm going to need more time if you want a thorough translation."

"Can you tell me what you have so far?"

"Got an email address?"

Sturm rattled it off, fished the carrying case with her laptop from under the passenger seat, and opened it on the seat beside her. While she waited for the old Dell to boot up, she told Perriera about where they had found the etchings, but shared only the details he absolutely needed to know about the circumstances surrounding her discovery.

"I'm starting to think this might be an elaborate hoax, officer," Perriera said when she was through. "If you're telling me the truth, then someone could have just carved the symbols in hopes of generating a little publicity or a spectacle of some kind. They could have found the words I was able to translate in any number of texts and simply made up the rest."

"It's a possibility, doctor. However, for the time being, I'd like to approach this as though they're genuine."

"You know something you're not telling me."

The expectant silence on the line was interrupted by the chime of her email program downloading her mail. She opened the file Perriera had attached and stared at the document. The characters she had photographed formed continuous rows of arrows and lines without any apparent breaks for words or letters, but Perriera had chopped them into smaller segments. The words he had identified were highlighted in yellow, and reproduced at the bottom of the page beside their translations. Early in the paragraph, he had highlighted ⟩⊤⊢⊣ ⊨⊺ ⎾⎾ ⌐⊧⊧⊺, which translated to "mother die."

⊱—⟨ was repeated several times throughout the message. Any icy finger traced Sturm's spine when she read its meaning.

"Blood," she whispered.

Another word was repeated over and over, a good dozen times in just the sections she had photographed: ⊶⊧⟨⊼⟩ .

It meant "scared."

She remembered how the little girl had curled up in her lap and cried in her arms, how helpless she had seemed, how like any other child who simply couldn't handle the terror of the world around her.

The worst was the very end of the excerpt, where the same word was repeated at least twenty times in a row. The uniformity of height and the clarity of the lines deteriorated with each instance

to the point that the final occurrence trailed off the bottom of the
wood.

   ⊢≛𝖸𝖸𝖸≺

She stared at the translation and felt the warmth of tears on her
cheeks.

Alone.

Sturm closed her eyes and could see the little girl crying as she
knelt naked in the darkness, scratching the word that summed up
all of her fear and feelings of isolation and hopelessness into the
wood again and again, before crawling through the rubble, curling
up against the wall and covering herself with the cold dirt that was
no substitute for a dead mother's embrace, and trying to sleep in a
frightening tomb far from her home.

"Officer Sturm?" Perriera said. "Are you still there?"

"Yeah." Sturm looked out through the front windshield at a
mother leading her daughter through the parking lot from the
grocery store. Red ribbons flowed from the child's pigtails, her
mouth blue from the Ring Pop on her thumb. "I'm going to have to
get back to you, doctor."

"You're going to tell me what's really going on when you do,
right?"

"Thanks for your help. I really appreciate it."

"You can't just leave me wondering—"

Sturm ended the call and watched the woman lift her child into
the back seat of a Volvo and buckle her into a booster seat, but in
her mind, she saw her own mother and a little girl in dusty overalls
who was everything she could no longer be. She averted her eyes
before she started to cry again and dialed another number on her
cell phone. When the voice on the other end answered, she spoke
without bothering to identify herself.

"There's something you need to see."

TWENTY-EIGHT

Seattle, Washington
4:36 p.m. PST

Porter stood on the end of the commercial pier, watching the waves roll in from the distant, cloud-blanketed horizon, bringing with them the dots that would grow into the ships that would soon enough dock in front of him and unload the day's catch. The sandwich on the rail beside him was only partially consumed, the coffee long since cold. An ambitious seagull hopped a little closer to his food every time he looked away, until it eventually made its big move and, with a shriek, snatched his sandwich from the wrapper, which spun lazily down toward the water. A boy and his father baited their hooks from a bucket of tiny squids and cast their lines out into the chop over the rail behind him. He tried not to look to the south, where he could see the gold of the Bertha Knight Landes Cultural Center through the outrigger booms of the *Dragnet*. He tried not to think about his SAC's words, about how his concerns had been dismissed without the slightest pause for deliberation or the opportunity to state his case. His orders had been explicit, the consequences implied.

Stay the hell away from the waterfront development tonight…*or pack your bags for the field office in South Dakota.*

How had it come to this?

Seventy-two hours ago, he had been a shooting star in the department, the go-to guy when things needed to be handled quickly and quietly. And now here he was, an outsider in his own investigation, one that no one appeared to want him to solve; a pawn in a political game with rules he couldn't figure out, let alone understand. Men had *died*, but no one seemed to remember that inconvenient little detail. Or care, for that matter. There was a child who could write in a dead language living in the ruins, and a private defense contractor preparing to unleash a team of mercenaries into the subterranean warrens. And who could forget the mayor's fundraiser tomorrow night, which apparently was the only thing that actually mattered…

He flashed back to a thought that had just crossed his mind, but grasping its importance was like trying to grab an eel by the tail.

Men had died…

Before he even realized he was going to do it, he grabbed the brown barrel trash receptacle from the pier beside him and hurled it over the rail. It hit the ocean with a booming splash and bobbed against the pylons before sinking with a belch of air. He heard the zip of fishing lines being hurriedly reeled in and then the clamor of footsteps rushing away from him on the weathered planks.

He buried his face in his hands and then looked out upon the sea again, as though waiting for a ship he knew would never arrive.

He'd never felt so alone, so…displaced. All of the rules he'd devoted his life to enforcing no longer mattered to the men who wrote them. The ideals he cherished were worth nothing on the open market, where money and power were commodities worth far more than trivialities like justice and human life.

A warm breeze that smelled of sea salt and schooling fish raced ahead of the coming storm. He allowed it to caress his face and felt a preternatural sense of calmness settle into his very soul.

Porter smiled, removed his phone from his pocket, and dialed Sturm's number.

He had agonized over his situation, but there had never really been any decision to make, had there?

"I hear South Dakota's beautiful this time of year," he said when she answered.

*   *   *

Sturm met him at the pier twenty minutes later in faded Levi's and a black hoodie, and together they had picked their way through the abandoned buildings and vacant lots, and watched the development until it was safe to sprint across the street and scale the fence. She had called in sick for her shift, which had pissed off the watch commander to no end, but, since her days there were numbered, she was impervious to his threats. Besides, the waterfront rousting had been cancelled, which didn't come as a surprise in the slightest. The entire area needed to be cleared for the big night ahead. Porter had tossed his cell phone into the back of a panel truck with Oregon plates and replaced it with a disposable unit. They were now off the grid and skydiving without parachutes. If anyone found out what they were up to, they'd be hung out to dry by their departments and run out of town by the political machine. And he couldn't have felt more at ease. He could see it in Sturm's eyes, as well.

That, and a generous helping of fear.

He wasn't sure exactly what he thought about the child. All evidence pointed to the fact that she was a brutal killer, more animal than human, and yet this was the same little girl who had cried into Sturm's chest and carved her heartbreaking tale of her mother's death and her own feelings of helplessness into the walls around her. She was an enigma: a doll-carrying victim of circumstances beyond her control who ripped out the throats of her prey and consumed their blood. He didn't know what he was supposed to think or which course of action to take. On one hand, this child was a monster that had killed at least sixteen people that he was aware of and needed to be taken out of play by whatever means possible. On the other, she was just a frightened little girl who'd obviously been abducted from her home after watching her mother die and transported across the ocean into a terrifying world beyond her limited comprehension. Part of him knew he should either subdue her or put her down—if they even found her at all—while the part that seemed to be in control at the moment thought they should do whatever they could to save her, especially considering her value to the men who had smuggled her out of Russia, the same men who would soon descend upon the ruins under the cover of darkness, mere hours from now. He put aside the internal debate and made a firm decision, one that he was confident he could live with.

He was just going to have to wing it.

The sky was gray when they crawled down into the warrens, the lightning that stabbed from one storm cloud to the next imbued with red from the setting sun as though made from electrical flame. They didn't have a whole lot of time to attempt Sturm's plan. If they couldn't find the girl quickly enough, they were going to have to get the hell out of there regardless. The last thing they could afford was to be down there in the darkness when Spears and his men arrived. Following last night's failure, they will have adjusted their plan of attack, and Porter had a sour feeling in the pit of his stomach that insisted he didn't want to learn firsthand what they intended to do.

"I'll follow the route to the left," Sturm whispered, shining her flashlight through the dust motes toward a collapsed section of the brick wall. "You go—"

"The hell if I'm letting you out of my sight."

"I can take care of myself. And I know these tunnels far better than you do."

"We can't risk getting separated. When the time comes to get out of here, we're going to have to do so in a hurry. And you'd better believe I'll drag you out of her kicking and screaming if I have to."

She opened her mouth to argue, but glanced at her watch and simply shook her head.

"We need to get moving," she said. "How long do you figure we have before our company arrives?"

"Not nearly long enough to do what we need to do."

"Then we'd better get this show on the road."

She turned away from him and started deeper into the ruins. He grabbed her by the arm and spun her around so that their faces were only inches apart.

"I need to make sure you understand what will happen if the forces that are coming find us down here. These aren't the kind of men who are going to just let us walk away."

She drew her pistol from its holster, chambered a round with a *snick*, and offered a crooked grin that answered his question. Unfortunately, he still had one more.

"And what if we find this girl and she's not the helpless innocent that you think she is?"

Sturm's smile faltered.

That was all the answer he needed.

*   *   *

It was all he could do to keep from glancing at his watch every few seconds. Time was slipping away from them far too quickly. The sun had set at 5:44 p.m. That was just over two hours ago when he last checked, and they still hadn't encountered any sign of the child. They were living on borrowed time now. He tried to convince himself that the men who were coming would wait a while to minimize their chances of being seen, but he knew better. They were in an abandoned industrial district, in a closed construction site hidden from the road by the fence and the artwork. There were no houses nearby, and the closest potential witnesses were nearly a mile away at the commercial wharf where even cannon fire would be masked by the roar of engines, the booming of offloaded containers, and the beeping of forklifts. The powers-that-be had ensured that there would be no law enforcement presence or intervention and had given Phobos the green light to do whatever needed to be done to resolve this situation before the ribbon cutting ceremony tomorrow night. He knew for certain that the men wouldn't walk blindly into the rubble on a hunting expedition as they had last night. They will have amended their plans to compensate for their failure and ensure there would be no repeat performance. They had to know they had a short window to make this happen or it would be closed to them forever. Whatever they had planned, it was going to be big. Porter wished he had an inkling of what was in store. He was gambling on the child's importance to these men. If he was wrong, then they just might be willing to incinerate the ruins, with Sturm and him inside.

They had cleared the main passages first, before following the conveyor chute into the heart of the honeycomb. The girl hadn't been in her den as they had hoped, and every tunnel they explored led them to another dead end without any indication that she was even still down here. She had the advantage of familiarity with her surroundings, while it felt as though he and Sturm were merely bumbling through the maze, their flashlights about as effective as fireflies in the oily darkness. Every so often, he stopped and listened, but never heard anything more than the grumbling of the settling rubble, the skittering of pebbles through the debris, and the occasional distant rumble of thunder that shook loose cascades of dirt and dust. Once he thought he heard a scuffing sound in the tunnel behind them, but there had been nothing there when he turned around.

He rounded a bend and felt his knuckles scrape the soles of Sturm's shoes.

She lay prone in front of him, her flashlight beam muted by her palm, which glowed faintly red.

"Did you hear that?" she whispered.

He was about to ask what she had heard when what sounded like a muffled gunshot echoed from somewhere above him. Then another. And another.

Sturm looked back at him, her eyes wide, her face made stark-white by his light.

They weren't gunshots, he realized.

Those were the sounds of car doors closing.

They were out of time.

"They're here," he whispered.

III

In order to get power and retain it, it is necessary to love power;
but love of power is not connected with goodness
but with qualities that are the opposite of goodness,
such as pride, cunning, and cruelty.

—Leo Nikolaevich Tolstoy

TWENTY-NINE

Seattle, Washington
8:57 p.m. PST

There was no point in being quiet now. They were about to go in full-bore and there was nothing anyone or anything could do about it. The three black SUVs were parked side by side, tailgates open. He and his men donned their backpacks, clipped their flashbangs to their hips, and the "special" canisters to the harnesses on their chests so they would be within easy reach. They were dressed in black, from their stocking caps to their boots, and had painted their faces to match. Their night vision/thermal fusion goggles stood from their brows like a third insectile eye. They wore gas masks over their noses and mouths, their voices made tinny by the filters and the rebreathing apparatuses.

His men all knew their assignments and struck off toward their positions without a word. They had gone over the plan in painstaking detail until Spears was certain there would be no mistakes and synchronized their watches the second they stepped out of the cars. Once their assault commenced, everything was going to move at lightning speed and there would be no room for error. This would not be like last night. They were going to swoop in and out like an eagle falling upon a mouse, and then this operation would be over and they could get down to the real mission, the one that would change the world and make him the richest man alive in the process.

They all assumed their posts and blended into the shadows while they waited for the prearranged moment to arrive. Spears crouched in the tall weeds beside the northernmost, and, judging by the riot of footprints, the most oft-used, entrance to the underground warrens. When the creature came charging out of there, he prayed to God it would come right at him. He wanted to be the one to bring it down. Not in hopes of using it as leverage to weasel out of paying the men their promised bonuses, but because, from the very beginning, it felt as though events had conspired to place him at this particular point at that this precise moment in time. Call it fate, destiny, kismet, whatever. His entire life had built up to this one defining event, and he would finally achieve the greatness to which he had always aspired. The cost had been great, but the reward would be even greater. History was written by men who had the courage to seize the world by the throat and throttle it like the thrashing serpent that it was. This was his hour, his time. His name would be written in the annals of time with the likes of Patton and Truman, the khans and the Caesars, men who had conquered the world, or, as his son might have said, made it their bitch.

He pictured Nelson, and imagined the awe his son would have expressed had he known the enormous evolutionary leap that was about to be taken thanks to his magnificent discovery.

Spears wiped a tear of pride from his lashes before it could form and stared down at his watch.

Five.

He gripped a flashbang in each fist and crawled toward the dark opening.

Four.

He crouched just outside the orifice and peered inside.

Three.

No heat signature. No movement.

Two.

He glanced to either side and watched his men peel from the shadows.

One.

He pulled the pins and tossed the canister in his right hand first, then the one in his left, straight ahead into the tunnel.

Showtime.

Brilliant golden light exploded from the orifice with a loud *whoomph* that echoed across the waterfront.

He lowered his goggles, scurried through the hole, and dropped down into the sublevel. Smoke swirled and eddied around him. There was no heat signature waiting for him, no sign of movement. His respirator made a mechanical wheezing sound. Gravel crunched underfoot. Loose concrete and pebbles rained from the ceiling. He unstrapped the tear gas gun, which looked like a sawed off shotgun with an absurdly wide barrel, from his right thigh, loaded a canister of CR gas, and fired it down the corridor to his left. He broke the breech and loaded another and another and another and fired them off into the darkness, trailing swirling vortices of smoke behind them. They clattered out of sight and then exploded into toxic aerosol clouds that filled the tunnels. Before the gas reached him, he spun, hauled himself back into the tunnel and scurried toward the fresh air.

In a matter of moments, the dibenzoxazepine agent would filter through the ruins, following any air passage through the rubble. The lachrymatory gas was ten times more powerful than ordinary tear gas. Even the most transient exposure would cause intense skin irritation, especially to the mucus membranes, temporary blindness, gasping, coughing, and overwhelming panic. There was a risk of immediate incapacitation, but with the resilience the creature had already demonstrated, he wasn't overly concerned. The instant that thing felt the searing pain in its eyes and throat, it would make a mad dash for the nearest egress to the surface.

And they would be waiting.

It would stumble in blind agony right into their clutches. A bullet through both kneecaps and there would be no possibility of escape. Quick and easy. In and out. Spears had this mission planned perfectly, right down to the smallest detail. If the agent overwhelmed it, then all they would have to do is go in there after it and drag its flailing carcass back out. It would be in so much pain that he couldn't imagine it would put up any kind of fight at all. He'd seen the damage the CR gas could do. It had been used for riot control in South Africa two decades ago, and it had worked like a charm. The only problem was the mass casualties by asphyxiation and pulmonary edema in the weak and infirm segments of the population, which was why it was now classified as a combat class chemical weapon and such a challenge to procure.

He crawled out of the tunnel and assumed his post. Tendrils of yellowish-white smoke spiraled up out of the rubble. A glance to either side confirmed that his men were ready and waiting.

It was only a matter of time now. That monster was going to come flying out of the ruins at any second, tears streaming from its sightless eyes, unable to breathe through its closing throat.

He seated the butt of his assault rifle against his shoulder, assumed his shooter's stance, and scrutinized the black orifice through the wisps of smoke.

He squeezed his finger into the sweet spot on the trigger and prepared to fire at the first hint of motion.

"Come on, baby," he whispered. "Come on."

THIRTY

Seattle, Washington
9:02 p.m. PST

Sturm crawled as fast as she could. Porter goaded her from behind, pushing her rear end whenever she started to slow. The second they had heard the distant whoosh of the canisters being fired into the tunnels behind them, Porter had shouted for her to move and nearly hurled her into the nearest tube. She had recognized the sound, as well, but had only experienced the tear gas drills at the academy years ago. The sound had been incongruous to her surroundings. Never in a million years would she have thought the men would use such drastic measures to flush the girl out of the warren. Neither of them had been prepared for this kind of assault. She'd seen the debilitating effects of the gas and knew that they either got the hell out of there before they were temporarily blinded and went into bronchospasms, or they were in deep trouble. It was hard enough to navigate these passages with their eyes open. It would be impossible with them closed. And if they became trapped in one of these small chambers while the gas grew thicker and thicker, they might never make it out at all.

"Hurry!" Porter yelled. He shoved her haunches and she tumbled out into what she had come to think of as the central hub. Fingers of chemical gas already reached through some of the honeycombs. Her eyes immediately started to sting as though squirted with lemon juice.

"Which way?" she nearly screamed. It felt like shards of glass tore at her lungs when she coughed.

"They'll be covering every exit. If we crawl through the smoke into their line of fire—"

"That bootlegger's tunnel we found earlier—"

"Wouldn't be on any blueprints."

"But if they do know about it—"

"Then we're dead." He retched and pulled his shirt up over his mouth and nose. "We're probably dead already anyway, but it's our only chance."

She scrabbled up the wall toward the opening of the tunnel. They all looked alike and she couldn't be entirely sure she'd chosen the correct one. She pulled herself inside and crawled for everything she was worth. The knees of her jeans tore and she felt sharp fragments of concrete bite into her palms. She was certain she was leaving a trail of blood, but she forced the thought out of her mind. Her flashlight beam jerked from side to side with her exertions to such a degree that she could hardly see where she was going, let alone if she was headed in the right direction. The stinging sensation in her eyes grew exponentially worse. She could barely keep them open. The tears that flooded her lashes burned on her eyelids and cheeks.

The ground fell out from beneath her and she felt the pointed corners of broken bricks stab her shoulders, then her back. She landed squarely on her side and slammed her head against the ground. Porter tumbled down onto her a heartbeat later. She could barely summon the strength to open her eyes. She saw dried seaweed clinging to brick walls, felt just the faintest hint of a cool breeze on her face, and smelled the ocean and the rain.

"We have to keep moving," Porter said.

He rolled off of her, grabbed her by the arm, and tried to wrench her to her feet. She grabbed her flashlight and tried to stand—

Twin golden circles reflected her beam back at her.

She knelt and held perfectly still.

"Hurry up!" Porter snapped. He was already half a dozen paces ahead of her, his silhouette hazy through the thickening chemical fog. He barked a cough and took two strides toward her before she held up her hand to signal him to stop. "There's no time for…"

His words died when he saw what her flashlight had found.

The girl was huddled in the corner where the tunnel above had collapsed down onto this one. She had drawn her knees up to her chin and wrapped her arms around them. Her face glistened with tears and her pale skin was a stark contrast to the blood and grime caked to her bare flesh. Sturm raised the beam into the girl's face and she quickly turned away. She swatted at the light as though she could brush intangible column away. Her fingernails were more like talons than anything resembling human nails.

"It's all right," Sturm whispered. "We aren't going to hurt you."

The girl's entire body trembled.

"Just grab her and let's get—"

At the sound of his voice, the girl's head snapped around and she bared the set of teeth Sturm had cast from the neck wounds of the dead men on the *Scourge*. They looked infinitely sharper in person, like so many enlarged rattlesnake fangs fitted into a gorilla's jaws. Her mouth opened so wide it appeared to unhinge. Her pink eyes fixed on Porter and she lunged at him. Without thinking, Sturm stepped between them and took the brunt of the girl's attack in her midsection. She tumbled to the ground with the girl's weight on her chest. The girl's arms struck like vipers, with such strength and ferocity that Sturm couldn't get a grip on them. She felt claws slice through her sweatshirt and part her skin so cleanly that she didn't feel the pain until a second later. The girl was too strong for her, yet Sturm continued to pull the child tighter and tighter against her body until the struggling ceased and she felt nails curl into the back of her sweatshirt and loop under her skin like fishhooks. The small body trembled against hers.

Sturm coughed and tasted blood in her mouth. Her eyes had passed from stinging into a zone of pain that felt like hot needles were being driven through her corneas. She couldn't make them open any more than she could close them tightly enough to seal out the chemical fog that settled over them like a toxic blanket. The little girl coughed so hard her nails nearly flayed the skin from Sturm's back.

This definitely wasn't ordinary tear gas.

"Get up!" Porter shouted. His voice broke and she felt warmth drip from his nose or his mouth onto the back of her neck as he grabbed her under her arm and tugged her forward. "We have to keep moving!"

Sturm knew he was right. The fumes grew more intense with each passing second. It was only a matter of time before they were overwhelmed and would no longer have the ability to escape.

She wrapped her arm around the girl's back, cradling her to her own chest with as much strength as she could muster. The child squeezed her legs around Sturm's waist and squeezed like an anaconda. Sturm half-crawled, half-stumbled in the direction of the fresh air, which was now more of a memory than an actual physical sensation. She could hear Porter's staggering footsteps ahead of her, splashing in the water that bisected the floor, slapping from the smooth stones. He collapsed repeatedly, yet somehow managed to right himself and even drag her to her feet when she didn't think she could do so on her own.

The gas thinned and she tasted the ocean breeze, felt its cool currents working into the corners of her teary eyes and down her throat, stoking the flames she was certain burned inside her chest. She recognized how close she was, but feared she wasn't going to be able to make it. The fire spread from her eyes and lungs throughout her entire form. Every inch of her body hurt in a way she'd never imagined. She thought she was still crawling when Porter grabbed her by her hoodie and dragged her on her side thought the water. She heard a thump, then the squeal of hinges as he hauled her over the metal lip and right down into the tide.

She sputtered and gasped for air, choking on a mouthful of brine that seemed to lodge in her constricted throat to the point that she could neither swallow it down or spit it out. Her vomit reflex solved the dilemma for her and she dropped back under the sea right behind it. She pawed at her eyes, at her nose, at her mouth, the salt only aggravating—

The girl.

Sturm tried to open her eyes, but managed only a red, watery sliver through which she could barely discern the hazy outline of the ruined pier. She dove under the water and ran her palms across the sand and rocks, searching for an arm, a leg, an ankle, a handful of hair, anything at all by which to drag the girl back to the surface. She hadn't felt those sharp nails disengage from her skin or the weight fall from her arms to even know where to begin.

"Where is she?" Sturm cried, the words tearing through her trachea like barbed wire.

"Quiet!" Porter whispered directly into her ear. "We can't let them hear us."

"I can't find her! She could have been pulled under and swept out to sea. We have to—"

He clasped his hand over her mouth and drew her to him, pinning her arms to her sides in an awkward embrace.

"She's okay, Layne," he whispered. "You have to calm down before you get us both killed."

Sturm nodded and waited for him to remove his hand before she spoke.

"Where is she?" Sturm could barely see the silhouettes of the pylons around her, jagged with barnacles, the collapsed wooden planks, the shoreline where the rain-dimpled waves crashed into the rocks and threw up flumes of foam. "We can't let them get her."

And then she saw her, a hunched shadow momentarily illuminated by a strobe of lightning, sprinting low to the ground across the elevated ground to the north.

Then the darkness swallowed her.

When the lightning flared again, she was gone.

THIRTY-ONE

Seattle, Washington
Saturday, October 20th
12:42 a.m. PST

Spears and his men had waited until all of the gas rising from the rubble dissipated, and then waited some more. No one had seen the creature crawl from the ruins, and Spears had made sure that every man maintained his position. It must not have been as intelligent as he had thought. It must have tried to hide down there and become overwhelmed by the CR gas. Spears imagined it clasping its small fingers over its mouth and nose, trying desperately not to breathe as the chemical fog swirled around it. He pictured it baring its teeth and pinching its eyes shut as it held its breath, waiting for the fumes to disperse while the sensitive membranes in the corners of its mouth, nostrils, and eyelids started to sting. Then finally opening its mouth and involuntarily gasping the gas, igniting the flames that rushed through its body, a pain like no other lighting up its nerve tracts. He envisioned it clawing at the debris, unable to see, its throat constricting tighter and tighter with each attempted breath until it realized there was no way it would ever escape and panic set in. He could almost see its nails bending back and tearing from the cuticles as it attempted to clear the obstruction in its trachea by tearing open its own windpipe. It was the image of the monster bleeding out into the dirt from its self-inflicted mortal wound that was the source of the smile he now wore as he picked his way through the underground warrens.

They'd already been down here for close to three hours and had yet to find it, but Spears knew it was only a matter of time before they did. There was no way it could have broken through their perimeter, not without someone seeing the colorful blur of its heat signature like a streaking comet. No, it was down here, all right. They just hadn't found where it had crawled off to die.

Trofino would be incensed, but he'd get over it. He'd just have to work harder to earn the ungodly amount of money Spears was paying him. And he'd happily endure the doctor's wrath for the opportunity to kick the beast's face into a shattered crater.

He had just wriggled through a tunnel that felt as narrow as the womb and crawled into a small chamber still hazy with gas when his earpiece crackled.

"This is Morgan topside," a disembodied voice said. *"There's something you need to see up here."*

Spears acknowledged the message and cleared the room before turning around and squirming back toward the main passage. He didn't like the tone of Morgan's voice. It wasn't the way a man sounded when he found something his superior was actually going to want to see. Spears felt the acids burble in the cauldron of his belly and understood on an instinctual level that they had made a tragic mistake.

When he reached the main branch, he sprinted through the maze to the west where he had stationed Morgan. He climbed out through a widened crack in the foundation, but didn't immediately see his man.

"State your position," he said into the microphone retrofitted into his mask.

A shadow rose over the rocky edge of the shoreline, silhouetted against the dark sea, which flashed with reflected lighting, and hailed him with a single wave of its arm.

Spears picked his way through the proliferation of weeds toward the remains of a fallen pier. The decline grew steeper and he had to negotiate loose stones, trash, and detritus that had both washed in from the ocean and tumbled downhill from the demolition.

Morgan greeted him with a curt nod, and, without a word, ducked down under the collapsed framework of the pier. Spears followed and splashed down into shin-deep water that he could now clearly hear echoing inside an underground passage of some kind. He closed his eyes when he saw the rusted grate and fought the urge to lash out at Morgan. He drew several deep breaths to regain his composure, then threw the grate wide open with a scream of the rusted hinges. The remainder of the garbage and seaweed that had once concealed it fell into the tide when it struck the bank. He found himself staring into a long, dark tunnel that ran directly under the ruins.

"This wasn't on any of the blueprints." It was all he could think to say. The words sounded pathetic, even to his own ears. Had they been given the time to properly reconnoiter the area, they would have eventually found it. This was the kind of colossal blunder that tanked missions and ended up getting men killed. In this case, it was an unforgivable oversight that had just cost him his last shot at his prey. "Walk me through it."

"I was scouring the shoreline when I heard the water funneling underground. I climbed down the bank and saw what at first looked like a wall of seaweed. When I pulled off a handful of brown kelp and saw the iron rails, I knew we were screwed."

"You didn't see any sign of it in there?"

"No, sir. I called you first."

Spears ducked and entered the tunnel in a crouch. The gray water line on the walls was nearly to the rounded ceiling. At high tide, this tube might have been nearly filled. He cursed his luck and timing and sloshed deeper into the darkness, searching for any indication that the creature had passed through here. For all he knew, it could still be lying dead in the ruins, but a soldier didn't reach his age without trusting his gut, and right now his gut was telling him that he'd just fucked up worse than he ever had in his entire career. He saw the mouth of a tunnel where it had collapsed down upon this one and shambled as quickly as he could toward it. He was just about to pull himself up over the jagged metal lip when he saw tatters of fabric clinging to the sharp slivers. He peeled them away, turned them over between his fingers, and then removed his gloves. The very tips of the metal tines were crusted with something dark. He scraped some off with his fingernail and tasted it.

Blood. There was no doubt.

He looked at the fabric again and furrowed his brow. Something bothered him about it, but he couldn't quite grasp the thought. And then it hit him. He pulled down his mask and sniffed the cloth. Beneath the acrid tang of the gas, he smelled filth, and something else, something that should have surprised him and yet somehow didn't. It was some kind of perfume, or maybe just detergent or fabric softener. Only the faintest hint, but the

homeless who had been run out of here hadn't been the kind to
regularly launder their wardrobes and any clothes the creature
could have scrounged would have been every bit as filthy.

Someone else had been down here tonight. Someone who now
knew a lot more than he or she should.

Spears dropped the fabric and quickly donned his mask again.
Even in diminished concentrations, the gas made his nostrils and
throat feel as though he'd scoured their delicate linings with
sandpaper made of cracked pepper corns.

He nearly barreled through Morgan, who he hadn't even heard
approach, on his way back to the outside world. The rain whipped
inland from the sea, making the rocks even slicker to climb back
up to the shore. He stood and turned in a slow circle.

No one had seen the creature—or whoever else was down
there—emerge from the tunnel, which meant they had to have
either attempted to swim out into the ocean before doubling back
to land, which in this weather was patently absurd, or they had
stayed low against the bank and headed either directly north or
south.

He fixed his gaze to the north, where the lights from the wharf
flickered through the mist and the sheeting rain. That was where
the creature had first come ashore. It would have sensed an
element of familiarity and instinctively chosen that route. Maybe
this night wasn't over just yet. He could leave a handful of men
under Ritter's command to clear every last inch of the ruins, then
head south when they were certain it hadn't attempted to return to
the warrens, while he led a team into the shipyard. It had probably
climbed onto one of the moored ships and hidden down in the
hold, shivering and cold, its eyes and lungs seared, licking its
wounds.

He had underestimated it, but it was still just an animal, after
all. And there was no animal on this planet that was a match for
him.

Come hell or high water, he was going to find it.

And then—with apologies to the good Dr. Trofino—all bets
were off.

He wouldn't let it slip through his grasp again.

THIRTY-TWO

Seattle, Washington
3:49 a.m. PST

Porter watched the men systematically searching one boat after another, all pretense of discretion abandoned. With the slicker and the rubber boots he had "borrowed" from the harbor master's shack when no one was looking, he blended right into the background, sitting on a cable spool with a Styrofoam cup of coffee and the air of a man trying to dodge his work. He and Sturm hadn't had nearly enough time to properly search the wharf before she had seen the men materialize from the darkness to the south. There were too many ships and too much activity all around them to perform more than a cursory inspection. Besides, Porter was convinced that the girl wasn't here anyway. A naked girl sprinting up the shoreline and onto one of the piers would have attracted someone's attention, no matter how secretive she had been. And with her reaction to even the dim light from their flashlights, he couldn't imagine she would have sought refuge here under the towering banks of overhead spotlights. But someone needed to keep and eye on these men, who had cowed the harbor master when he had confronted them and sent him slinking back into his shack with his tail between his legs. They now moved from one pier to the next with the kind of impunity that positively infuriated Porter.

He opened his disposable cell and dialed Sturm's number. She had worked her way back inland and approached the construction site from the east, taking up position in the vacant lot across the street. The half of the team that stayed behind had searched the waterfront to the south and returned to their vehicles to await their rendezvous with the unit Porter now covertly observed.

Sturm answered in a whisper and quickly gave him an update before hanging up.

The men had gone back underground in full battle gear and gas masks. Porter knew what that meant. He could see the frustration in the men up here, even from a hundred yards away. Their body language and clipped shouts betrayed the fact that they were resisting the only inevitable conclusion. They had lost the girl and were running out of options. The men kept their distance from Spears, who stormed up and down the piers, barking orders and threats. He had lost control of the situation and even the work crews unloading the canisters from a massive freight ship with oriental letters on the hull recognized it. They tried not to gawk, but their foreman had to repeatedly get on the air horn to refocus them on their tasks.

Spears sending his men back into the ruins was a last ditch effort, confirmation that they hadn't found any sign of the girl either to the north or to the south and were hoping that she had doubled back once they had vacated the vicinity around her home. If not, she could be anywhere in the countless acres of warehouses and ramshackle neighborhoods where they would never be able to find her.

The eastern horizon was already melting from black to blue. Spears and his men were just about out of time and they knew it. This place would come to life before dawn, and there was no way they would be able to bully their way through the bustle under the full light of day. He and Sturm, on the other hand, were just two lowly law enforcement officers who wouldn't attract an absurd amount of attention, and their badges would allow them to come and go as they pleased.

There was still one glaring flaw with the plan that was slowly taking shape in Porter's head. If they did find the girl, what were they supposed to do with her? There was obviously something physically different about her, some mutation that had turned her into the kind of monster that could wipe out the entire crews of the vessels that had brought her across the sea, the kind of predator that stalked the ruins in search of prey to bleed to death. At the same time, though, he had seen this bloodthirsty killer crawl right into Sturm's embrace without a hint of malice on her face. If they somehow captured her and turned her over to the corrupt authorities, it would be just like handing her over to these men, who wanted to do God knows what to her. But what other alternatives were there? Drive her out into the country and turn her loose in the woods like a dog? Try to keep her hidden from the world and raise her like a normal child? Force her into the system and make her face the consequences of her crimes? Christ. For all they knew there wasn't a shred of humanity in her.

There was another option, but the mere fact that he even perceived it as such made him question whether or not he still held the deed to his soul. When an animal attacks a human, there's no hesitation. It's put down quickly and decisively. And that's when it merely bites someone. What does one do with an animal—despite the fact that it looks like a normal human child—when it's responsible for the slaughter of so many?

He tried not to envision himself holding this little girl to his chest, pressing the barrel of his pistol against her temple, and feeling the warmth of her fleeing life on his face and her body shuddering against his. But was that any worse than what these men had planned for her?

His phone rang and he answered it in the middle of the first ring, thankful for the diversion from that line of thought. He tried to look nonchalant as he spoke to Sturm and watched the men on the dock from the corner of his eye.

"*Something's going down,*" Sturm whispered. "*Two of the men had returned to their vehicles. They just hauled balls back underground.*"

Porter heard Spears shout, and then he and his men were on the move. They sprinted down the dock toward him and veered to the south.

"Talk to me, Layne. What do you see?"

"*Nothing. I can't see anything from here.*" Sturm's phone clattered in his ear as though she dropped it. "*I have to get closer.*"

"Stay where you are. I'm on my way."

Porter leapt up from the spool, kicked off the boots, and took off at a run.

"*I...see...the fence.*" Sturm's voice broke by static. "*...going over...*"

"Damn it, Layne! Don't you even think about going in there until I get there!"

There was a burst of static, then the line went dead.

THIRTY-THREE

Seattle, Washington
3:54 a.m. PST

Specialist Judd Ritter eased down the corridor, sweeping his rifle slowly in front of him. A rat scurried from the rubble and he barely recognized it in time to keep from shredding it with bullets.

"McCloskey," he whispered into his mic. "Acknowledge, goddamn it."

He didn't have to look at his watch to know that too much time had elapsed since McCloskey had radioed in that he'd seen movement down the tunnel ahead and was moving to intercept. His last communication rang in Ritter's ears.

Sweet Jesus. It's just a—

And then only silence.

No echo of gunfire. No screams.

Only that same awful silence that stalked them through these godforsaken tunnels.

He had dispatched McCloskey into the western side of the main building, via the newly discovered tunnel under the pier. Ritter didn't know precisely where McCloskey was when he reported, but it couldn't have been very far from where he was now. Stadler was converging on his position from the south and should be stepping into sight at any minute. Ritter had to pause to dial down the volume on his earpiece. Spears was in his head, demanding a second-by-second account, but he needed to focus right now. He'd seen what this thing could do. Any distraction could prove fatal.

Ritter pressed his back against the brick wall and glanced through a crumbled section into a makeshift corridor crisscrossed with broken timber and iron framework. He sensed movement ahead of him and recoiled. Lowering himself to the floor, he peered over the cracked mortar rim and saw the midnight blue outline of a rifle, then the golden crescent of Stadler's face below his night vision goggles. The long aperture turned toward him and Ritter quickly identified himself into his microphone before the other man could line him up in his sights, then stepped through the wall and into the hallway. He ducked under a wooden beam and joined Stadler, who motioned with his rifle toward a small room to his right. Through what was left of the doorway, Ritter saw a rusted trough urinal, broken pipes protruding from the walls where the sinks and toilets had once been, and in the center of the floor, on the cracked tiles and heaped debris, was a Colt IAR just like the one seated against his shoulder.

Ritter motioned for Stadler to guard their flank and cautiously entered the bathroom. He nearly slipped on the tiles. Something slick was smeared all over the floor and an arc of it traced the wall to his left, right up to where the ceiling should have been. One of the conveyor chutes had fallen at an angle through the floor above, snapping its rivets and exposing a warped orifice. A droplet swelled from the sheared metal and dropped right between his feet with a *plat*. He stepped up onto a chunk of plaster and wood and peered inside. At the very edge of sight, he could barely discern the outline of a pair of boots. A rivulet of dark blue blood ran toward him from between the heels.

He stepped back down and turned to tell Stadler, but instead found himself staring through the empty doorway into the dusty corridor.

"Stadler?" he whispered.

Leading with his rifle, he stepped out into the hallway and looked first to his left, then to his right, where purplish spatters glowed on the floor like radioactive waste.

He hadn't heard a sound.

"Stadler's down! I repeat, Stadler's—!"

Warmth poured onto his head and slithered down his neck. He instinctively looked up and the purple fluid washed over his vision. He raised his rifle and tried to clear his lens with his forearm.

An orange-red shape plummeted down onto him, knocking his goggles from his face and sending his rifle clattering across the floor.

He tried to cry out, but the noise that came from his mouth was foreign to him, almost like the burbling sound one made when trying to breathe underwater.

A face the color of the flesh around a peach pit leaned over him. It was smeared with gold from its chin all the way up past its forehead. He saw his fate reflected in its eyes, the mechanism of his demise glinting in its mouth.

And then it was upon him.

*   *   *

Chaos erupted in his earpiece as Spears sprinted past the cultural center, his feet sinking in the new sod. He heard shouts and cries and disjointed and contradictory orders, but not a single gunshot. These were professional soldiers. And they were dropping like flies. By the time he reached the ruins and dove headfirst into the narrow tunnel, there was only silence from the men inside. Four highly trained soldiers, and they'd lasted less than the six minutes it had taken him to run just over a mile from the shipyard. His blood flowed hot with rage and an emotion he hadn't experienced in so long that he had forgotten what it felt like. He'd been helpless to stop the slaughter, and that was one thing he'd sworn long ago that he would never be again.

He squirmed through the darkness and dropped down into the sublevel. There was no visual sign that any gas still lingered in the warrens. There was only a pall of dust that seemed to fall like a curtain from the inexhaustible supply tenuously braced overhead. Ritter and his men had been ambushed in the western half of the cannery. He resisted the urge to charge headlong in that direction and waited for his remaining three men to gather around him. He needed to formulate a plan. The creature held the home field advantage and charging blindly through the countless bottlenecks would only play into its hands. He could positively feel the bloodlust radiating from his men. They had just listened to their friends die horrible deaths without being able to do a blasted thing to stop it. If they were as anxious to exact their revenge as he suspected, he could use that to his advantage.

Spears motioned for Morgan to crawl back out and go around the building to enter from the west. He scurried off without a backward glance. Spears gestured for Austin to head south, then wend his way back through the maze. The moment he took off, Spears directed Evans to the shortest route to the point of ambush. He waited until he could no longer hear Evans's footsteps, then followed in his tracks. Evans would be the first to arrive, and when the creature attacked him, Spears would be right there to take it down. Any good strategist knew that sacrificing a pawn was vastly preferable to risking the king. It was the whole reason armies had infantries.

The silence crackled softly in his earpiece. He lightened his tread on the gravel and broken bricks and eased cautiously through the puddles of rainwater that dripped ceaselessly through the rubble. His respirations whirred mechanically through his mask. He focused on slowing his heartbeat each time it attempted to accelerate. This was the endgame. He could feel it. The air tingled with violent potential. This was the feeling a combat soldier lived for. The attack could come at any second now. It was kill or be killed. No second chances. No regrets. The way Spears saw it, this is how it must feel to be a god.

He approached an oblong hole in the brick wall that had once separated the buildings. Beyond, he could see only the black nothingness. As he ducked through, never once lowering his rifle, he heard a muffled grunt in his ear. He readjusted his grip on the IAR and advanced slowly, waiting for bright color to appear against the deep blue and black night vision contrast. The doorway to his right was choked with debris. The one to his left opened upon a room stuffed full of antiquated equipment, the tarps that had once covered the machines strewn on the floor amid the broken bottles. He rounded a bend to the right and saw a sight like nothing he had ever seen before. Droplets of fuchsia rained from the rafters that slanted across the corridor. They faded to purple as they fell and alighted in fluorescent blue puddles.

There were only three of them left now, and all Evans had managed in his defense was a grunt.

Spears felt the man's blood drip onto his head and shoulders as he pressed on. He found Evans's body hidden behind an avalanche of timber and concrete. What little skin showed was mottled with pink and light blue. The wound on his neck was the purple of an overripe plum.

There was no other color. No movement. The only sound, the thrum of his pulse in his ears.

He veered left, then right through the winding corridor. He didn't see Ritter's body on the ground in the doorway to his left until he was on top of it. There was another facedown just inside the old bathroom. Both of them had already cooled to the point that their heat signatures were barely distinguishable from the rubble around them. He noted the shaft of the conveyor tube near the ceiling and innately understood how the ambush had occurred. Instead of climbing up to peer inside the broken halves of the tube, he fired a burst of three shots into each side. When nothing bled or crawled out, he returned to the corridor in time to see Austin creep into the hallway from the south. The soldier rose to his feet and stared directly at Spears through the horn-like apparatus.

Spears glanced at his shoulder and upper arm, which were still spattered with blue blood, then back at Austin.

"Evans," he whispered into the microphone.

Austin swelled with a deep breath, repositioned his grip on his rifle, then nodded resolutely. He had just taken his first stride into the corridor when Spears saw a flash of orange behind him through the mouth of a tunnel. Before he could call out a warning, Austin doubled backward as though impaled from behind by a pike. A geyser of gold burst from his mouth. He turned his head. That was all the opportunity the creature needed. It tore into his neck in an explosion of yellow and white, then wrenched his body sideways.

Spears opened fire. Golden starbursts blossomed from Austin's chest and abdomen as the bullets struck him with the sound of ferocious body blows against a heavy bag. He shot round after round into Austin's corpse, which the creature used as a shield to cover its retreat. He could only hope that one of the bullets would pass through Austin and hit it in the head. He hurried down the hall, still firing as he went. When he reached Austin's body, it was crumpled on the other side of the hole in the wall, spilling pink and purple onto the paving stones.

He looked up and saw two violet handprints on an iron beam, above which was an alcove of darkness that was undoubtedly the mouth of another infernal tunnel.

"*Jesus,*" Morgan's voice whispered in his ear.

Spears turned to see his man framed by the collapsed section of bricks, looking down at the ground where Austin's spattered blood still glowed a bluish-lavender. Morgan glanced up and their stares locked through the lenses. Morgan's apparatus shifted to the side so that he was looking not just past Spears, but above him. Morgan started to raise his rifle and Spears turned as fast as he could. He saw a blur of orange-red the color of lava scurry across the suspended rubble, clinging upside down to the girder, heard the triple-tap of automatic fire behind him, felt the heat and wind from the bullets cut the air beside his left ear. The bullets sparked and rang from the metal, but the creature was too fast. It had already disappeared into the rubble by the time Spears sighted down the point where it vanished. Another three shots whipped past his right ear, ricocheted from the iron beam, and careened off into the darkness.

Spears watched the girder shift and heard the groan of something buckling overhead. Debris tumbled down on him. He whirled and dashed toward the passage between buildings. Sharp stones struck his back and rang from his head. His vision blurred. He concentrated on the brick-lined gap and dove—

The impact drove him to the ground. His teeth clattered when his head struck the ground. The goggles shattered and it felt as though a spike were being driven through his forehead. The weight of the fallen ceiling on his back made it nearly impossible to breathe. His appendages were unresponsive, and not even the pain that lit up seemingly every nerve ending could hold back the cold black tide of unconsciousness he could feel rising inside of him. He tasted blood in his mouth, and with his last conscious effort, turned his face so that it would drain out of his mouth.

Yellow flashes in the corner of his vision were punctuated by echoing reports.

Morgan's screams trailed him onto the dark, insensate pit that awaited him.

THIRTY-FOUR

Seattle, Washington
4:12 a.m. PST

Sturm moved through the darkness, navigating the treacherous corridors by memory and instinct. She'd lost the flashlight Porter had loaned her during their escape from the gas and now followed her Beretta, the sights of which she couldn't even see. The gunfire had ceased and the ruins had once again settled. No longer did chunks of rubble rain from above. She had thought for a moment that the whole works was going to come down on her head. From where she'd crouched in the doorway to a room that smelled of urine, body odor, and alcohol, she'd listened to the debris shatter in the corridor and felt the entire building shift, but eventually the world had stilled and she'd been able to resume her approach through the stirred dust that caked in her nostrils and on her lips.

Her only thoughts were of the little girl. Did the cessation of gunfire mean she had been captured? Or, worse, killed? Had she somehow eluded her pursuit and escaped back out into the night? Why had she even come back here and how had she done so without being seen? Was she hurt down here and in desperate need of help? Sturm knew there was no hope of salvation for the child. She had killed people and for that there could be no absolution, but she couldn't forget how she had felt when the girl had crawled into her lap and clung to her like any other frightened child would. The girl was lost and alone, half the planet away from her home, and could probably understand her surroundings no better than they could understand her. She was an animal who could nearly pass for human, a savage who could read and write a primitive language that had confounded scholars for years, and a stone-cold murderer with the emotional frailty of any child her age. On one hand, Sturm wanted to do whatever she had to do to save her, but on the other, she knew Porter was right. There was no place for the girl in the world they lived in, no chance of assimilating her into civilized society, no hope of saving her from the men who wanted to exploit her…shy of death.

The bottom line was that Sturm didn't know what to do with the girl. All she knew was that right now she needed to find her. Let the chips fall where they may from there.

Dust turned the tears on her cheeks into mud. Her teeth were gritty, her tongue and throat parched. Her phone continued to vibrate in her pocket. She had silenced the ringer after deciding to follow the men underground, knowing full well that Porter would call incessantly. He probably would have been able to talk her out of making such a rash decision if given the opportunity, which was why she hadn't waited for him. Instead, she'd walked around to the access point farthest from where the men had entered in such a hurry and worked her way back toward them, hoping they would drive the child ahead of them and she would be able to snatch her up and extract her from the ruins before anyone even guessed that she was there. But so far, she hadn't heard so much as the patter of bare feet or any sound at all other than her haggard breathing and occasional curses when she tripped over the dislodged debris that hadn't been there before. Her plan was foolish and she knew it. Not only could she stumble blindly into the line of fire of a man with night vision goggles, an assault weapon, and a quick trigger finger, but she could encounter the girl, who she might have caught in a moment of weakness earlier and would now view her as a threat. She was willing to take that chance, though. Had the girl truly wanted to kill her, she'd had two perfect opportunities already, and hadn't taken advantage of either. It was hard to believe she was capable of killing all of the others. For whatever reason, she'd allowed Sturm to see her vulnerability. Maybe it was only because Sturm had found her half-asleep the first time, or perhaps there was a better reason. But after killing so many men…

She stopped dead in her tracks.

"Men," she whispered aloud.

The girl had gone after Porter the moment she saw him, and yet when Sturm had stepped between them, the child had given up the fight and allowed herself to be whisked from the gas in Sturm's arms. Was it possible that there was something about men specifically that triggered her aggression? Did they remind her in some way of the reason she was now in this desperate situation? If that was the case, then maybe Sturm *could* get her out of here safely after all.

She was about to start walking again when she heard a clicking noise from somewhere ahead and to her right. At first, she thought it might be the rubble preparing to shift again and braced herself for another debris storm, but then it faded. A few moments later it repeated, then stopped again.

Sturm inched forward, following the sound through the warrens. Each time it ceased, she paused and waited for it to begin again before pressing on.

The intermittent sound grew louder and louder until it sounded like she was right on top of it. She crawled through a collapsed section of a brick wall and remained on her hands and knees, listening. It was right in front of her now. It wasn't so much a clicking noise, but rather the sound of something wet and sticky being repeatedly peeled from whatever it was stuck to, and between occurrences, another much softer sucking sound. She crawled closer and smelled the coppery scent of—

Light flooded across the chamber from behind her, casting her shadow ahead of her onto the paving stones and the supine form of a man dressed entirely in black. The pale shape crouched over him, its face buried in the man's neck, slurping from a ragged wound and then slapping its lips contentedly. It looked up in surprise and the light reflected from a pair of pink eyes. Blood glistened on the girl's face and torso. She was positively drenched with it. She bared her teeth and snapped at the beam of light, then, in one fluid movement, leapt to her feet and darted into the shadows, using her hands to propel her like a jungle cat.

"Wait!" Sturm called after her, but she knew it was already too late. She whirled to face Porter, who just stood there holding his flashlight, his face ashen, staring at the point where the girl had been only a moment prior. His light reflected from a wide crimson puddle on the ground. Sturm stood up and rounded on him. "What do you think you're doing? She wasn't frightened until you stormed in here. I was just about to—"

"About to what? Did you see what she was doing? She was drinking his blood right out of his goddamn neck!"

"And now she's gone and we don't have a chance in hell of finding her?"

"Finding her? Can you hear yourself, Layne? Look around…" He shined his beam from one side of the corridor to the other. There had to be at least half a dozen bodies sprawled on the floor. All of them wore the same black utilities and boots. Their faces were turned to one side, their necks twisted away from their bodies to expose the massive gouges in their throats. "She killed all of these men. We walked in on her sucking the blood right out of them. What part of this are you not getting?"

"She's just a little girl, for God's sake. You saw what she wrote. She's scared and alone and far away from home. Her mother was killed and people with guns keep coming in here after her. How do you think she's going to react?"

"By nearly tearing their heads off with her teeth? Of course. That's how any normal child would react."

"When faced with the men who killed her mother? Presumably before her very eyes? What would you expect her to do?"

"Not practically decapitate and exsanguinate them for starters!" Porter took a deep breath, blew it out slowly, and resumed in a more rational tone. "She can't stay down here, Layne. You know that as well as I do. They're going to keep sending men in here after her until they either get her or cut their losses and just firebomb the place. If you have some brilliant idea of how to deal with her, I'm all ears. Otherwise…otherwise we have no choice but to neutralize the threat. Can you see any other alternative?"

She turned away and stared off into the darkness. He pointed his light at her to gauge her reaction. Her shadow wavered on the exposed timber and wiring in the wall. She watched it nod from the corner of her eye as though it belonged to someone else entirely.

His hand closed over hers and he drew her into an embrace. She shuddered against him, then hurriedly wiped the tears from her eyes before he could see them. She was so tired that whatever control she had once had over her emotions was long gone.

"Whatever she may be," Sturm whispered, "she's still just a child."

Porter nodded, but said nothing. His brow furrowed and he glanced up into the rubble. He craned his neck and listened for a long moment.

"Time to go," he whispered.

"Wha—?"

And then she heard it. A distant rumble of engines. The ground trembled almost imperceptibly. Dust cascaded down on their heads.

"Get moving," he whispered, and pushed her ahead of him.

They were running when they heard the muffled bang of a car door closing outside the ruins.

THIRTY-FIVE

Seattle, Washington
4:28 a.m. PST

Spears drifted in and out of consciousness, from one black realm to another. His mouth and sinuses were full of blood and his lungs made a rattling sound when he breathed. Even the slightest movement speared him with a sharp pain from the broken rib that prodded his insides. Pins and needles assaulted his hands and feet. He'd barely been able to activate his emergency beacon, or maybe he'd just dreamed that he had. It was so hard to tell the difference anymore. The darkness grew colder with each passing second, or was it a consequence of losing so much blood? At one point, he was certain he heard the soft patter of footsteps, but it could just as easily have been the irregular tapping of his pulse in his ears. All of his men were dead. That was the one certainty. And if the men he had left at the compound on standby didn't retrieve him soon, he would be too, whether the creature returned to finish him off or not. The weight of the rubble was slowly compressing him to the floor, making it harder and harder to steal even a whiff of the dust-riddled air. If the broken rub shifted and punctured a lung, even that futile effort would be beyond his physical capabilities.

His blood stung his eyes, but he blinked them clear, if only for a few seconds at a time. He heard indistinct noises, somewhere far away, but they subsided and again gave way to the silence of the grave. He tried to claw his way out from beneath the rubble, blood streaming down his face from the laceration across his hairline and dribbling from the corner of his mouth. Grabbing any handhold he could find, he pulled himself through the slick puddle of his own blood. His arms trembled, but at least the feeling had returned to his fingers, even if he only felt pain. By the time he pried his legs out from under the debris, he could already hear the sound of footsteps echoing down the corridor from somewhere ahead, disembodied sounds that seemed to originate from everywhere and nowhere at once. With a roar of agony, he freed himself, crawled through the gap in the brick wall, and fell onto his side in the hallway crisscrossed with wood and iron beams.

He could smell the blood of his men all around him, and, beneath it, the faint residue of wasted gunpowder.

The footsteps grew louder and he pinpointed the source. His men were closing in on him from the north. The hell if he was going to allow them to find him like this. It took superhuman effort, but he managed to rise to his feet, where he swayed, gripping his broken rib, until he found his equilibrium. When his men finally arrived, the anger on his face masked the pain and he staggered toward their indistinct silhouettes and the clomping sound of their boots. With their night vision goggles, he knew they could see him just fine, while he was at a distinct disadvantage. He gritted his teeth, lowered his hand from his ribs, and stood defiantly before them.

"Are you all right, sir?" one of the men asked. Spears didn't immediately recognize the man's voice, but it didn't matter.

"I need a pair of goggles." There was a clattering sound as the man picked up something from the ground. The cold metal was damp and sticky when he pressed it into Spears's hands. "Preferably a pair not covered with Morgan's blood, if you wouldn't mind."

The man swapped the pair in his hand from those on his face and passed them to Spears, who seated them over his eyes. After so long in complete darkness, even the odd blue and black contrast was a godsend. He looked at the soldier before him and watched the expression of revulsion crinkle his face when a ribbon of blood trickled down his cheek from under the lenses. Spears recognized him as Darby Keenan, a section leader in Phobos's Search and Detection Division. Had he really burned through so many of his best men that he was this far down the organizational chart? Behind him stood two more men, their backs to him as they covered the corridor down the sights of their IARs. A fourth man knelt on the floor beside an open tackle box. He rummaged around until he found what he was looking for and rose to his feet. He couldn't have been much more than five feet tall. When Spears saw the field dressings in the man's small hands, he realized that it wasn't a man at all. Kate Newland was a trained medic and long-range rifle shooting champion. He had hired her away from the Marines for both specialties. He liked the idea of a sniper who could pluck off enemies from a distance and then sneak in and tend to any members of his advance team if they fell. Right now, though, he didn't require any of her skills. He swatted her hands away when she reached for his face with a roll of gauze and cringed at the resultant pain in his side.

"You're going to need to get that rib taken care of," she said, and turned away without another word. She retrieved her case and loaded it into her backpack.

"What happened down here?" Keenan asked. He was staring at a wall spattered with long arcs of blood that looked like they could have been sprayed there by a garden hose. He nodded to himself as though confirming an inner theory he hadn't shared out loud. "What are you orders, sir?"

"Collect the remains, load them up in the cars, and get them the hell out of here." Spears paused. "How long do we have before sunrise?"

"Roughly an hour, sir."

Spears looked at Newland. Despite her diminutive size, she projected an aura of quiet strength. The way she held her rifle. Her slender arms and legs, corded with muscle like high-tension cables strung under her smooth skin. She was every bit as intimidating as any of his men. Yes, she was definitely an impressive physical specimen. He thought about her body under those fatigues and imagined exactly what he wanted to do to it.

A smile played at the corners of his lips.

"Sir?" Keenan said.

Spears realized the man had been talking and was waiting for a response. He spit a gob of clotted blood onto the ground and turned away from Newland.

"Keenan. You and the other men are in charge of retrieving the bodies. How many did you pass on your way in here?"

"I didn't stop to count, sir."

"But there were plenty of them, weren't there?"

"Yes, sir."

"Then you'd better get on it, soldier."

"Sir, yes, sir." Keenan spun on his heel and ushered his men off in the direction from which they had come.

"Newland," Spears called. She had fallen into step behind the others, but stopped when she heard her name. He closed the distance between them and tried not to study her body too overtly. "One of my men might still be alive. I could see him through the hole in the wall over there when the ceiling collapsed on me. The creature attacked him, but I thought I saw him make a break for one of the tunnels over there in that room."

She glanced at the blood-streaked wall, then back at him.

"Leave no man behind," Spears said. "If there's a chance he survived, we can't just abandon him."

"Which man was it, *sir*?"

She made no effort to hide the note of incredulity in her voice.

"I couldn't tell. The whole goddamn ceiling had just fallen down on my head, in case you didn't notice." He smeared the blood from his temple with the back of his wrist for effect. "If you aren't coming, then fine. Give me your kit and I'll go by myself. Just don't bother showing up for your final check unless you want it shoved straight down your throat."

He reached for her pack, but she grabbed his hand before he even got close.

"What about that thing you came down here to hunt?"

"If you see it, drill it through the eye."

She smirked and turned away from him. He followed her through the nearly collapsed doorway into the room he had been in before. The orifice at the back led to the broken branch that would deposit them in the bootlegger's tunnel. She looked him up and down, removed her backpack, and looped one of the shoulder straps around her ankle. Leading with her rifle, she crawled into the dark tube. Spears scurried in behind her and tried to stay right on her heels. As she was so much smaller, she moved through the narrow chute with admirable speed and agility. Had he been thinking rationally, he would have brought her down here from the start. Perhaps they would have even accomplished their mission by now.

At the end of the tunnel, she tucked her head, rolled down the heap of broken bricks, and alighted on her feet. She waited from him to tumble down and stood over him with an amused expression on her face. The pain from his broken rib must have been obvious. She hardly had to duck to stand erect in the tunnel.

"So what's it going to be?" She still wore the smirk on her face as she stared down at him through the aperture. "You and I both know damn well whoever lost all that blood didn't go running off in this direction. Don't think you're the first to run this game on me."

Spears attempted to stand, but she braced her boot on his shoulder and shoved him back down.

"You obviously have the wrong idea," he said.

"Do I?" She grabbed him by the collar and jerked him to his knees. He looked up into her face, and then at her right hand as it slowly lowered the zipper on her jacket. She wore a tank top underneath, one so tight that it clung to her like a second skin. He could see the sharp points of the nipples on her small breasts. "I've done it in some crazy places, but this beats all. This do it for you? Knowing that men have died down here, that death could come for you at any second. That what gets you off?"

"What do you want?" Spears asked.

He had to be careful how he played this.

"Same thing you do." She opened her jacket all the way, then popped the top button on her pants so he could see the smooth taper of her abdomen and the silky rim of her panties. "And, you know, a seat at the table. A more prominent position within the organization."

"I think that can definitely be arranged," Spears said.

"Then it sounds like we have a deal. Can you think of the right way to consummate it?"

Spears rose to his feet, threw the flaps of her jacket aside, and studied her chest and belly. Yeah, she would work perfectly. With the broken rib and his overall weakened state, he was going to have to do this quickly. He searched her face for any sign of recognition, then gripped her roughly by the hips and spun her around. She braced her hands against the stone wall and shifted her rear end against his hips. He wrapped his left arm around her lower belly and pulled her tighter against him. With his right, he reached for the object in the sheath on his belt.

"Hurry up," she whispered, grinding against him. "I'm ready. Just do it."

Spears withdrew the knife from his pocket and opened the blade in one motion. With the next, he drove it into the side of her neck. Her heat flooded over his hands and her body thrashed against his. He squeezed her around the belly and shoved her flat against the wall as he jerked the blade hard enough to cut through her trachea. Her dying scream whistled from the bloody opening. He held her, facing the wall, until the blood no longer fired in arterial bursts, but merely poured over his hand, then lowered her to the ground.

He rolled her onto her back, stripped off her clothes, and studied her naked body for a long minute, evaluating every curve. It wasn't the perfect setup, but it would do. He removed her medical kit from her backpack and tossed the contents until he had everything he needed, then rummaged through Newland's clothes until he found her com-link, seated it in his ear where his had been before it was presumably lost in the cave-in.

"Report," he whispered into the microphone.

"We're still loading bodies into the first vehicle. Once we have the first half in the trunk, I'll send it back to base with either Tillman or Niederhoffer, then start on the second."

"Keep pushing it. We don't have much time left."

Spears silenced his microphone and went back to work. He turned Newland's face to the side, raised the butt of his rifle, and slammed it down on her cheek. Her teeth skittered across the floor. He pounded the stock down, again and again, grunting with the exertion, his broken rib stabbing him like a knife. Newland's cheek was split all the way back to her ear, her cheekbone and mandible pulverized, the outer rim of her orbital socket flattened in such a way that her eyeball hung from the socket and somehow seemed to look back at him. He drove the butt down twice more for the sake of thoroughness, then tilted her face upward and opened her mouth. There were several white nubs where the teeth had broken off at the gum line, but the majority had popped out cleanly. He tugged her shattered jaw down and swept his finger behind her tongue and down into her throat, but didn't find any more teeth. If Trofino were to find one hidden back there, Spears's deception would be spoiled too soon. All he needed was twenty-four hours, and then it didn't matter what anyone else knew. He ground his heel on the mess of teeth and listened to them crack with a distinct sense of satisfaction.

He returned to the supplies he had procured from Newland's kit and grabbed the bottle of isopropyl alcohol. Once he had splashed it all over her body, in her hair, and in her mouth, he cast the empty container aside, rolled her onto her stomach, and repeated the process with the chloraseptic scrub and the betadine, then returned her to her back. With the high-pressure butane lighter, which was stocked to serve as a cauterizing torch, he lit the fluid in the hair on her head and then between her legs, and watched the blue flames race across her body, meeting over her breasts and rising from her toes. The skin beneath the nearly translucent flames turned stark white through the goggles, then started to blister. Her hair singed quickly back to her scalp and pubis. The fire scorched her gums and her tongue as it followed the path of the alcohol down her trachea toward her lungs. Blood boiled from the gash in the side of her neck. Smoke wafted from her nostrils, harbinger of the flames that burned through her sinuses and fed on the cartilage in her nose, shriveling it to a skeletal hook. Her skin eventually crisped, then cracked like a dry riverbed. Pustulates seeped out from the fissure before hardening to the consistency of tree sap. Her fingers curled into claws and her toes folded backward. The tendons in her appendages tightened, drawing her arms and knees to her chest. When there was nothing left to burn, the flames extinguished themselves and left the body smoldering golden in his vision. Wavering pink heat rose from it. He watched them fade to blue and then finally out of the thermal spectrum.

But there was still one crucial detail that required his ministrations.

Spears aimed his rifle at what remained of her right eye and pulled the trigger. The IAR coughed and produced a crater where the socket had once been. He did the same thing to her other eye, then stood back to admire his work. Hair, eyes, teeth, fingerprints…all obliterated. A thorough autopsy and blood tests would give him away in a heartbeat, but he knew how Trofino worked. He was slow and methodical, meticulous to a fault. He would spend the majority of the morning stomping his feet about the condition of the corpse. When he eventually buckled down, it would take him forever to work his way through the charred flesh, layer by layer, to reach the undamaged subcutaneous tissues, bones, and organs from which he would quickly be able to ascertain genetic samples.

And by the time he did, it would be too late.

It was a shame about Newland, though. She did have potential. Spears only wished he felt badly about what he had done, but in the end, a commander had to do what was necessary to win the war, even if it meant sacrificing his own troops along the way.

"*The second vehicle just left, sir,*" Keenan's voice crackled in his ear. "*Seven bodies total, cross-checked against the mission log. Everyone's accounted for.*" He paused to let Spears know that he recognized the significance of finding all of the men from the log. It blew Spears's story about the potentially injured man out of the water. "*What are your orders?*"

"We're at the end of the tunnel leading west from the point where you found me," Spears whispered. He unscrewed the suppressor from the barrel of his rifle as he spoke. "There's something down here with us. I can't quite see it from where I...Jesus Christ!"

He fired a trio of bullets down the long tunnel toward the sea with a staged war cry that he could hear even over the deafening report. His ears ringing, he tugged the com device out of his ear, spiked it on the ground, and stomped it into a jumble of components.

That would bring Keenan running.

No doubt about it.

Spears studied Newland's carcass for a moment, then walked back toward the smaller chute above the hill of fractured bricks. Within five minutes, he heard Keenan's elbows and knees banging on the metal as he scurried toward Spears's position, his rifle clattering ahead of him.

Spears seated his IAR against his shoulder and sighted down the end of the tube. He saw the barrel of Keenan's rifle first. The moment Keenan peeked his head out to survey his surroundings, Spears fired straight into the aperture of his goggles.

It was the least he could do for Keenan.

A warrior deserved to see his fate coming.

THIRTY-SIX

Seattle, Washington
5:04 a.m. PST

Porter felt more impotent than he ever had in his life. There had been no choice but to watch the men retrieve the corpses from the ruins, toss them into their trucks, and drive off into the night. He had no backup. He and Sturm were outnumbered and outgunned. A direct confrontation would be suicide, and he couldn't help but wonder if they were even still on the side of the right. There was no support from his superiors. Both the FBI and the police were in someone's pocket, and the Department of Defense had given a private contractor license to turn the waterfront into a war zone.

If his count was right, they were now down to no more than three men in the ruins. He was going to have to make a decision soon. Those odds weren't insurmountable, especially if they maintained the element of surprise. But if push came to shove and he and Strum took out Phobos's men, while they were going against direct orders, they would be crucified.

And, he was ashamed to admit, there was a part of him that hoped these men would handle the girl for him so that he wouldn't be forced to do so himself.

For Sturm's sake, as well as his own.

They crouched side-by-side against the rocky edge of Salmon Bay, a hundred yards to the north of the pier that hid the westernmost exit. From this vantage point, they could see both of the western egresses and the one to the north, where the SUV was parked. He held Sturm's left hand in his right, more to prevent her from breaking cover and bolting back into the ruins than as a gesture of any kind of physical or emotional support. For a moment, it had smelled like meat roasting on a barbecue, but that had faded around the time the first shots were fired. After the sudden spat of gunfire had ceased several minutes ago, there had been only one more shot. Both he and Sturm recognized the sound of a *coup de grâce* when one was dealt. She feared it meant that the men had found the girl and finished her off. He wondered if it wasn't the other way around and that none of the men would be returning to the surface to reclaim their vehicle.

Either way, they could only wait so much longer. If the men didn't emerge soon, they were going to have to go in after them, regardless of the consequences.

He could feel Sturm's stare on the side of his face. Her patience was gone and he could almost hear the gears clanking in her head as she formulated her words. It would be an ultimatum, he knew. She was going to go down there, with or without him.

She had just drawn a breath to speak the words when there was movement in the shadows under the pier. Porter pulled her down, flat against the rocks beside him, and watched a solitary figure draw contrast from the darkness. At first, it appeared hunched and misshapen, its gait staggering and uneven. When it stepped out into what little moonlight permeated the rain clouds, he saw why.

Sturm gasped beside him. He rolled on top of her and used his body weight to hold her in place. She struggled against him, but he secured solid leverage.

A flash of lightning illuminated the figure. The aperture of the man's night vision goggles pointed toward the black SUV as he ascended the incline. He wore a sagging backpack and his rifle slung over his shoulder, but it was what he carried in his arms that drew Porter's attention. He glanced down at Sturm and saw her expression of anguish, the tears glistening on her cheeks. A sound that positively broke his heart crossed her lips, and he had to look away.

The man carried a small body against his chest. Even from this distance, Porter could tell it had been burned to a crisp. Its thin arms were retracted to its chest, its wrists furled under as though palsied. Its knees were bent at a sharp angle, its feet hooked back upon themselves. The ligaments and tendons had contracted to such a degree when they cooked that the body was contorted into a hellish construct that barely resembled human. It looked so small in his arms, so diminished. It was hard to believe it had ever contained a life force at all.

"We can't let him get away with this," Sturm said through bared teeth. Her sorrow had metamorphosed into rage in the blink of an eye. Her voice rose in volume, but the man was far enough away that he didn't appear to hear. "We have to do something."

The trunk of the SUV opened and spilled light onto the ground at the man's feet. He heaved the remains into the back, drew a tarp over them, and slammed the door closed again.

"There's nothing we can do," Porter whispered.

"The hell there isn't."

She pushed against his chest with one hand and tried to draw her pistol with the other. He grabbed her wrist before she could do anything she'd regret and looked directly into her eyes when he spoke.

"She's gone, Layne. You can't change that now. The only thing you can do is avenge her—"

"That's the plan."

"—and wind up in prison for the rest of your life."

"That's all up to you, Porter. You do what you have to do. My decision's already made."

She struggled against him again. He wasn't going to be able to hold her down indefinitely, and he wasn't entirely convinced that he should.

"We need to do this by the book," he said. The driver's side door closed and the engine started with a roar. The taillights cast a red glow over the rubble. "We can still take him down. You and me."

She bucked her hips against his and tried to raise a knee into his groin when he shifted his weight. She knew her window of opportunity was closing fast.

"We won't be able to touch him if we allow him to leave," she nearly screamed. "No one's going to let us near him. You've already seen what kind of power he has at his disposal."

The SUV's tires grumbled over the gravel and weeds. It was nearly to the fence and the main road beyond.

"Do you trust me, Layne?"

"Let me go before it's too late!"

He leaned his face down over hers until their noses touched and their lips were only a breath apart.

"Do you trust me?"

Her eyes searched his, probing deep inside him, reaching into the very core of his being.

The chain link fence closed with a resounding clank. A moment later the tires splashed through the gutter and onto the wet asphalt.

And then the SUV was gone.

Porter released her wrist and slowly rolled off of her, his eyes never straying from hers.

She averted her stare, crawled up the hill, and spoke with her back to him.

"You'd better be right." She climbed over the crest and started across the weeded lot. "I'll never forgive you if you aren't."

Porter stood and watched her walk away, her head hung in misery.

He wouldn't be able to forgive himself if he was wrong either.

He only hoped he would be able to figure out a plan soon, because right now, he didn't have the slightest clue. Phobos had a seemingly impenetrable shield. He was going to have to get creative.

Sturm slipped through the gate and disappeared from sight, leaving him standing all alone in the ruins, wondering how in the hell he was going to make this right.

THIRTY-SEVEN

Seattle, Washington
7:52 a.m. PST

It was going to be a banner day for the city of Seattle. In a matter of hours, they would be able to secure the funds they needed to make his vision come to life. From where Mayor Elgin Marten stood on the patio behind the Bertha Knight Landes Cultural Center, his jet-black gelled hair glistening under the sun and his wintergreen eyes on the horizon, he could see into the future. The high rise lofts, the statuary along the waterfront, the sun reflecting from the steel and smoked glass, the trees, the families, the restaurants and coffee houses, live music spilling out onto the street from trendy clubs, all of it. This was his dream, and soon it would be his reality. All of these decrepit buildings would be gone, memorialized in the center behind him through the rose-colored glasses of revisionist history. Gone would be the crumbling docks where his grandfather had slaved for next to nothing right up until the point where he had dropped dead, the stench of a century's worth of decomposed fish, and a past that might have defined the city as it was, but had no place in the modern era. This development would be his crowning glory, a feather in the cap of the governor who had once upon a time been a lowly mayor. The thought of his grandchildren playing in a green park beneath the shade of elm trees and at the foot of a statue dedicated to him and his vision made him smile.

But there was still much work to be done.

The project was already seven-figures in the black and all they had to show for it was this one, albeit glorious, building and about two hundred thousand tons of rubble they couldn't afford to clear. They could probably raise enough money through the sale of municipal bonds to finance the roads and foundations, but it was going to require a massive infusion of private funding to build up

into the sky. Promises would need to be made, tax credits dealt like
playing cards, and future considerations guaranteed. And all it
would cost him personally was his soul. His advisors had already
game-planned the night ahead: what they should offer to whom,
how much they should expect from specific businessmen, and what
each potential contributor would require in return. Selling their
overpriced plates of salmon, chicken, and steak wouldn't raise
enough money to put a Porta-John on the boardwalk. This dinner
was about networking. He liked to think of it as a big game hunt.
He was going to stalk a herd of some of the richest and most
powerful men and women in the country and pick them off one by
one. Of course, they undoubtedly looked at him the same way.
They wanted to gauge not just him personally, but his future value.
Ten million dollars was an enormous amount of money to invest,
but the cash would be well spent if they wound up with an eventual
senator in their pockets.

He supposed that should have bothered him on some level, but
there was a price one must be willing to pay for greatness.

And he was prepared to pay it in spades.

It was still early and he had a thousand things left to do. He
had only swung by long enough to see with his own eyes that
everything was progressing at an acceptable pace, motivate the
various supervisors and planners in charge of the event, and make
sure that there was nothing that was going to complicate this, his
finest hour.

The grounds looked sharp. Better than that. They looked
spectacular. He had been warned that the patrons would need to
stay off of the fresh sod, but that was of no consequence. They
could always buy more. It was just grass, after all. And the fences
had been rearranged to his exact specifications. The painted banner
with the future skyline looked perfect from here. The partygoers
would be able to look to the south and see his vision as it would
one day appear. The massive piles of rubble were hidden in their
entirety, and the only thing that one would be able to see beyond
the fences after dark would be the lights of the skyscrapers
downtown.

There was just one final detail he needed to confirm. One last
item to check off his list. And then he would never again have to
think about how close he had come to ruin, but rather how he had

triumphed over the kind of adversity that would have destroyed lesser men.

And this situation had better have been resolved to his satisfaction or heads were going to roll.

His among them.

The mayor dug his cell phone out of his jacket pocket and was just about to dial the dreaded number for what he hoped would be the final time when a group of workers rounded the side of the building. He nodded in greeting, flashed his megawatt smile, then ducked around the portico into an alcove where a scarlet maple sapling had been planted. A sparkle in the grass caught his eye.

"Damn it!" He turned and stormed back out to where he had just seen the work crew. "Hey! One of you! Come over here and look at this!"

One of the men hesitantly broke away from the others. Marten recognized the man, or maybe it was just his generic coveralls, as one of the countless supervisors with whom he dealt. The man removed his paint-spattered ball cap when he neared and nervously wrung the bill in his hands.

"Look at this!" Marten said, pointing back into the alcove. "Was anyone planning to take care of this or do I have to do everything for myself?"

"First I've heard of it, sir." The man crouched beside the shards of broken glass and stared down into the basement of the building through the empty frame. "I'll get this taken care of right away."

"See that you do. This is entirely unacceptable. I was under the impression that the citizens of Seattle cared about this fine city."

Marten didn't wait for the man to formulate an excuse. The beads of sweat blooming from his forehead assured Marten that the job would be done in time. He walked back to the patio before he was surrounded by the thirty men it would take to replace the broken window. City workers. Was there a lazier bunch on the planet?

He ducked inside the main exhibit hall and was blasted with frigid air. There were dozens of industrial fans positioned around the room to force out the rank smell of fish guts, which seemed to be somehow fused to the oxygen molecules themselves. They would be the last things to be put away before the ribbon cutting if Marten had anything to say about it. His footsteps echoed from the pristine marble floor. Gold-framed black-and-white photographs lined the walls behind Plexiglas-encased displays of maritime relics. The skylights admitted columns of sunshine that cast long shadows from the red steel girders, from which replicas of historical seafaring vessels were suspended by cables. The exposed ductwork pumped heat down through vents the size of manholes in an effort to counteract the fans. Several matronly women were being schooled in the proper presentation of the various displays. By tonight, they would be dressed as though they had just stepped out of the nineteenth century.

He passed them with his most chivalrous smile and ducked down the hallway into the anteroom of the main convention hall, where he finally found himself alone beside a bank of chrome elevators. He plopped down in a faux velvet chair and sighed like an old man.

"No time like the present," he said, and dialed the dreaded number.

*   *   *

Spears let the private line in his office ring until it went to voice mail and waited for the man he knew was on the other end to call again. Let him sweat it. Spears had learned to seize every possible advantage in any given situation. By the time the mayor called back, the panic would be tickling at the back of his skull and he would be desperate to believe whatever Spears said.

He stood at the mirror, the reflection of a man he hardly recognized staring back at him. He picked the crusted blood from the creases in his forehead and watched fresh crimson dribble down from the gash on his hairline to replace it. Both of his eyes were swollen and purple, deeply set into pools of black around slits through which he could barely see. He didn't even bother washing the grime from his face. He bared his teeth and tongued the bloody gap where his right upper incisor had been. Everyone who saw him gave him a wide berth. Even Trofino, who had come storming into his office, face red, finger raised in accusation, had tucked tail and retreated the moment he saw Spears's face. Or maybe it was the look in Spears's eyes, which seemed to drift in and out of focus independent of one another. Regardless, the good doctor had what he wanted and the rest of Spears's men were busy taking care of the remains of their fallen comrades. They all knew to leave him alone and would do so right up until the moment his deception unraveled. And then they would come for him. They were soldiers; such was their lot. But he would be long gone by the time that happened. Before the sun rose again, this situation would be resolved.

Damn the consequences. This was personal. It was high time he admitted that it had always been.

He could compartmentalize his feelings all he wanted. The money didn't matter. He already had more than he could ever spend. And the genetic engineering possibilities fell a far cry short of the heart of the matter. There was no point in attempting to rationalize it. This creature was responsible for his son's death and he was going to destroy it. He was going to paint himself with its blood and carry its head on a pike through the center of downtown. The men he had lost were soldiers. This was the life they had chosen, and whether they died here or in some remote godless desert or in a Third World coup was irrelevant. They had been extremely well compensated for their skills and had been slain in the course of the service into which they had willingly enlisted. His son, and the other hand…his son was a gentle soul who had chosen a far different life than the one his father had offered. While Spears had originally fought tooth and nail to make a man of his son, to make a hero out of him, in the end he had been forced to settle for the happiness of the child who meant more to him than anything else in the world.

And that choice had cost Nelson his life.

No. It was because of Spears's intervention that his son was dead. Nelson would never have been able to join the doomed exploration party on his own. Spears had pulled strings, called in favors, and thrown an absurd amount of money at a long list of people to make his son's dream come true. It was his fault that Nelson was dead. That was the reality he now needed to accept.

He had killed his own son.

And now it was up to him, and him alone, to do something about it.

He changed out of his tattered, blood-crusted shirt, tightened the dressings that compressed his ribs, and sat down at his desk to await the inevitable call.

His plan was the most simple and practical ever devised. If one wanted to kill a monster, then one needed to lure the monster from its lair. To do so, one needed three things. One needed an unobstructed view through the scope of a high-powered rifle, the courage to pull the trigger, and the most important thing of all.

He needed bait.

Fortunately, in less than ten hours, he would have all he could hope for. And then some.

He smiled and his face lit up with pain. It was worth it, though. For after tonight he knew there would be no future for him. Not that there ever could have been without his son. Everyone would be coming for him. The FBI, the DoD, the police. All of the people who had made him rich by paying him to do their dirty work when they hadn't had the stomachs to do so themselves.

"Fuck them," Spears said aloud. "Let them come."

All that mattered now was that the creature suffered, and that it ultimately died by his hand.

The phone rang. Once. Twice. He waited until the fourth ring and snatched it from the cradle. The voice on the other end was every bit as panicked as he had expected. Maybe more so. Spears waited out the windbag's tirade and then said the words the man needed to hear.

"Yes, Mr. Mayor. There is nothing to worry about. The threat has been neutralized."

The sigh of relief was so great that Spears could almost feel the mayor's breath in his ear. Marten had never known exactly what was down there in those ruins. For all he knew, the prevailing theory with the investigators was still some sort of mutated animal, or even more ridiculous, a serial killer who wore blood thinner-impregnated dentures. It didn't matter. No one would ever truly know what was down there.

But it would be a long time before the city would be able to forget the coming night.

Spears slammed the phone onto the cradle, jumped to his feet, and heaved his desk into the air with a roar. It landed on its back and splintered into a dozen pieces. Pens and paperclips skittered across the floor. His computer monitor and his lamp shattered. He kicked the broken debris and released another roar that he was certain could be heard throughout the complex.

Blood seeped into the bandage on his side and he could feel the bone fragment poking through the skin. Warmth flowed from his hairline down into his eyes. He tasted salt in his mouth.

He didn't care.

"Ready or not!" he bellowed in a sing-song voice. "Here I come!"

THIRTY-EIGHT

Seattle, Washington
2:04 p.m. PST

Porter sat on the hood of his Crown Victoria in the parking lot across the street from the Phobos compound. He no longer cared if he was seen. His superiors may have been controlled by powers higher up the food chain, but he was beholden to no one. This was still America—his America—and no one was going to turn it into a free-fire zone. Not on his watch. He had signed on to protect the people of this great nation, even if it meant protecting them from the very government to which he'd sworn his allegiance. It didn't matter how far up this conspiracy went or who all was involved. No man was above the law. Not even the president himself could be allowed to cover up the murders of so many people. This was about the ideals upon which this country had been built. No more of this cloak-and-dagger nonsense. He was going to expose the parties involved and ensure they were brought to justice. Never mind his career. This was personal, and he'd be damned if he was going to walk away without a fight.

He caught the reflection from a pair of binoculars through the window of the guard shack. With the biggest smile he could muster, he raised his arm and waved to the guards. Things were finally about to get interesting. By the time the security guard crossed the street, Porter was lying with his back against the front windshield, his fingers laced behind his head. He didn't bother removing his sunglasses.

"Is there something I can help you with, sir?" the guard asked. He wore a standard security guard uniform: navy blue slacks and a lighter blue button-down with epaulettes on the shoulders. His cap was pulled down low to hide his eyes. The muscles in his square jaw bulged when he attempted a smile that suggested he had no intention of being helpful in the slightest. His name badge read: E. Pahlson.

"Just catching some rays before the next storm rolls in." Porter smiled and tilted his face to the sky. "You can never tell where it's going to come from until it rolls right over you."

The guard's smile faltered.

"There are plenty of places out there that are much nicer than this parking lot. You should really try one of those."

"Like down by the waterfront? I hear the new cultural center is beautiful."

Pahlson shook his head and looked back across the street. The other guard now stood outside the shack, cupping his hand over his brow. Pahlson gave him a subtle wave and the man stepped back into the shack.

"Time to move on, pal. This is a private lot."

"Thanks, but I'm good." Porter pulled his badge from his jacket and flashed it at the guard. "I'm actually looking for a missing person. Hey…maybe you can help me after all. I don't suppose you've seen a little girl around here. She'd be hard to miss. Short. Kind of pale. Bald. Big teeth. Not the cutest kid on the planet, but definitely one you wouldn't forget if you saw her. You haven't seen anyone like that around here, have you?"

Porter stared up into the sky with an amused smile. He could feel the guard's stare burrowing into the side of his face.

"You have a good day, sir." Pahlson took several steps toward the street, then stopped and turned around. "Better enjoy the sun while it lasts. Funny thing about the weather this time of year…you never do see those storms coming until it's too late."

"Don't worry about me." Porter patted his shoulder holster through his jacket and gave his most charming smile. "I always pack my umbrella."

Pahlson nodded and struck off across the street. Porter watched him talk to the other guard, who couldn't help but glance back at Porter. He offered a mock salute.

That was fun.

Maybe this day wasn't going to be a total wash after all.

He could still have plenty more fun before the day was through. He'd poked the hornet's nest here. He could almost hear the men inside already starting to buzz. Only time would tell what would boil out. In the meantime, he had a couple of calls to make. It wasn't fair that he should be having all of this fun by himself. He could think of at least one other person who'd be happy to join in.

*   *   *

"That can't be right," Dr. Trofino snapped. "Run the tests again."

"We've already run them three times," his lab assistant, Carla Stewart, said. "The results came out exactly the same each and every time."

"But they can't be accurate. You must have contaminated the samples or improperly calibrated—"

"Fine. We'll start the whole process over again with new samples. Will that make you happy? And when the results come out identical—"

"They won't. Somebody obviously screwed something up. Just make sure it doesn't happen again."

Trofino turned his attention back to the work at hand, but the seeds of doubt had taken root. He didn't employ ordinary assistants with trade school educations prone to making such ridiculous errors. Carla had a master's degree in microbiology and had spent the better part of a decade at the CDC in Atlanta. His frustrations aside, he knew better than to question her results. But no one was infallible, not even the venerable Dr. Amon Trofino, loath as he was to admit it. Prudence dictated that new samples be obtained and run through the gamut of tests again. Only then would he allow himself to contemplate the ramifications. Of course, that didn't mean he intended to sit on his hands in the interim.

The whirring drone of the ventilation fan overhead lulled him into a state of total concentration. The clean room was the perfect laboratory environment. Everything, from the autopsy table to the implements at his disposal, was cast of stainless steel that glinted under the high-wattage lights on armatures mounted to the ceiling. The air was sterile and heavily oxygenated, the temperature just cool enough to heighten his focus. He absolutely loved every minute he spent in here. It was his own idyllic world of order, the eye in the hurricane of chaos that swirled relentlessly two stories above him.

He adjusted his plastic face shield and shot the sleeves of his isolation suit. He wasn't working with the kind of pathogenic agents to which he was accustomed, but part of the joy he derived from his work was in the ceremony. There was nothing quite as exhilarating as the feeling of walking into a room knowing that the only thing separating him from the miasma of potentially virulent microorganisms he prepared to unleash from the corpse before him was a thin layer of polyvinyl-impregnated fabric.

Thus far, his investigation had been on a purely macroscopic level. He had meticulously photographed every inch of the burned body, which was curled into fetal position at the mercy of the contractures that were only now slowly beginning to relax, and sampled the epidermal and subcutaneous tissues. He had grudgingly allowed Carla to draw a few ccs of cerebrospinal fluid and what little blood she could from deep within the wound on the cadaver's neck, but had insisted that visceral tissue and bone marrow extractions wait until he had properly examined the body and reached the appropriate stage in the process. He was anxious to get on with it, as well, but he wanted to savor every single moment of this. There was no telling when an opportunity like this would come along again. The corpse was far less useful than a live specimen would have been, but it would more than suffice. Adding the knowledge he gleaned from this fresh body to that of the other degraded samples from the Siberian remains that had nearly gone to rot during their long journey across the Pacific would surely give him everything he needed to launch the groundbreaking gene-splicing project that would not only allow him to stamp his name on the field, but to change the world in a way that no man ever had. This was bigger than Columbus proving that the world was round, bigger than the discovery of genetics itself in Gregor Mendel's garden, bigger even than putting a man on the moon.

This was the kind of revolutionary project that would allow him to see the universe through God's eyes and remake it not just in his image, but in any image he chose.

He tried not to consider Carla's words as he rolled the small corpse onto its back and began pulling its arms and legs away from its chest in anticipation of creating the Y-incision. They were still waiting on formal DNA sequencing, but the preliminary blood tests, which should have been a mere formality, were more than a little troubling.

"The CBC showed RBCs and WBCs well within the normal range. Hemoglobin and hematocrit levels are marginally high," she had said.

Trofino had looked curiously at her and tried to interpret the expression on her face.

"That's impossible."

"And yet that's precisely what the tests showed."

She had crossed her arms over her chest as though to physically defend herself from the argument ahead.

"If that's true—and I find your results dubious at best—then you're suggesting that—"

"There's no way this blood is anemic in the slightest, let alone to the degree of thalassemia."

Trofino understood the implications of what Carla was saying. All of the other bodies had exhibited identical signs of thalassemia. She could run the blood and CSF samples all day if he wanted her to while they awaited the genomic profile, but there was one surefire way to answer the question right now.

He cut two diagonal lines from the clavicles to the sternum and another from the point of their intersection to the pubis, then carefully reflected the crumbling black skin to expose the discolored and desiccated musculature. Breaking his own rules of proper dissection protocol, he carved through the upper abdominal muscles so he could gain access to the tenth anterior rib, at the bottom of the right side of the cage.

"*Dr. Trofino,*" Carla said through the intercom from the anteroom.

He tried to ignore the intrusion before it broke his concentration.

"*Dr. Trofino. I know how you feel about being interrupted while you're working and wouldn't even dream of doing so unless I felt it was of the utmost importance.*"

Trofino sighed in resignation. He left his index finger inside the incision to mark his place.

"Get on with it," he said.

"*One of the front gate guards is down here. He needs to talk to you.*"

"You interrupted me because a gate guard—a *gate guard*—needs to talk to me?"

"*You really should listen to what he has to say.*"

"Whatever it is, he should take it up with Spears, not me."

"*That's part of the problem...*"

There was a rustling sound and a man's voice came over the intercom. He cleared his throat and then spoke with his mouth too close to the microphone so that his words were unnecessarily garbled.

"*Dr. Trofino. Pahlson here. There was a federal agent in the parking lot of the warehouse across the street, just sitting there watching the compound.*"

"And just how does this pertain to me?"

"*He said he was looking for a little girl.*"

"Again, I ask how—?"

"*He described her as pale and bald with big teeth.*"

The guard now had his full attention.

"How could a federal agent possibly have gained access to those details?"

"*No way that I can think of.*"

"You didn't tell him—"

"*Not on your life, sir.*"

"What did Spears have to say?"

"*I couldn't find him. His office is trashed and no one seems to know where he is. All I could confirm was that he had signed out a field kit from the armory.*"

"A field kit?"

"*It's a case equipped with a disassembled M24 Sniper Weapon System, a Beretta M9 semiautomatic nine-millimeter, a pair of night vision/thermal fusion goggles, a gas mask, and a pair of both fragmentary and incendiary grenades.*"

"Why in the world would he—?" Trofino closed his eyes when the answer hit him. "Who was on the mission with Spears last night?"

"*Austin, Morgan, Stadler, Keenan, Newland—*"

"Damn it!"

Christ. The blood tests had been right. Spears had set them up.

He gripped the edges of the sliced muscle in both hands and jerked them apart to expose the ribs. One of the key distinctions of thalassemia was a thickening of the ribs where iron deposits continued to amass throughout the lifetime. All of the Siberian bodies had ribs that had widened to such a degree that he could hardly squeeze a scalpel between them. The ribs he stared down at now were normally spaced and showed no indication of increased cortical density.

His heart hammered in his chest and his hands started to shake.

The blood tests were normal.

The physical examination was unremarkable.

He'd met Newland, and she couldn't have been much more than five feet tall.

The FBI knew about the girl and already had surveillance in place.

There was no doubt in his mind.

Spears had hung them out to dry.

He hadn't gotten the creature last night so he had used Newland's remains to create the illusion that he had, while he enacted another plan of his own. He must have rolled over for the FBI and let them know exactly what was inside this compound. Was it possible he had done so just to buy himself more time to go after the creature on his own? And hadn't last night been their final opportunity to hunt it because of the ribbon-cutting ceremony tonight?

"Oh, no," he whispered. He knew exactly what Spears intended to do, and he would end up taking each and every one of them down with him in the process.

"*Dr. Trofino?*" Pahlson asked. "*What should we—?*"

"Code Meridian," Trofino interrupted. "Initiate the countdown sequence."

"*Are you out of your mind?*" Carla said. "*We'll lose everything—*"

"Just do it, goddamn it!"

A klaxon blared and the red emergency lights bloomed from their housings on the walls.

"Grab the samples, Carla!" he shouted as he raced across the clean room.

He wasn't about to go down with the ship.

The sublevel walls were fortified with a solid foot of asbestos-insulated lead and iron baffles. They had been built to withstand a nuclear detonation outside, and then reinforced through the years for a different purpose entirely. The moment he activated the code, the failsafe protocol had been set in motion. In less than five minutes now, these corridors would be flooded with a complex mixture of natural gasses propelled by pressurized oxygen. At the same time, the heptafluoropropane waterless fire suppression system lines would be diverted to a secondary system of pipes that drew gasoline from the storage tanks under the motor pool. In barely longer than it would take for the system to generate the lone necessary spark, the entire basement of the building would be consumed by a fireball that would burn at more than five thousand degrees Kelvin, hot enough to incinerate everything down to the atomic level, while the floors above remained unscathed. No one would ever be able to tell what they had been doing down here. Every last shred of evidence would be vaporized.

Everything but the samples that Carla had hurriedly gathered from her station and packed into the liquid nitrogen-cooled briefcase he had ready and waiting for just this contingency. She handed him the case and they ran together toward the door.

There was no way he was going to lose his research.

It might take several years longer, but he would eventually be able to pick right back up where he left off.

THIRTY-NINE

Seattle, Washington
5:18 p.m. PST

Sturm awakened abruptly to a sound at odds with her dream, which vanished the moment she tried to recapture it. She was confused and disoriented. The darkness surrounding her was oddly unfamiliar. Her eyes closed of their own accord, then snapped back open when she heard banging from somewhere nearby. It took several seconds to recognize the blankets draped over the blinds to block out the light, the heap of dirty clothes in the corner, and the cluttered dresser, all of which were stained red by the numbers on the digital clock. Try as she might, she couldn't arrange the numbers into a coherent pattern that would allow her to tell the time. Her brain was pudding and each thought seemed to peter and die in the gooey morass. The base of her skull throbbed. She felt somehow detached from her warm body, which stretched away from her under the covers.

She vaguely remembered stumbling into the precinct just before dawn, slapping her badge and her gun down on the watch captain's desk, and storming back out without a word. Had she called the CSRT to let them know she wasn't available today? She couldn't recall. Somehow, she had raced her exhaustion home and passed out under the covers. At least she knew that much. When she had seen the girl's cooked carcass, every last iota of strength had fled her. Sleep had come bearing down on her like a freight train, and run right over her with a vengeance.

The banging sound again.

She swung her legs over the side of her bed and buried her face in her hands. More than anything else in the world, she just wanted to crawl back into bed and sleep clear through to the next day. Maybe even the day after. What day was it anyway? How long had she been asleep? It felt like no more than five minutes.

Banging. Louder.

"Christ," she croaked. Her throat was bone-dry. "I'm coming already."

She staggered into the hallway and crossed through the living room to the front door.

The thin wooden slab shook with a solid blow from the other side.

"This had better be really flipping important."

She opened the door and found herself a foot away from Porter, his fist raised to knock again. He stared at her face and her mussed hair, then his eyes traveled down her body. She glanced down and realized she was only wearing her bra and panties.

"I'm thrilled to see you were expecting me," he said with a wink, and brushed past her through the doorway. He had what could have been a dry cleaning bag slung over his shoulder. It almost looked to her sleep-addled mind like he was wearing a cape.

"Please. Come right in." She glanced out upon the gray day and saw just the faintest hint of scarlet through the clouds to the west. "You mind if I grab some clothes or have you come to ravish me now that our partnership is officially over?"

"Yeah," he said. She raised an eyebrow at him. "I mean, yeah...I would mind if you got dressed. I have something special for you instead."

"You certainly know how to charm a girl. How about this? I go back to bed, write this whole thing off as a bad dream, and maybe we can try again some other day when I've actually caught up on a little sleep. Maybe start off with dinner and a movie and see where things go from there."

"I have a better idea."

"You already mentioned that."

"No, no. You've got it all wrong." He lowered the bag from his shoulder. "I mean I have a better idea than dinner and a movie. But I have to admit I dig the direction you were going with that last part."

He pulled the wrapper off of the hanger to reveal a stunning iridescent blue evening gown that perfectly matched her eyes. She stared at it for a long moment, unsure exactly what to make of it. The dress was a long strapless number that looked as though it was designed to cling to every curve. It shimmered even in the dull light that filtered through her curtains. She looked up at Porter and tried to read his intentions on his face. The corners of his lips cocked upward into a sly half-smile and she realized what he had in mind.

"We're going to be run out of town, you know," she said.

"At least we'll get to enjoy some dinner and dancing first." His smile widened and lit up his eyes. "Is this more along the lines of what you had in mind for our first date?"

"I thought we already had our first date."

"Then if this is our second, a guy's entitled to have some expectations, especially if he's shelling out a month's salary for dinner."

Sturm smiled and snatched the dress out of his hands. She ran her fingertips over the silky fabric and then looked directly into his eyes.

"Thank you," she whispered.

He stepped closer and tipped up her chin. Their lips were only inches apart.

"I told you we weren't about to let this one go."

He leaned in and brushed his lips against hers. Softly. She parted hers in anticipation and inhaled his breath.

"Save that thought," he whispered. "We'd better hurry up and get ready. We don't want to miss out on any of the entertainment."

Sturm draped the dress over her arm and turned to head for her bedroom. She stopped and peered back at him.

"Why are you doing this? Your career will be over."

"Now that I've seen how easily power can corrupt justice, maybe that's not such a bad thing," he said. "Or maybe I just wanted to spend a little more time with the most beautiful woman I've ever met. Either way, it's going to be a night to remember."

FORTY

Seattle, Washington
5:56 p.m. PST

Spears crouched inside the old smokestack that lorded over the ruins on a grate coated with lifetimes of accumulated carbon and ash. He was more than a hundred feet above the rubble to his right. From this vantage point, he could clearly see over the chain link fence and onto the patio to the south of the cultural center, where all of the tables had been set up under a series of white gazebo-like tents. The places were already set and the waiters were milling about the wet bars and ice sculptures, killing time. He smelled garlic and peppers and meat roasting somewhere out of sight. Searchlights crisscrossed the sky from in front of the building at the end of the circular drive, where red-vested valets awaited the first arrivals. The mayor and his entourage were inside, presumably making last minute preparations. The Seattle Philharmonic had just finished warming up their instruments in the main exhibit hall.

It was almost show time.

Soon enough, more than two hundred men and women would be gathered around the building for the formal ribbon-cutting, and the drinking and schmoozing to follow.

Spears, on the other hand, already had everything in place and ready to go. His M24 was assembled and loaded, and he'd already sighted in the patio at just under three hundred yards. At this distance, he could put a bullet through a hoop earring without grazing the lobe. Piece of cake. The M9 was loaded and holstered under his arm. His goggles rested on the grate beside him. The grenades were clipped to a diagonal belt across his chest. He had isolated the main power line on the street and rigged it with a small charge of C4 rigged to a timer. At precisely ten o'clock, the charge would blow, killing the power to the center, extinguishing the lights.

And then, he knew, the creature would come.

Complete darkness.

Prey huddled together.

Helpless.

Simply waiting for the lights to come back on.

Spears would be able to see it all perfectly.

The moment the screaming started, he would be able to sight the monster down the barrel of his rifle and put a bullet right through its skull. And if that failed? He was armed with enough firepower to engage an entire platoon. He would wade into the fracas and take it down at close range. Regardless of the civilian casualties. If he had to blow up the whole damn cultural center with him inside, then so be it. There was no future for him beyond this final mission. This all ended tonight.

His son would be avenged.

He slumped down on the grate, closed his eyes, and allowed himself to drift into a state of perfect awareness, where he was neither asleep nor awake, where time passed in a blur as he visualized the siege to come.

And come it would.

Of that there had never been any doubt.

FORTY-ONE

Seattle, Washington
7:03 p.m. PST

Porter glanced at Sturm from the corner of his eye. She was positively radiant. The shimmering dress. The smooth white skin above her neckline. The perfectly styled hair. The smirk on her face that betrayed her thoughts. She was ready to confront the mayor, ready to make him squirm in front of hundreds of the most powerful people in all of the Pacific Northwest. Maybe whoever had applied the pressure to all of the law enforcement agencies would be here and they could put the squeeze on him, too. There were so many possibilities, but only one real outcome. They would have to take their shots quickly, because it was only a matter of time before they were run off and presumably taken into custody, where they would have the honor of watching the careers they had worked so hard for flushed down the toilet right before their very eyes. But would it be worth it? Oh, yeah. At this moment it felt like the culmination of all of his hopes and dreams. He would undoubtedly reevaluate again in the morning under the light of day and realize what a titanic mistake he had made, but right now, there was nothing he wanted more.

"You ready to do this?" he asked as he followed the procession of luxury vehicles into the circular drive toward the waiting line of valets.

"You'd better believe it." Sturm smiled at him from the passenger seat and he knew they had made the right decision, come hell or high water. "I've been ready for this since my first night rousting those poor homeless people."

"We're going to pay for this, you know."

She stared straight through the windshield as they coasted to a halt at the curb. The valet opened her door and helped her out, then jogged around to the driver's side door and swapped spots with

Porter. The Crown Vic drove away behind them, leaving them standing on the sidewalk, awed by the spectacle before them. Music blared from inside the main hall over the din of seemingly thousands of competing voices. There was laughter in the air, and yet, at the same time, an aura of refinement.

Porter offered his arm, and guided Sturm up the front walk to where men in tuxedos collected their invitations and ushered them into a different world. Waiters circulated with glasses of champagne on sparkling serving trays. The philharmonic played from the back of the massive hall, beyond a cluster of silver-haired men and their younger wives, who sloshed golden fluid from their glasses as they danced. Older women, dressed in period costumes, guided smaller groups through tours of the displays. There were impromptu gatherings all around. Deferential men laughing haughtily at bad jokes. Women with predatory eyes swirling their champagne as they eyed their next step up the social ladder from across the room. Everything reeked of unchecked ambition and entitlement.

Porter surveyed the sea of faces, searching for anyone who would potentially identify them too soon and put an end to their game before it even started. He recognized a senator and two congressmen, a pair of corporate magnates he'd seen on television, a couple of actors whom he couldn't immediately place, and in the rear right corner, the district attorney and the chief of police trading stories with his SAC and two other men he had seen paraded through the field office on more than one occasion.

"We should keep moving," Porter said, and guided Sturm across the floor to a hallway that led to the smaller exhibit halls, careful to keep his face turned from the law enforcement contingent.

"I still haven't seen the mayor," Sturm said.

"Don't worry. It's only a matter of time. He's around here somewhere."

"You know...I was thinking. If we're going to go down, we should do it in style."

"What do you propose?"

She smiled and he could have sworn she actually giggled.

"Oh, no," he said.

"Hear me out first," she said.

By the time she finished telling him her idea, he couldn't hide the grin on his face either.

*   *   *

The actual ribbon-cutting had gone off without a hitch. It had been somewhat lackluster, and less a ceremony than a photo op. Only a small crowd had gathered in front of the center, where the patrons were outnumbered by photographers from the local papers and the news wires. A two-foot wide red ribbon had been strung between columns. After a brief and uninspired speech, the mayor had raised a comically large pair of scissors and conferred the honor upon a famous software developer. It was surely an arrangement brokered behind closed doors, but one that added a necessary bit of levity. The software developer had struggled to make the scissors work and ended up delivering a one-liner about how hard it was to cut through American red tape that had left the audience in stitches.

Every face was lit with a smile and flushed with the glow of alcohol. These men and women were in their element. This was a completely different world than the one Sturm knew. She imagined that in this one building, she could undoubtedly find the president of the bank that had foreclosed on her family farm and all of the brokers who had denied her father's loan applications. These were people separate from the rest of their species, people who lived inside a bubble of affluence that couldn't be popped by the realities of the suffering around them, an opaque sphere that blinded them to the deterioration of the society from which they had excepted themselves.

They were seated under the gazebo tents, all business set aside. Soft music drifted across the patio from inside the building, a pleasant undertone to the clanking of serving trays and the more subdued rumble of conversation. Stewards tipped cloth-wrapped bottles of champagne with their trademark flair, never once making eye contact. The steaming cuts of meat and fish smelled positively divine. A cool breeze flowed inland from the sea with barely enough strength to ruffle the tablecloths. The stars shined down upon them from a night sky so clear it appeared incapable of ever producing rain.

Sturm twisted Porter's wrist so she could see his watch.

9:53 p.m.

Sturm and Porter sat at an out-of-the-way table at the eastern periphery, on the wrong side of the aisle the servers used to usher the meals from inside the building, where they could hear the caterer barking orders like a drill sergeant. It was obvious they would be the last to be served, but neither of them cared. They hadn't come for the food. From their vantage point, they could barely see the mayor at the head of the central table, flanked on either side by ice sculptures of ancient frigates bursting through cresting waves. There was a podium between them, and behind it an enormous rectangle draped with velvet like a stage curtain. The mayor appeared to be preening for invisible cameras as he talked and laughed with the others at the table of honor. His wife sat at his left shoulder, demure and petite, her blonde-highlighted hair drawn up on top of her head to showcase her slender neck. Her face was taut with Botox, her lips plump with collagen. The senator sat to his right, a more impressive presence who tipped the balance of power in such a way that the table seemed to lean. Around the circle were the chief of police, Red Gardener—whom Sturm now understood fancied the commissioner's office—and two software designers who looked like mannequins in their tuxes beside stunning companions who looked like they were probably being paid by the hour.

Once all of the food had been served, the mayor rose from his seat, straightened his tie, and assumed the podium. He held up his glass and tapped it with a spoon. Conversation trickled to silence and the music ceased inside. The only sounds were provided by the waves rolling in from the timeless Pacific.

Sturm caught a glimpse of Porter's watch when he checked the time.

9:56 p.m.

They were running ahead of schedule.

She looked up and met Porter's eyes. His expression was calm and confident. She wanted to borrow some of his strength, because right now her heart was pounding so hard it felt like it might leap out of her chest. She clenched her hands into fists to keep them from shaking. She closed her eyes and pictured the despondent souls she had run out of their home for just this occasion, so that their suffering wouldn't spoil anyone's appetite. She pictured the little girl who might have been a monster, but never should have been hunted down and burned alive. She could still feel the child crawling into her lap and trembling in her arms. There was no doubt that the girl was different and that she had been responsible for the horrible deaths of so many, and yet Sturm couldn't help but feel as though the blame should be shared by all in attendance. A government-sanctioned private defense contractor was responsible for turning her loose on her victims, for all of the bloodshed she caused, and the people sitting around her had helped to cover it up. None of this should ever have come to pass. None of it. And now here these people sat in their expensive clothes, as though the deaths of sixteen men and one little girl they had turned into a savage killer had never even happened…

Her face flushed with anger. It was all she could do to keep from streaking across the patio and grabbing the mayor by his throat. She focused on her breathing, on clearing her mind. When she made her move, she needed to be in complete control.

"I'd like to start by thanking all of you for joining us on this most beautiful and historic evening," the mayor said into the microphone. His voice was amplified by small speakers mounted high up in the tents above them. "It's because of people like you that Seattle is indisputably the greatest city in the country, and because of your generosity that it will remain that way for the foreseeable future. So why don't you all give yourselves a hand." He stepped back from the podium and led the applause. When he stepped back up, he raised his glass. "Now, before we all share a glimpse into that future, I want to propose a toast."

The mayor scanned the gathering and waited until every glass was held high.

Sturm's legs tensed and her pulse accelerated.

This was the moment she'd been waiting for.

"To each and every one of you, for—"

"Driving the homeless back into the streets," Sturm shouted. She leapt to her feet, glass held high, and made her way toward the podium. "For conspiring to cover up murder, and—"

"Who is this woman?" the mayor shouted. His expression shifted from surprise to anger.

"—for killing a little girl!"

"Someone shut her up!"

Sturm felt hands grab her right arm and jerk her backward. From the corner of her eye, she saw Porter lunge from behind the table and the pressure abated. She turned her focus on the chief of police.

"Tell them, *sir*. Tell them all how you had us down there, night after night, running the homeless out of this area so that no one would have to even look at them while eating these overpriced meals."

She slapped a plate of steak from the table beside her for emphasis.

When she caught the senator's eye, she held it.

"Tell them how you sanctioned a private defense contractor to unleash toxic nerve gas on this very site just twenty-four hours ago!"

The strobe of flash bulbs behind her was disorienting. The news crews had obviously stuck around in case anything interesting actually happened.

"I want this woman arrested!" the mayor shouted.

A man leapt from his seat, grabbed Sturm around her waist, and lifted her into the air.

"Let go of me!" she screamed. "I'm not finished yet!"

There was a loud cracking sound behind her head. The man grunted and released her. She spun around in time to see Porter flinging blood from his knuckles.

"You think all of your money makes you untouchable?" Sturm shouted. "None of you are above the law!"

There was a loud explosion, like the sound of a head-on collision.

The ground trembled.

The lights died with a resounding thud.

Someone grabbed her and wrenched her arm behind her back. She was driven forward and lost her balance. She hit the ground flat on her chest with someone's weight on her back, knocking the wind out of her.

Men shouted for someone to turn the lights back on. Voices rose in tumult. Chair legs scraped the paving stones. Tables crashed to the ground. Plates shattered. A woman cried out.

Sturm couldn't see a blasted thing. She couldn't move her arms and could only thrash her head from side to side. She kicked at the ground for leverage only to find out that she'd lost her shoes.

When she caught her breath, she expelled it as a scream.

FORTY-TWO

Seattle, Washington
10:00 p.m. PST

Spears inched the scope slowly from left to right, watching the chaos for what he knew was soon to come. Men and women trampled each other in their hurry to distance themselves from the melee. The mayor still stood at the podium with the same dumb expression on his face, frozen in place. Screams echoed across the overgrown lot. Bedlam reigned. He kept an eye on the edge of the rubble and the fence line, knowing that at any second a pink and gold form would come streaking across his field of view.

He tensed his finger against the trigger, eased his cheek down onto the stock, and readied himself for the kill shot.

This time, he would not miss.

*   *   *

Frances Mueller stood perfectly still in the middle of the main exhibit hall. She had just changed out of her period costume and was on her way to the front door when the explosion killed the lights and the screaming commenced. After wearing the heavy garments for so long, it felt as though every vertebra in her spine had been compressed. Her hips ached, her knees and ankles throbbed, and her feet had swollen to the point that they threatened to burst out of her shoes, but her ears seemed to be working just fine. She heard hollow thumping sounds and the crumpling of the aluminum ductwork overhead, then the crashing noise of something heavy falling into one of the replica ships suspended above her. The guy wires screeched in protest, then snapped with a twang and the crack of a whip. Something struck the ground behind her, something large and yet simultaneously soft, that made a slapping sound. She felt the change in the air as it passed beside

her, smelled filth and rot in its wake, and heard the whooshing
sound of the model boat plummeting down toward her. It crashed
to the floor mere feet behind her and threw her forward into a
display case. Her head impacted the glass and her vision filled with
sunbursts. She was mercifully unconscious before her forehead
bounced off of the marble tiles.

*   *   *

Marty Knapp tucked the champagne bottle under his vest as he
peered out through the doorway, curious as to what had transpired
while he ducked off to enjoy a little of the bubbly himself. There
was barely enough starlight to show him a herd of stampeding
bodies, all of them shouting and wailing as they shoved through
each other, stomping those who fell before the human tide. He
shrugged, stepped to the side again, and tipped back the bottle.
Shame to let this expensive stuff go to waste. He belched and
crinkled his nose. Something reeked. He smelled a godawful
stench like a turned compost heap a heartbeat before someone
collided with him from behind. Nails pierced his back, lancing
right through his skin and between his ribs. Something scurried up
his jacket, tearing the fabric as it went. Searing pain in his neck.
And then the weight was gone. When he raised his trembling hand,
the pulsing heat drove it away from the wound.

*   *   *

Senator James Hawley lowered his shoulder and bulled his way
through the scrum. The woman in front of him shrieked as she
tumbled to the ground. He stepped up onto her back and used her
to lunge forward, grabbing two men by the shoulders and knocking
them down in the process. One of the tent's support posts fell
sideways and the whole works started to come down. He juked
right, then left, just like in his old football days, and saw the
opening to the end zone. A door leading inside. All of the others
were fighting their way along the side of the building. If he could
slip inside and make a break for one of the other exits—

A shadow, nearly indistinguishable from the darkness, fired up at him from near the ground, striking him high up on his chest. His legs ran out from beneath him and he knew he was going down. Pressure under his chin, driving his head back. Something sharp clamped down on his throat like a bear trap, probing under the flesh, through the muscles, and then it was gone. He hit the ground on his back. His own blood rained down on him.

*　　　*　　　*

Porter fought through the surge toward where Sturm had fallen, following the sound of her cries. His mind was racing at a million miles an hour, trying to rationalize the situation. Either the main power line had overloaded and exploded, or someone had sabotaged it. None of the men they had come to expose had been prepared for it, which meant that they were undoubtedly every bit as surprised as he was. It was either the most perfectly timed accident ever, or someone had rigged the power to be cut at precisely ten o'clock. And if all of the higher powers were in attendance, then that left only one wild card for which he couldn't account, one faction that could ill afford to have its activities brought to light.

Phobos.

And if he was right, Spears was out there right now, prepared to do whatever it took to keep his involvement secret. This was only the first phase of the assault. Spears and his men couldn't allow any of them with knowledge of the events to survive long enough to talk. They would be coming in fast and hard. Their willingness to openly attack could mean only one thing. They fully intended to make sure there were no survivors.

But there was one glaring flaw in his stream of logic. Why would they initiate this siege now? It was all too public, too visible. Even if they did manage to kill every last one of them, there would be no way the slaughter would go unnoticed. It didn't fit. All of the men who were ultimately responsible for keeping the secret had too much invested personally to risk any kind of exposure. They would have taken it to the grave with them, regardless. He could only think of one reason for killing the lights and causing such chaos.

The girl.

With her night vision and predatory instincts, she would have been drawn to the commotion like a lion to a herd of wounded gazelle. But he had seen Spears carrying her corpse out of the ruins last night. Unless that had all been for show and the girl was still—

Something hot and wet spattered his cheek. He tasted copper on his lips. A man plowed into him from the side, driving him to the ground. The man was limp. Dead weight. Spilling blood onto Porter's head, down under his collar.

He shrugged out from beneath it and crawled toward Sturm.

A small foot stepped squarely on the center of his back.

He felt it clearly.

A small, bare foot.

Jesus Christ. The girl was still alive.

Spears was using them all as bait.

"Layne!" he shouted, and scrabbled forward as fast as he could, trying to separate her screams from all of the others.

*   *   *

Mayor Elgin Marten shook off the shock and stumbled out from behind the podium. Every inch of his body was numb. His brain threatened to shut down. He was witnessing the end of his career. By the time this catastrophe hit the news in the morning, the entire city will have rallied to build the cross they would use to crucify him. The screams were horrible, and they were everywhere. The tables were toppled, the dishes destroyed, the tents coming down like the final curtain on his mayoral tenure. Everyone had shed their gentility in favor of self-preservation, and now attempted to crush one another to death in their mad rush for freedom. How had this happened? He had planned everything meticulously. How had he allowed—?

The woman.

This was all her fault. She had seized control of events in an effort to publicly crush him. She had verbally attacked him for the whole world to see and had sabotaged the electricity in hopes of producing just this kind of bedlam.

Well, he would definitely have to deal with her.

He crunched over the broken ice from the shattered sculpture and worked his way through the jostling bodies toward where he had seen the chief of police take her down. In the midst of the chaos, no one would see him close his hands around her scrawny neck and wring it like a dishrag. No one would ever know. He could think of nothing else.

Marten stepped on a woman who cried out in pain. Somewhere, deep down, he knew it was his wife, but he kept on going.

He was nearly to the point where he had watched Gardener tackle the woman when he heard the chief's voice.

"Hold your goddamn hands still!"

"Let go of me!" the woman cried.

Marten smiled. He could already feel her windpipe compressing in his grip.

Something unbelievably sharp pierced his left cheek and nearly flayed the skin from his face as it spun his head roughly to the side. Teeth on the side of his neck. Digging, ripping, wrenching. He felt a mouthful of himself tear away and tried to scream, but he was already falling. His chin ricocheted from the paving stones before a pathetic whimper crossed his split lips.

*   *   *

Sturm struggled to roll out from beneath the chief. He had already cuffed her right wrist and had the leverage to keep it pinned up near her shoulder blade. It was all she could do to keep her left out of his reach or the game would be over. In her mind, she knew it already was, but her heart insisted there was a whole lot more that needed to be said. These men needed to not just pay; they needed to be ruined.

She kicked and bucked to no avail. She heard Porter calling her name, closer now. Feet stomped past her head. One came down on her free hand and she screamed in agony.

Gardener took advantage of the opportunity and grabbed her by the wrist. He nearly had it twisted up by her other hand when the pressure suddenly abated. Something warm and wet splashed down on her back and slithered across her bare skin. Her first thought was that a bowl of soup must have sloshed from one of the tables, but she quickly remembered they hadn't served soup. She realized exactly what it was at the same time that the chief's lifeless body flopped onto her.

Sturm cried out and dragged herself out from beneath him. She rounded on him and was prepared to scream again when she caught a quick flash of reflected light in twin spheres and smelled the ghastly aroma of the underground warrens.

A tiny, cold hand closed gently around her wrist where the cuff was clamped. The girl's entire body trembled as she crawled closer to Sturm and buried her face into the bare skin above the neckline of her dress. Sturm felt the warm dampness on the girl's face, smelled the metallic scent of blood, and heard the soft whimpering as the girl started to cry.

Sturm wrapped her arms around the child's narrow shoulders and drew her into an embrace. The girl's shoulders shook and she squeezed so tightly that Sturm gasped. She stroked the back of the girl's bald head and felt the heat of tears on her own cheeks.

The entire episode was surreal. She had seen Spears removing the girl's scorched remains from the underground warrens, and yet here she was, alive and in her arms.

"Shh...Everything's going to be—"

A burst of pain in her shoulder and she pitched forward onto the girl. Pain raced down the length of her right arm and up her neck into the base of her skull. She felt a sudden chill, deep inside, like an icicle grinding against the underside of her scapula.

A sound like thunder split the night and echoed across the waterfront, drowning out even the screams.

*   *   *

Spears ejected the spent brass and chambered another round. He had tracked the creature along its bloody rampage until it finally held still long enough for him to get off a shot. Granted, he had been forced to take it straight through the woman's shoulder, but even at this distance it should have passed through her cleanly with enough residual velocity to hit his target. The creature had moved so fast that it had appeared as little more than a blur through the goggles. He had expected it to come from the ruins, but it had surprised him. It had already been inside the building. Clever little demon. He should have been prepared for that contingency, and yet he was also thankful for his rare lack of foresight. Watching it move through the crowd was breathtaking. Darting first one way and then the other, nearly separating men from their heads with the grace of a striking cobra, then speeding off in a different direction entirely before the golden arterial spray even hit the ground. It was awesome observing it in its element. If there was one consolation for him, at least Trofino would be smart enough to recognize the net closing in on him and would bolt with his research and destroy any evidence that he had ever been there. The project would live on, but this was the end of the road for Spears.

He lined up the next shot, slowly blew his breath all the way out, and thought of his son as he sighed down the monster through the nightmare frenzy.

And pulled the trigger.

*   *   *

Porter was in motion the moment he heard the bullet pound Sturm's back. He dove of top of her as the hornet-whine of the second bullet sang past his ear. They tumbled to the side and he used their momentum to roll her behind an overturned table. He felt her blood on his hands, on the side of his face, soaking through his shirt. Hot and wet. She screamed when she came to rest on her back. He tried to keep her left hand from exploring the crater of the exit wound. Blood boiled out between her fingers. He jerked off his tie, wadded it up, and pressed it to her shoulder to stanch the bleeding. She cried out with the application of pressure.

"Hold this right here." He placed her hand on the tie and slid his away. "Press down as hard as you can."

She moaned something he didn't hear. He was already crawling back out from the behind the table. He peered around the edge just in time to see the distant strobe of muzzle flare, about three hundred yards out and a hundred feet up. There was a spark to his right as the bullet ricocheted from the ground and careened off into the building with the sound of shattering glass.

The majority of the guests had made it around to the front of the center, where their screams echoed under the colonnade. The injured still back here groaned and whimpered as they attempted to limp and drag themselves through the wreckage of the ruined tables and chairs and across the path of broken glasses and dishware.

He heard crying behind him and turned to reassure Sturm that everything was going to be all right, but froze when he caught the glare of eyeshine above where she lay. He stared into those small, wide eyes for a long moment. They glistened with tears. It was the girl who was crying. The sounds she made were full of such palpable pain that Porter instinctively reached out to her. He touched her softly on the side of her face. She leaned her damp cheek into his palm.

The table jumped with a *crack* and peppered his face with splinters. He yanked back his hand and ducked lower as the report echoed off into the night.

Something changed in the girl's eyes. They somehow narrowed and sharpened, and he recognized the predator lurking behind them. He could barely see the silhouette of the girl's bald head when she leaned down toward Sturm's face.

"No!" he shouted and dove to try to stop the girl from finishing off Sturm, but she was already gone.

He ran his hand over Sturm's neck, felt her slow, thready pulse, smoothed his fingers over her unbroken skin. If the girl hadn't gone for Sturm's throat, then what—?

Another crack of gunfire, but he couldn't tell where the bullet struck.

He peeked back around the side of the table and saw a small dark shape scale the fence and leap down onto the other side.

And then it was gone.

"Don't..." Sturm whispered. "Don't let...anything happen...to...her."

Her cold hand found his and squeezed ever so softly. The blood on her fingers was already crusted. He squeezed back, then replaced her hand on the sopping tie.

He had no weapon. No backup. They were pinned down by rifle fire and she was bleeding to death. Attempting to move her was a risk, especially though the field of fire, but he needed to get help. If he didn't at least try, she could die right here.

There was no other choice.

He swept her up in his arms, pulled her as tightly as to his chest as he could, and sprinted out into the open, knowing full well that he would feel the bullet tear through his flesh long before he heard the report.

*   *   *

Spears saw the fuchsia and gold shape alight on his side of the fence and sprint toward the ruins. He managed to get off one quick shot before it vanished from sight. He leaned over the edge of the smokestack and tried to take aim, but it was too close and he had lost his angle. It must have gone back underground, where it assumed he would have to give up his advantage and face it on its own turf. He cursed his misfortune as he watched the rubble through the scope for several long moments. He had wanted to see the expression on its face when the first bullet hit, and then the explosion of pink mist when the second destroyed its skull.

It was only a matter of time before this entire area was swarming with cops. It was one thing for the men down there to cover for him from afar; another entirely when they were down there in the bedlam with blood spattered all over them. Fortunately, he had prepared for this eventuality. In addition to the small, shaped charge he had rigged to the main power line, he had spent the better part of the afternoon planting bricks of C4 throughout the warrens. There was enough down there that when he pressed the button on the remote detonator, the whole waterfront would crumble into the Pacific. Both he and the creature would be enveloped in the firestorm. He would take his vengeance with him to the grave.

Spears studied the ruins for nearly a full minute longer. There was no sign of the monster.

The men and women at the cultural center had found their way to the front of the building. If anything, their screams seemed to have grown louder. Beyond the building, he could see red and blue lights in the distance, approaching fast. The shrill sound of sirens reached him a heartbeat later, and beneath them, what could only have been the mechanical pounding of helicopter rotors.

It was now or never.

He cast aside his rifle, removed the detonator from the inner pocket of his jacket, and rested his thumb on the first in the series of triggers. From his first day in Basic, he had always known that his destiny was to go out in a blaze of glory. He felt neither shame nor sorrow, only vindication. This was how it was meant to be. He clung to the image of his son's face as he pressed the first button.

The ground shook and the northern edge of the ruins dropped from sight. Smoke and dust chased a fireball into the sky. Debris rained from above like massive hailstones. He pressed the next button, and the one after that. The smoke and flames billowed toward him, forcing him to duck down behind the lip and onto the grate. He coughed and retched as clumps of concrete pummeled his back. The smokestack began to lean. He could already hear the crackling sound of bricks breaking apart and the mortar that had held them together for a century crumbling to powder. He could barely see the red glow of the final button through the suffocating cloud. When he pressed it, the ground would open up directly beneath him and swallow him into its fiery depths.

He covered the light with his thumb, drew the deepest breath he could through the smoke and dust, and—

A reddish-orange flash below him. Through the grate. Its shape distorted by the swirling smoke. But he knew damn well what it was.

The creature clawed its way straight up the crumbling inner wall of the smokestack toward him.

He leaned over the access hatch in the grate and locked eyes with it.

"I'll see you in he—!"

The creature fired up through access hatch. The iron rim struck him in the face and knocked him backward. The detonator fell from his hand and clattered to the grate.

It was upon him before he could react.

Claws hooked into his face: through his cheeks, the soft crescents beneath his eyes, inside his ears, and under his chin. Teeth bit right through the flesh on the side of his neck. He felt them scrape against his vertebrae, felt his lifeblood rushing out into its mouth.

The smokestack shuddered and tilted to the side. He slid across the grate with the creature still perched on his chest, ripping his neck from side to side, refusing to let go. His fingertips brushed against the detonator and he managed to flatten his hand across it, pinning it to the grate. He smashed his palm onto it with the last of his strength, pressing every button at once.

The creature tore away a strip of flesh and stared down at him, his muscles and tendons dangling from its bared teeth, its face a golden mask of his pain.

"Boom," he sputtered through a mouthful of blood.

*   *   *

Sturm could barely see through the film of tears over her eyes, but she wouldn't allow herself to so much as blink for fear of losing consciousness. Smoke boiled toward them from across the field, crashing over the fence like a tidal wave. She coughed and cupped her functional hand over her brow in an effort to shield her eyes from the dust. The smokestack was a vague black column toppling to the right, until a fireball shot straight up its height, blowing apart the bricks even as the structure tumbled toward the ground. Flames blasted up into the sky.

And then they were gone.

The earth shuddered one final time as the smokestack's bulk collapsed upon it, then stilled.

Sturm sobbed and leaned back against Porter's chest. He wrapped his arms around her from behind to both support her and keep pressure on her gunshot wound.

Tires screeched behind them. Sirens squawked as they died. Swirling red and blue lights diffused into the smoke and made black silhouettes of the terrified men and women who converged upon the emergency vehicles.

"You did everything you could," Porter whispered into her ear. "She didn't suffer."

Sturm tried to squeeze his hand, but she lacked the strength. She merely grazed her palm across the back of his hand.

The darkness swept up from inside her and drew her down into its cold depths. Her last thought was of a child consumed by fire reaching out to her before disintegrating into a cloud of embers.

                    *   *   *

"I need medical attention over here!" Porter shouted.

He carefully lowered Sturm to the grass and leaned over her so he could keep as much pressure as possible on her wound. His tie was saturated. Rich black blood poured out from beneath the compress, wetting his hands and soaking through her dress. There were standing puddles in the recesses of her clavicles and her jugular notch. Her pale face was freckled with crimson. Her eyes seemed to be sinking into the dark pits of her sockets. He could feel her breath slowing in her chest and prayed that he could pass his life force through his hands and into her.

"Goddamn it! I need a doctor over here! This woman's been shot!"

He felt warmth on his cheeks but couldn't be certain whether he was crying or covered with her blood.

More and more emergency vehicles arrived behind him, their sirens creating a carnival of lights. Surely one of them was a mother-loving ambulance.

"Out of the way," a man said, and bodily shoved him to the side.

Porter was about to take a swing at the man when he recognized the blue-on-blue of the paramedic's uniform and the case of medical supplies he slammed onto the ground beside him. Porter looked up and saw another paramedic running toward them with an orange backboard on a gurney.

"You do whatever you have to do to save her," Porter said, "or, God help me, I will track you down and make sure—"

"I said get out of the way!"

Porter scooted around toward Sturm's head and leaned down over her face.

"You hang on. Do you hear me? Don't you dare quit on me."

He kissed her on the forehead. Her skin was cold against his lips. He watched her eyes for any sign of acknowledgement, but saw none. There was a smear of blood on her cheek that almost looked like...

"Back away!" the first paramedic shouted. "We need to get her on the rig right now!"

Porter leaned closer. The girl hadn't been going for Sturm's throat or the blood gushing from her shoulder.

The paramedics slid the board under her back and strapped down her legs, hips, and chest.

Porter stared off through the settling smoke toward where the smokestack had once lorded over the ruins and felt a sense of loss he couldn't quite define.

The men hefted Sturm up from the ground and set her, board and all, on the gurney.

"I'm coming with you," Porter said. He took Sturm's hand and ran beside the cart as they wheeled her toward the waiting ambulance. "I'm right here, Layne. I'll be with you all the way."

He watched her face in the alternating red and blue glare, hoping for some miraculous sign that she was going to make it, but he couldn't tear his eyes from the bloody kiss on her cheek that could only have been made by the small lips of a child.

EPILOGUE

Ships that pass in the night, and speak each other in passing,
only a signal shown, and a distant voice in the darkness;
So on the ocean of life, we pass and speak one another,
only a look and a voice, then darkness again and silence.

—*Henry Wadsworth Longfellow*

1400 Defense Pentagon
Washington, DC
Monday, October 29th
10:36 a.m. EST
(6:36 a.m. PST)

Nine days later…

Dr. Amon Trofino sat in the anteroom of the Deputy Under Secretary of Defense for Science and Technology's office, tapping a happy rhythm with his feet. He was not only on the verge of becoming one the wealthiest men on the planet, he was about to make all of his professional dreams come true. He'd have his own lab, equipped precisely to his specifications with no expense spared, the finest staff in the world, and carte blanche to conduct whatever experiments his heart desired. And he was about to change the world in a way that no man shy of God Himself had ever even imagined. Once the DoD scientists verified the legitimacy of the samples that Carla had saved from the lab under the Phobos compound before they permanently sterilized it, the Secretary of Defense himself would undoubtedly stroll in here with a beaming smile on his face, clap him on the shoulder, and offer him the key to Fort Knox.

Today was the day when his real life began. Too bad Carla couldn't be here beside him. She had been the best assistant he had ever seen. Unfortunately, she had known nearly as much about the project as he did and he couldn't risk being cut out of his own deal. He could still clearly remember the sound of her fists pounding on the closed door from inside the sealed lab. Perhaps she hadn't been as smart as he had thought after all. She should have waited until they were clear of the sublevel before handing him the case. He'd be surprised if there was enough of her left to fill a thimble.

The hallway door opened and a man Trofino hadn't seen before entered. He wore a crisp black suit, a matching tie, and sunglasses on his impassive face. Even though Trofino couldn't see the man's eyes, he could feel his stare crawling all over him like the legs of so many spiders.

This wasn't how he had envisioned his moment of triumph, but he should have expected that the Deputy Under Secretary would want to keep his hands clean for culpability's sake. He smiled his broadest smile and gestured for the man to go ahead and make the offer they both knew was coming.

Two more men stepped into the room behind him. Trofino didn't recognize either of them, but he definitely recognized their uniforms. Olive green. Bulky utility belts. Side arms. Muscular physiques. The brims of their caps worn low over their eyes. Both of them had bands around their right biceps that featured two letters.

MP.

Military police.

"What's going on here?" Trofino asked.

He tried to rise from the chair, but the man with the glasses dissuaded him with a shake of his head. That was fine by Trofino since his legs were trembling so badly that he wouldn't have been able to stand up anyway.

Something was wrong. Something was terribly, terribly wrong.

"Dr. Amon Trofino," the man said. His voice was surprisingly high-pitched, but not lacking in confidence or authority. "Please allow me to introduce myself. My name is Davis Walls, Chief Security Officer. And you are under arrest for suspicion of murder in the first degree."

"What in the name of God are you talking about?"

"Those samples you brought us?"

"What about them? Surely you understand the significance of what's contained within them."

"That we do, Dr. Trofino. We ran the standard battery of tests several times. The results were indeed conclusive. Those samples were taken from a former Marine First Sergeant Katherine Newland, honorably discharged. We were able to ascertain with just a few phone calls that she was listed as MIA in a recent DoD-sanctioned mission. And now you bring us proof that at least someone might actually know what happened to her."

"You're wrong. Those samples…"

The words died on Trofino's lips. In all of the chaos before the lab was destroyed, Carla had run off with the case to collect the various tissue, blood, and genetic samples. She hadn't been gone long enough to have made it to the cryogenic freezer. He should have realized it at the time.

"Anything you want to say before these men read you your rights, *doctor*?"

Trofino closed his eyes. He could almost see Carla running into the adjacent room and sweeping all of the samples from the cooked body Spears had brought back during the night in an effort to deceive them into the case. All of the ordinary human tissue samples that they had used to determine exactly what these men just had. And if these weren't the samples from the creatures, then he himself had incinerated every bit of corroborative evidence when he initiated the self-destruct sequence.

He was screwed.

Walls slapped him on the cheek and he opened his eyes in shock.

"Nothing to say for yourself? Fine. Then I'll have the last word. I hope they lop off your nuts and shove them straight down your throat. I served with First Sergeant Newland in Afghanistan. She was worth a dozen men like you. I will make it my life's mission to make sure that you pay for whatever you did to her."

Trofino shook his head back and forth and whimpered. This couldn't be happening.

"Get him out of my sight," Walls said, and turned away.

"Dr. Amon Trofino," the first MP said. "You have the right to remain silent…"

Seattle, Washington
3:45 p.m. PST

Elena Sturm leaned on the railing at the end of the southernmost commercial pier, staring across the cresting waves to the south toward Salmon Bay. The entire waterfront renovation had been sealed off from public view following the assault of negative publicity and the resultant investigations by every law enforcement agency from the state to the federal level and undoubtedly beyond. She had watched the aftermath on the news from her hospital bed. Officially, a lone militant, former Air Force Brigadier General Franklin Spears, had waged a one-man war of terror on his own country, a country he felt had failed him along the way. It was speculated that the death of his son had pushed him over the brink. He had taken his revenge on society as a whole by opening fire on its elite, killing a senator, the mayor, and a half-dozen other guests. He'd even shot a police officer, which was about the only part of the sanitized story that was actually true, but if even the medical examiner insisted that they'd been killed by the same 7.62 x 51 mm NATO rounds that had hit Sturm, then who would ever argue that the wounds looked more like ferocious bites. Spears had killed the power and the lights. No one had seen a little girl with fangs, but everyone had definitely seen the muzzle flash and heard the repeated gunshots. Too bad no one could ask Spears or examine his weapon. They had both been either incinerated in the blast or lost under tons of debris. He was being compared to Timothy McVeigh and Ted Kaczynski. No one from the FBI to the DoD had any knowledge of his plans or his deteriorating state of mind leading up to that fateful night, when he had obviously snapped. Or so they said. The same agencies had visited her to make sure she said the same thing. None of them knew anything about a girl living in the ruins. Neither did she, they said. And what did it matter anyway? The girl had been vaporized in the explosion that had dropped more than two acres of land into the Pacific, along with the western half of the Bertha Knight Landes Cultural

Center. From out on the ocean, one could see straight into the building like the back side of a doll house.

Sturm had no idea which entities actually knew the entire story, but they had doled out different versions of the truth to each of the different agencies that had participated in the investigation. The FBI had led the raid of the Phobos compound, but had found only sublevels that had been sterilized by fire and chemicals and Spears's demolished office. And a rambling, psychotic tirade detailing his plans for vengeance, which he had apparently typed before setting off for the shootings. The CSRT had been convinced it had been a mutated man-eating tiger from the Sunderbans region of India that had killed the crews of the *Scourge* and the *Dragnet*, and the homeless man with the green eyes. Lord only knew where they procured the tiger they dragged out from the rubble, live on CNN, or how they altered its teeth to match the cast that Sturm herself had created. All of the killing had been blamed on a tiger, not a little girl. Or so they told her to remember. Not that she could ever forget. They'd described the consequences in explicit detail should she ever remember it differently. She had asked for two concessions in return, with which they had readily complied. She had asked that none of them ever come near her again or she would tell the truth to every journalist who would listen. She hadn't so much as sensed their presence since. The second request would have to wait until the center was razed. Once it was, the city would create a homeless shelter where it had stood, surrounded by a park with playgrounds and trees, and the statue of a little girl that would be sculpted to Sturm's exact specifications.

Her arm was still immobilized in a sling, and the Erector Set the surgeon had used to cobble her scapula and shoulder girdle back together felt like it had been fitted to her bones with railroad spikes. It hurt like the dickens, but she was tired of taking painkillers. She wanted to think clearly and, most of all, she wanted to be able to feel.

She'd barely been discharged an hour ago, and here she was already, with no idea of what she was supposed to do. The little girl had been a monster, no doubt. She had killed people in the worst possible ways, and yet at the same time there was no denying her humanity. Maybe this area was safer now that she was gone, but Sturm couldn't help but think that they, as a whole, had gotten what they deserved. They had taken a child who had been lost and alone, who had watched her mother die, and turned her loose in a frightening land where her survival instincts had been the only thing she could trust. Sturm could only hope that wherever she was now, the girl had found her mother and the peace that every child should know at all times.

Sturm removed the roses she had bought from the florist on her way out of the hospital from inside her sling, unwrapped them, and scattered them upon the sea.

"Godspeed, little one," she whispered, and wiped the tears from her eyes.

"I thought I might find you here," a voice she immediately recognized said from behind her.

She leaned back into Porter and he wrapped his arms around her. He had been right there by her side throughout her convalescence. Holding her hand. Laughing with her. Crying with her. Joking that she could finally catch up on her sleep. He was the one good thing to come from this whole mess. More than anything, she looked forward to finding out what the future held for them.

"What do you say we get the largest cups of coffee we can find and take a stroll on the beach?" he said.

"It's like you can read my mind."

She took his hand and leaned against his shoulder. Soon enough they would have to determine what was left of their professional lives, but, for now, they fully intended to enjoy every moment exploring each other.

They walked down the pier toward the early morning hustle and bustle. They were nearly to the fish market when Sturm stopped and stared down toward one of the smaller berths at the bottom of a slanted walkway.

"Do you see that?" she asked.

"What?"

Sturm tugged him by the hand down the walkway toward a line of pylons crusted with barnacles and whitened by salt. Had she really just seen—?

There.

She released his hand and ran across the planks toward a vacant commercial dock. She dropped to her knees, leaned awkwardly over the side, and nearly toppled into the ocean as she tried to get a better look at the fresh carvings on the post, near the water line.

The wood was lighter on color where it had been carved with a sharp nail by someone hiding beneath the dock, waiting for the right moment to arrive. She recognized a pattern. It appeared to be one symbol, repeated over and over.

She glanced back over her shoulder at Porter and smiled.

Seattle, Washington
5:00 p.m. PST

"Are you certain?" Porter said into his cell phone.

"Without a doubt," Perriera said.

Porter ended the call and stared out across the sea toward where a bank of thunder heads swelled against the infinite horizon.

"Well?" Sturm asked. She allowed the steam piping from the lid of her cup to tickle her lips and nose. "Are you going to tell me or am I going to have to beat it out of you?"

Somewhere out there, bad things were about to happen.

"What?" she asked again. She walked over and hugged him from behind. "What does it mean?"

"It means 'home,' Layne. She's trying to go home."

Pacific Ocean
86 km North-Northwest of the Washington Coast
10:58 p.m. PST

The able seaman thundered down the stairs into the hold. There was definitely something wrong with the engines, and they hadn't been able to raise the engineer on his com link. They weren't slowing down fast enough. If they didn't decrease their speed in a hurry, they risked running aground in the San Juan Archipelago, which would peel the underside of the ship open like a sardine can.

He sprinted down the corridor toward the engine room, his heavy tread echoing in the close confines.

From somewhere ahead of him, he heard the captain's static-riddled voice shouting for the engineer.

He burst into the room and stopped. A pair of legs with black galoshes stretched across the floor from underneath a workbench. What looked like oil was spreading in a pool around them. He took a single step forward and caught movement from the corner of his eye.

"Jesus. You scared the crap out of me."

He took a step closer and reached out for the poor child. She was naked and shivering, and drenched with a dark fluid that shimmered crimson under the lights on the console beside her.

"How the hell did you get on this boat?"

She looked up at him when he neared and golden spheres reflected in her eyes, like those of a dog. Her skin was blistered and webbed with thick scars, as though she'd been badly burned, but he didn't fully realize how much trouble he was in until he saw her teeth.

MICHAEL McBRIDE

is the bestselling author of *Ancient Enemy*, *Bloodletting*, *Burial Ground*, *Fearful Symmetry*, *Innocents Lost*, *Sunblind*, *The Coyote,* and *Vector Borne*. His novella *Snowblind* won the 2012 DarkFuse Readers Choice Award and received honorable mention in *The Best Horror of the Year*. He lives in Avalanche Territory with his wife and kids.

To explore the author's other works, please visit www.michaelmcbride.net.

60219877R00168

Made in the USA
San Bernardino, CA
09 December 2017